East of the Sun
and West of the Moon

East of the Sun and West of the Moon

by
PETER ASBJØRNSEN

WORDSWORTH CLASSICS

This edition published 1995 by Wordsworth Editions Ltd,
Cumberland House, Crib Street, Ware, Hertfordshire SG12 9ET.

ISBN 1-85326-164-5

Typeset in the UK by Antony Gray.
Printed and bound in Denmark by Nørhaven.

The paper in this book is produced from pure wood
pulp, without the use of chlorine or any other substance
harmful to the environment. The energy used in its
production consists almost entirely of hydroelectricity
and heat generated from waste materials, thereby
conserving fossil fuels and contributing little to the
greenhouse effect.

❄

Contents

An Old-Fashioned Christmas Eve   7

*The Lads who Met the Trolls
in Hedale Forest*   21

Matthias the Hunter's Stories   25

The Lad and the Devil   34

*The Man who was Going to
Mind the House*   35

The Cormorants of Udröst   38

The Giant who had No Heart   45

The Pancake   53

A Day with the Capercaillies   57

The Greedy Youngster   79

The Seven Fathers in the House   91

Brave Old Bruin   94

Mother Bertha's Stories   97

The Smith and the Devil   109

The Three Billy-Goats who went up
    into the Hills to get Fat   116

Peter Gynt   118

Legends of the Mill   124

The Lad and the North Wind   135

Ashiepattle and the King's Hares   139

Mackerel Trolling   148

Peik   160

Foolish Men and Scolding Wives   169

The Parson and the Clerk   172

The Giant and Johannes Blessom   174

The Box with the Funny Thing in it   177

The Widow's Son   178

East of the Sun and West of the Moon   188

Ashiepattle who Made the Princess Tell the Truth   200

An Evening in the Squire's Kitchen   202

Hans who Made the Princess Laugh   221

A Summer Night in a Norwegian Forest   227

The Witch   243

※

An Old-Fashioned Christmas Eve

The wind was whistling through the old lime and maple trees opposite my windows, the snow was sweeping down the street, and the sky was black as a December sky can possibly be here in Christiania. I was in just as black a mood. It was Christmas Eve, the first I was to spend away from the cosy fireside of my home. I had lately received my officer's commission, and had hoped that I should have gladdened my aged parents with my presence during the holidays, and had also hoped that I should be able to show myself in all my glory and splendour to the ladies of our parish. But a fever had taken me to the hospital, which I had left only a week before, and now I found myself in the much-extolled state of convalescence. I had written home for a horse and sledge and my father's fur coat, but my letter could scarcely reach our valley before the day after Christmas, and the horse could not be in town before New Year's Eve.

My comrades had all left town, and I knew no family with whom I could make myself at home during the holidays. The two old maids I lodged with were certainly very kind and friendly people, and they had taken great care of me in the commencement of my illness, but the peculiar ways and habits of these ladies were too much of the old school to prove attractive to the fancies of youth. Their thoughts dwelt mostly on the past, and when they, as often might occur, related to me some stories of the town, its people and its customs, these stories reminded me, not only by their contents but also by the simple unaffected way in which they were rendered, of a past age.

The antiquated appearance of these ladies was also in the strictest harmony with the house in which they lived. It was one of those old houses in Custom-house Street, with deep windows, long dark passages and staircases, gloomy rooms and garrets, where one could not help thinking of ghosts and brownies; in short, just such a house, and perhaps it was the very one, which Mauritz Hansen has described in his story, 'The Old Dame with the Hood'. Their circle of acquaintances was very limited: besides a married sister and her children and a brother's little daughters, no other visitors came there but a couple of tiresome old ladies. The only relief to this kind of life was a pretty niece and her merry little cousins, who always made me tell them fairy tales and stories.

I tried to divert myself in my loneliness and melancholy mood by looking out at all the people who passed up and down the street in the snow and wind with blue noses and half-shut eyes. It amused me to see the bustle and the life in the apothecary's shop across the street. The door was scarcely shut for a moment. Servants and peasants streamed in and out, invariably pausing to study the labels and directions when they came out into the street. Some appeared to be able to make them out, but sometimes a lengthy study and a dubious shake of the head showed that the solution was too difficult. It was growing dusk. I could not distinguish the countenances any longer, but gazed across at the old building. The apothecary's house, 'the Swan' as it is still called, stood there with its dark, reddish-brown walls, its pointed gables and towers, with weathercocks and latticed windows, as a monument to the architecture of the time of King Christian the Fourth. The swan on the sign looked then as now a most respectable and sedate bird, with its gold ring around its neck, its spur-boots and its wings stretched out as if ready to fly. I was about to plunge into a reflection on imprisoned birds, when I was disturbed by noise and laughter proceeding from some children in the adjoining room, and by a gentle, old-maidenish knock at my door.

On my requesting the visitor to come in, the elder of my landladies, Miss Mette, entered the room with a curtsey in the good old style; she inquired after my health, and invited me without further ceremony to come and make myself at home with them for the evening. 'It isn't good for you, dear lieutenant, to sit thus alone here in the dark,' she added. 'Will you not come in to us now at once? Old Mother Skau and my brother's little girls have come; they will perhaps amuse you a little. You are so fond of the dear children.'

I accepted the friendly invitation. As I entered the room, the fire from the large square stove, where the logs were burning lustily, threw a red, flickering light through the wide-open door over the room, which was very deep, and furnished in the old style with high-backed Russia-leather chairs, and one of those settees which were intended for farthingales and straight up-and-down positions. The walls were adorned with oil paintings, portraits of stiff ladies with powdered coiffures, of bewigged Oldenborgians and other redoubtable persons in mail and armour or red coats.

'You must really excuse us, lieutenant, for not having lighted the candles yet,' said Miss Cicely, the younger sister, who was generally called 'Cilly', and who came towards me and dropped a curtsey, exactly like her sister's; 'but the children do so like to tumble about here before the fire in the dusk of the evening, and Madame Skau does also enjoy a quiet little chat in the chimney corner.'

'Oh, chat me here and chat me there, there is nothing

you like yourself better than a little bit of gossip in the dusk of the evening, Cilly, and then we are to get the blame of it,' answered the old asthmatic lady whom they called Mother Skau.

'Eh, good-evening, sir,' she said to me, as she drew herself up to make the best of her own inflated bulky appearance, 'come and sit down here and tell me how it fares with you; but, by my troth, you are nothing but skin and bones!'

I had to tell her all about my illness, and in return I had to endure a very long and circumstantial account of her rheumatism and her asthmatical ailments, which fortunately was interrupted by the noisy arrival of the children from the kitchen, where they had paid a visit to old Stine, a fixture in the house.

'Oh, auntie, do you know what Stine says?' cried a little brown-eyed beauty. 'She says I shall go with her into the hayloft tonight and give the brownie his Christmas porridge. But I won't go, I am afraid of the brownies!'

'Never mind, my dear, Stine says it only to get rid of you; she dare not go into the hayloft herself, the foolish old thing, in the dark, for she knows well enough she was frightened once by the brownies herself,' said Miss Mette. 'But are you not going to say good-evening to the lieutenant, children?'

'Oh! is that you, lieutenant? – I did not know you! How pale you are! It is such a long time since I saw you,' shouted the children all at once as they flocked round me. 'Now you must tell us something really jolly! It is such a long time since you told us anything. Oh, tell us about Buttercup, dear Mr Lieutenant, do tell us about Buttercup and Goldentooth!'

I had to tell them about Buttercup and the dog Goldentooth, but they would not let me off till I gave them a couple of stories into the bargain about the brownies at Vager and at Bure, who stole hay from each other and who met at last with a load of hay on their backs, and how they fought till they vanished in a cloud of hay-dust. I had also to tell the story of the brownie at Hesselberg, who teased the house dog till the farmer came out and threw him over the barn-ridge. The children clapped their hands in great joy and laughed heartily.

'It served him right, the naughty brownie,' they shouted and asked for another story.

'No, no, children! you bother the lieutenant too much,' said Miss Cicely. 'Aunt Mette will tell you a story now.'

'Yes, do auntie, do!' was the general cry.

'I don't know exactly what I shall tell you,' said Aunt Mette, but since we have commenced telling about the brownies, I think I will tell you something about them too. You remember of course old Kari Gausdal, who came here and baked bread and who always had so many tales to tell you.'

'Oh, yes, yes!' shouted the children.

'Well, old Kari told me, that she was in service at the orphan asylum some years ago, and at that time it was even more dreary and lonely in that part of the town than it is now. That asylum is a dark and dismal place, I can tell you. Well, when Kari came there she was cook, and a very smart and clever girl she was. When one day she rose very early in the morning to brew, the other servants said to her: "You had better mind you don't get up too early – and you mustn't put any fire under the copper before five o'clock." "Why?" she asked. "Don't you know there is a brownie here and brownies don't like to be disturbed too early," they said. "Before five o'clock you mustn't light the fire whatever you do." "Is that so?" said Kari; she was anything but chicken-hearted. "I want nothing to do with that brownie of yours, but if he gets in my way, why, by my faith, I will send him head over heels through the door." The others warned her, but she did not care a bit, and next morning, just as the clock struck four, she got up and lit the fire under the copper in the brew-house. But the fire went out almost at once. Somebody appeared to be throwing the logs about on the hearth, but she could not see who it was. She gathered the logs together over and over again, but it was of no use and the chimney would not draw either. At last, her patience exhausted, she took a burning log and ran round the room with it, swinging it high and low while she shouted: "Begone, begone whence you came! If you think you can frighten me, you are mistaken." "Curse you!" somebody hissed from one of the darkest corners, "I have had seven souls in this house; I thought I should have got eight in all!" But from that time nobody saw or heard the brownie in the asylum, so Kari Gausdal told me.'

'I am getting so frightened,' said one of the children. 'You must tell us some more stories, lieutenant; I never feel afraid when you tell us anything, because you tell us such jolly tales.' Another proposed that I should tell them about the brownie who danced the Halling dance with the lassie. That was a tale I didn't care much about, as there was some singing in it. But they would on no account let me off, and I was about to clear my throat and prepare my exceedingly unharmonious voice to sing the Halling dance, which goes with the story, when the pretty niece whom I have already referred to entered the room, to the great joy of the children, and came to my rescue.

'Well, my dear children, I will tell you the story, if you can get Cousin Lizzie to sing the Halling for you,' said I, as she sat down, 'and then you'll dance to it yourselves, won't you?'

Cousin Lizzie was besieged by the children, and had to promise to do the singing, so I commenced my story.

'There was once upon a time – I almost think it was in Hallingdal – a lassie who was sent up into the hay-loft with the cream porridge for the brownie – I cannot recollect if it was on a Thursday or on a Christmas Eve, but I think it was a Christmas Eve. Well, she thought it was a great pity to give the brownie such a dainty dish, so she ate the porridge herself, and the melted butter into the bargain, and went up into the hay-loft with plain oatmeal porridge and sour milk, in a pig's trough, instead. "There, that's good enough for you, Master Brownie," she said. But no sooner had she spoken the words, than the brownie stood right before her, seized her round the waist, and danced her about so vigorously and so relentlessly that soon she was gasping for breath and when the people came up into the hay-loft in the morning she was more dead than alive. And all the time they danced, the brownie sang . . .

Here Cousin Lizzie undertook her part, and sang to the tune of the Halling:

> ' "And you have eaten the porridge for
>   the brownie,
> And you shall dance with the little
>   brownie!

> ' "And have you eaten the porridge for
>   the brownie?
> Then you shall dance with the little
>   brownie!" '

I assisted in keeping time by stamping on the floor with my feet, while the children romped about the room in uproarious joy.

'Come now, you are turning the house upside down, children!' said old Mother Skau. 'If you'll be quiet, I have another story for you.' The children were soon quiet, and Mother Skau began.

'You hear a great deal about brownies and fairies and suchlike beings, but I don't believe there is much truth in it. I have seen neither one nor the other – of course, I have not been around much in my lifetime – and I believe it is all nonsense. But old Stine, out in the kitchen there, she says she has seen a brownie. About the time when I was confirmed, she was in service with my parents. She came to us from the household of a captain, who had given up the sea. It was a very quiet place. They never went anywhere, and nobody came to see them. The captain only took a walk as far as the quay every day. They always went to bed early. People said there was a brownie in the house. Well, it so happened that Stine and the cook were sitting in their room one evening, mending and darning their things; it was near bedtime, for the watchman had already sung out "Ten o'clock", but somehow the darning and the sewing went on very slowly indeed. Every so often "Jack Nap" came and played his tricks upon them! At one moment Stine was nodding and nodding, and then came the cook's turn – they could not keep their eyes open; they had been early up that morning to wash clothes. But just as they were sitting thus, they heard a terrible crash downstairs in the kitchen and Stine shouted: "Lor' bless and preserve us! it must be the brownie." She was so frightened she dared scarcely move a foot, but at last the cook plucked up courage and went down into the kitchen, closely followed by Stine. When they opened the kitchen door, they found all the crockery on the floor, but none of it broken, while the brownie was standing on the big kitchen table, with his red cap on, hurling one dish after another on to the floor and laughing in great glee. The cook had heard that brownies could sometimes be tricked into moving to another house, if they were told of one that was very quiet, and as she had long been wishing for an opportunity to play a trick upon this brownie, she took courage and spoke to him – her voice was a little shaky at the time – telling him he ought to remove to the tin-man's over the way, where it was so very quiet and pleasant because they always went to bed at nine o'clock every evening; which was true enough, as the cook told Stine later, but then the master and all his apprentices and journeymen were up every morning at three o'clock, and hammered away and made a terrible noise all day. From that day on they never saw the brownie again at the captain's. He seemed to feel quite at home at the tin-man's, although they were hammering and tapping away there all the time; but people said that the tin-man's wife put a dish of porridge up in the garret for him every Thursday evening; and that it was no wonder that they got on well and became rich when they had a brownie in the house. Stine believed he brought things to them. Whether it was the brownie or not who really helped them, I cannot say,' said Mother Skau, in conclusion, and got a fit of coughing and choking after the exertion of telling this, for her, unusually long story.

When she had taken a pinch of snuff she felt better and, becoming cheerful once more, began again.

'My mother, who, by the by, was a truthful woman, told a story, which happened here in the town one Christmas Eve. I know it is true, for an untrue word never passed her lips.'

'Let us hear it, Madame Skau,' said I.

'Yes, tell, tell, Mother Skau,' cried the children.

She coughed a little, took another pinch of snuff, and did as she was asked.

'When my mother was still in her teens, she used sometimes to visit a widow whom she knew, and whose name was – dear me, what was her name? – Madame, yes, Madame Evensen, of course. She was a woman who had seen the best part of her life, but whether she lived up in Mill Street, or down in the corner by Little Church Hill, I cannot say for certain. Well, one Christmas Eve, just like tonight, she thought she would go to the morning service on the Christmas Day, for she was a great church-goer, and so she left out some coffee with the girl before she went to bed, that she might get a cup next morning – she was sure a cup of warm coffee would do her a great deal of good at that early hour! When she woke the moon was shining into the room, but when she got up to look at the clock she found it had stopped and that the fingers pointed to half-past eleven. She had no idea what time it could be, so she went to the window and looked across to the church. The light was streaming out through all the windows and she thought she must have overslept herself. She called the girl and told her to get the coffee ready, while she got dressed. Then she took her hymn-book and started for church. The street was very quiet; she did not meet a single person on the way.

'When she went inside, she sat down in her customary seat in one of the pews, but when she looked around her she thought that the people were so pale and so strange, exactly as if they were all dead. She did not know any of them, but there were several she seemed to recollect having seen before, but when and where she had seen them she could not call to mind. When the minister came into the pulpit, she saw that he was not one of the ministers in the town, but a tall pale man, whose face was vaguely familiar. He preached very nicely indeed, and there was not the usual noisy coughing and hawking which you always hear at the morning services on a Christmas Day; it was so quiet, you could have heard a needle drop on the floor – in fact, it was so quiet she began to feel quite uneasy and uncomfortable.

'When the singing commenced again, a female, who sat next to her, leant towards her and whispered in her ear: "Throw your cloak loosely around you and go, because if you wait here till the service is over they will make short work of you! It is the dead who are keeping service." '

'Oh, Mother Skau, I feel so frightened. I feel so frightened,' whimpered one of the children, and climbed up on a chair.

'Hush, hush, child,' said Mother Skau; 'she got away from them safe enough; only listen! When the widow heard the voice of the person next to her, she turned round to look at her – but what a start she got! She recognised her, it was her neighbour, who had died many years ago; and when she looked around the church, she remembered well that she had also seen the minister and several of the congregation before, and that they had died long ago. This sent an icily cold shiver through her, she became that frightened. She threw her cloak loosely round her, as the female next to her had said, and went out of the pew; but she thought they all turned round and stretched out their hands after her. Her legs shook under her, till she thought she would sink down on the church floor. When she came out on to the steps, she felt that they had got hold of her cloak; she let it go and left it in their clutches, while she hurried home as quickly as she could. She reached the door as the clock struck one, and by the time she got inside she was nearly half dead – she was that frightened. In the morning, when the people went to church they found the cloak lying on the steps but it was torn into a thousand pieces. My mother had often seen the cloak before, and I think she saw one of the pieces afterwards, I'm not sure – it was a short, pink, woollen cloak with fur lining and borders, such as was still worn in my childhood! They are very rarely seen nowadays, but there are some old ladies in the town and down at the home whom I see with such cloaks in church at Christmas time.'

The children, who had expressed considerable fear and uneasiness during the latter part of the story, declared they would not hear any more such terrible stories. They had crept into the sofa and up on to the chairs, but still they thought they felt somebody plucking at them from underneath the table. When the lights were brought in we discovered to our great amusement that the children had actually put their legs up on the table. The lights, the Christmas cake, the jellies, the tarts and the punch soon chased away the horrible ghost story and all fear from their minds, revived everybody's spirits and brought the conversation to their neighbours and the topics of the day. However our thoughts took a flight towards more serious matters on the appearance of the Christmas porridge and the roast ribs of pork.

We broke up early and parted with best wishes for a merry Christmas, but I passed a very uneasy night. I do not know whether it was the stories, the substantial supper, my weak condition, or all these combined which was the cause of it; I tossed myself hither and thither in my bed and got mixed up with brownies, fairies and ghosts the whole night. Finally I sailed through the air towards the church, while some merry sledge bells were ringing in my ears. The church was all lit up, and when I found myself inside I saw it was our own church up in the valley. The pews were full of peasants in their red caps, soldiers in full uniform, country lasses with their white head-dresses and red cheeks. The minister was in the pulpit; it was my grandfather, who died when I was a little boy. But just as he was in the middle of the sermon, he turned a somersault – he was known as one of the most versatile men in the parish – right into the middle of the church; his surplice flew one way and his collar another. 'There goes the parson, and here am I,' he said, with one of his old familiar gestures, 'and now let us have a spring-dance!' In an instant the whole congregation was in the midst of a wild dance; a big tall peasant came towards me and took me by the shoulder and said: 'You'll have to join us, my lad!'

At this moment I awoke and felt someone pulling at my shoulder. I could scarcely believe my eyes when I saw the same peasant whom I had seen in my dream leaning over me. There he was with his red cap down over his ears, a huge fur coat over his arm, and a pair of wide eyes looking fixedly at me.

'You must be dreaming,' he said, 'the perspiration is standing in great drops on your forehead, and you were sleeping as heavily as a bear in his lair! God's peace and a merry Christmas to you, I say, and greetings to you from your father and all yours up in the valley. Here's a letter from your father, and the horse is waiting for you out in the yard.'

'But, good heavens, is that you, Thor?' I shouted in great joy. It was indeed my father's man, a splendid specimen of a Norwegian peasant. 'How in the world have you come here already?'

'Ah, that I can soon tell you,' answered Thor. 'I came with your favourite, the bay mare. I had to take your father down to Næs and then he says to me, "Thor," says he, "it isn't very far to town from here. Just take the bay mare and drive down and see how the lieutenant is, and if he is well enough, you must bring him back along with you," says he.'

When we left the town, it was daylight. The roads were in splendid condition. The bay mare stretched out her smart old legs and we arrived at length in sight of the dear old house. Thor jumped off the sledge to undo the gate, and as we merrily drove up to the door we were met by the boisterous welcome of old Rover, who in his frantic joy at hearing my voice almost broke his chain in trying to rush at me.

Such a Christmas as I spent that year I cannot recollect before or since.

The Lads who Met the Trolls
in Hedale Forest

Once upon a time in the olden days there lived a poor old couple, tenants of a small farm up in Vaage in the Gudbrandsdale. They had many children, and two of the sons, who were but half grown, had always to tramp about the parish begging. In consequence they knew all the roads and by-roads, and were familiar with the short cut to Hedale.

The two boys were bound for Hedale one day, but as they had heard that some falconers had built themselves a hut at Mœla, they thought they would just look in on the way and see the birds and how they were caught, so they took the short cut over the Longmoors. But it was so late in the autumn, that the dairy-maids had gone away from the dairies in the mountains and they could find neither shelter nor food anywhere. They had therefore to press on to Hedale. However, the path was so faint that when night set in they lost the track altogether, and to make matters worse they could not find the bird-catchers' hut either. Before they knew where they were, they were right in the thick of Hedale Forest. They knew they would not be able to get out of the forest that night, so as they had a hatchet with them, they set about cutting boughs off the pine trees with which to make a fire and build a hut. Then they gathered heather and moss and made themselves a bed. No sooner were they lying down, however, than they heard something which sniffed and snuffed very loudly through its nose. The boys put their ears to the ground and listened attentively to hear whether it was a wild beast or a forest troll. Just then the sniffing became louder and a voice shouted, 'I smell Christian blood about here!'

Whoever it was, was walking so heavily that the ground shook. They knew it must be the trolls who were about. 'Lord help us! what shall we do?' said the younger lad to his brother.

'Oh, you had better stand under the fir tree, where you are, and be ready to take our bags and make off when you see them coming; I will take care of the hatchet,' said the elder brother.

Just then they saw the trolls approaching; they were so big and tall that their heads reached as high as the tops of the fir trees, but they had only one eye among the three of them and this they used in turn. They had a hole in their foreheads, in which they put it and shifted it about with their hands. He who had the eye went first; the others followed behind holding on to him.

'Run away now,' said the elder of the lads, 'but don't run too far, so that you can see what happens. Since they have got their eye so high up, they won't be able to see me very well when I tackle them from behind.'

Well, the younger brother ran off and the trolls after him. In a trice the elder brother darted behind them and gave the last troll a cut with the hatchet in the ankle. The troll uttered a horrible shriek which gave the first troll such a start that the eye fell out of his forehead, and the lad was not slow in picking it up. It was larger than two pint basins put together, and it was so bright that, although the night was pitch dark, he could see as clearly as by daylight when he looked through it.

When the trolls realised that he had taken their eye from them and that he had wounded one of them, they began to threaten him with every kind of evil in existence if he did not return them the eye at once.

'I am not afraid of trolls or threats either,' said the lad, 'now I have got three eyes all to myself and you three haven't got any.'

'If we don't get our eye back this minute, we'll turn you into sticks and stones,' screeched the trolls.

But the lad was in no hurry; he wasn't afraid of witchcraft or their bragging words, he said. If they didn't leave him alone, he would cut away at them all three till they had to crawl along the ground like snakes.

When the trolls heard this they became frightened and began to mend their manners. They begged him very nicely to give them their eye back again and he should have both silver and gold and everything he wished for. Well, the lad thought that was very fair, but he wanted the gold and silver first. If one of them would go home and fetch as much gold and silver as he and his brother could fill their bags with, he told the trolls, and give them two good crossbows of steel into the bargain, they should have their eye back again, but until they did this he would keep it.

The trolls screamed and wailed, and demanded to know how one of them could go home when they hadn't an eye to see with. Presently, it occurred to one of them to bawl out for their old woman, for they did have an old woman among the three of them. After a while somebody up in the mountains a good way off to the north answered. The trolls shouted to her to come at once with two steel crossbows and two buckets full of gold and silver, and she came pretty smartly, I can tell you. When she heard what had happened, she too began to threaten them with witchcraft. But the trolls were afraid, and urged her to beware of the little wasp. She had better mind or he might take her eye as well. So she threw down the buckets with the gold and the silver and flung the crossbows at them, and made off towards the mountains with the trolls. And since that time no one has heard that the trolls have been walking in Hedale Forest sniffing for Christian blood.

❄

Matthias the Hunter's Stories

One fine Saturday in November 1836, I found myself at the house of my good friend the Squire, in Nittedale. It was a very long time since I had been there, and as he is not the sort of man to receive an old friend with a new face, I had to stay to dinner and to drink a cup of coffee afterwards, which was very acceptable after the long walk of fourteen miles from town. We were just settling ourselves around the coffee-table, when several friends from the parsonage arrived. According to the custom of the house, punch was brought in; the conversation became animate and we looked to our glasses so frequently, and I looked so oft into the dear blue eyes of the pretty daughter, that I almost forgot the appointment I had to shoot on the following day with a friend in Gjerdrum.

The sun stood already on the ridge of the mountains, and if I wished to reach my destination before my friend went to bed, it was of little use to think of taking the main road round by the church through the Midwood and over the moors, which at that time of year was sure to be in very bad condition after the chilly November weather we had had; so I went instead up to Nystuen, the nearest cottage under the hill, and got hold of Old Matthias, the hunter, who at once was willing to go with me and show me the short cut across the mountain. He only wanted 'just a chew of 'baccy' before he started.

It was a beautiful evening; on the western horizon

gleamed still the wintery evening sky. A slight degree of cold gave the air that freshness which makes many of our November days so delightful. A light mist rose from the little stream running close by, and covered the trees with a silvery rime, which made their branches glitter like crystal.

We were walking at a smart pace, and a sip from my pocket-flask soon set my old friend's tongue going.

He talked about hunting and shooting, and told me how unfair it was that Ole Gjörtler, who really belonged to Gjerdrum parish, should set his bird-traps on Solberg Common; next I was treated to the story about the nine bears which he was supposed to have shot, about his trip to Hallingdale when the parson moved there, to a number of remarks, which were only too true, about the careless way in which the Gjerdrum people looked after the public pasture grounds and much more which I cannot now remember. When we came to Askevangen dairy every trace of daylight had disappeared; the moon alone, which had just risen above the horizon, threw her unsteady light between the tops of the trees. As we passed the deserted mountain dairy, we must have crossed the fresh track of a hare, because the hounds became rather uneasy in the couples.

'Now much depends 'pon the strength of the couples,' said Matthias, who tried all he could to keep the dogs back, 'because it isn't as it should be about here!'

'I think you are right there, Matthias,' I said; 'it isn't as it should be, because it isn't light enough for shooting; were the moon clear of the trees yonder, we would be able to make out more, and the hounds would, as sure as I am here, treat you to the best music for a sportsman's car.'

'That may be,' he continued, and as he spoke he looked cautiously back at the dairy, 'but they do say the huldre is hereabouts at this time.'

'Ah, indeed, perhaps you have seen her yourself?'

'No, I have never seen her here,' he said.

'But where did you see her then, Matthias?' I asked curiously, 'for I see you believe that there are such beings as fairies and brownies.'

'Well, shouldn't I believe what there's written in the Scriptures?' he said. 'Why, when the Lord banished the fallen angels, some of them went down below there, of course,' and he pointed significantly downwards; 'but they who had not sinned overmuch, are up in the air, under the ground, or in the sea. Besides I have myself often heard them and seen them in the woods and glens about here.'

'You must tell me something about them,' I urged; 'we have nothing else to do while we walk along.'

'If you care to listen to it, of course I shall tell you all I know,' he answered, and commenced his story.

'Well, the first time I came across the huldre, I was about eight or nine years old, and it was somewhere up on the main road between Bjerke and Mo. I had been on a message for my father, and was walking home along the road, when I saw a tall, fine lassie coming over the bogland on the right-hand side of the road. That part of the bog is very full of pits and pools. I recollect her now as plainly as if she were before me this minute, it was just as light as it is now; she had on a brown skirt, and a light handkerchief over her head, and she had a skein of wool in her left hand. She was a pretty creature altogether. But she was walking right across the bog, and didn't seem to mind the pits or the pools; she came along as if there were not any there at all. I looked at her now and then, and when I had walked some distance and got to a cutting in the road, which hid her from my view, I thought it was wrong to let the lass go and trudge through the bog, and that I ought to run up on the bank and shout to her that she had gone astray from the road. Well, I did so, but there was nothing to be seen but the moon, which was reflected from every pool on the bog, and then I guessed it must have been the huldre I had seen.'

Although I thought he had scarcely seen sufficient to satisfy himself that this was the huldre, I kept my doubts to myself, as I could see that any objections on my part would not shake his belief but only silence him. I asked him, therefore, if he had not seen similar apparitions on other occasions.

'Yes, of course I have; I have seen a great many things, and I have heard many strange noises and sounds in woods and glens,' said Matthias. 'I have often heard talking, cursing and singing; at other times I have heard such lovely music that I cannot tell you how lovely it was. Well, once I went out bird-calling; it must have been at the end of August, because the bilberries were ripe and the cranberries were just beginning to redden. I was sitting by a path on a tussock between some bushes, whence I could overlook the path and the little valley to which it led down, and where nothing but ling and heather grew. At the foot of the hill you could see the mouths of several dark caverns. I heard a grey hen cackling among the ling, and I thought to myself, "If I could get a sight of you now, it would be your last cackle." Just then I heard something moving behind me on the path. I looked round and saw an old man, but strange to say he appeared to have three legs; one of them hung and swung backwards and forwards between the other two as he walked – though he didn't walk exactly, but appeared more to be gliding – down the side of the mountain and vanished into one of the darkest caves down in the valley. I was not the only one who had seen him, because directly afterwards the grey hen came creeping out from behind a tussock, with her head on one side and her neck stretched out looking cautiously in the direction of the old man, but then, as you may guess, in another moment I had the gun up, and bang, there she lay flapping her wings.

'So much for that; but another time at home in Laskerud – it wasn't very long after I had seen the huldre walking over the bog, a Christmas Eve, it was – my brothers and I were at play on the side of a hill, making snowmen and sliding down the slope on sledges. They used to say there were fairies in that hill but, nothing daunted, we were playing and running about as you know children can do. My youngest brother was only four or five years old, but he romped about and shouted and enjoyed himself thoroughly.

'It was getting very late, when all of a sudden somebody in the hill shouted: "Go home now." But we did not go; we thought it was still very early. Before long, however, we heard another shout, "Go home at once, now."

' "Just listen," said my youngest brother – he hadn't sense enough to know that he shouldn't take notice of their shouting – "they are shouting to us over in the hill to go home."

'We did not stop playing, however, but kept on sliding down the hill on our sledges, until we heard a shout which made our ears ring: "If you don't go home this moment, I'll – "

'We didn't hear any more, for we took to our heels and ran as fast as our legs could carry us, and didn't stop till we were outside our own door.

'Sometime after this – we were all grown up by that time – my brother and I were coming home one Sunday morning, after having been out all night fishing, when we all at once heard some hounds giving tongue over in the Solberg Wood. It sounded fine, I can tell you! Well, I was tired and went in to lie down, but my brother thought it was such a fine morning that he would stay up and listen to the dogs. All at once they ceased, so he went over there thinking he might come across the track of the hare and start it again. But when he came to a clearing in the wood, where the trees had been cut down, he discovered right before him a big, fine house, painted red, with the windows and the doors all askew. He wondered what building this could be; he had never seen it before, although he thought he was well acquainted with those parts. In front of the house was a big bog, but he thought he would walk across it and have a look at the house. There were no people to be seen. Afterwards he would go home and tell me about it and get me to go back with him.'

'It was a great pity,' said I, 'that he didn't fire his gun over the house – I suppose he had a gun with him – because by the time you got there, I suppose it was all gone?'

'You are right,' said Matthias, 'it was a pity he didn't fire into it. Had I been there, I should have done so, but he lost his senses entirely. But just listen, and you'll hear he fared worse than you would expect. When he got half-way across the bog, he met such a lot of people that he had to elbow his way through them. They were scantily clothed, and all were going north. He had scarcely pushed his way through the crowd, when they turned round upon him and felled him to the ground, where he was lying when my sisters came past on their way to bring the cow home in the evening. There he was lying with both his fists clenched and thrust into his face, which was quite black, and the froth was foaming out of his mouth. They were terribly frightened, as you may guess, but they got him home at last, and laid him on a bench, and then they fetched me. As soon as I saw him I guessed what was the matter with him. I knew of only one way to get him round. I took my gun down from the wall and I fired it lengthways over him, but although that's considered a good thing, he didn't move any more than that beam there, which the Gjerdrum people have placed across the road. He was as dead as a stone, he was!

' "Oh, no!" thought I, and loaded the gun again. "Come and give me a hand, lasses," said I, "and let us put him where you found him. It's no use trying here."

' We did so, and I fired again, and no mistake, he woke that time. If he didn't jump up the moment I fired the gun over him, may I never leave this spot alive! He glared and stared about him so horribly, that we were almost afraid of him. We took him home again, but he was very poorly and he was so queer and frightful-looking afterwards you would scarcely believe it. He would remain standing in one place, staring straight before him, as if his eyes would start out of his head; he wouldn't eat anything, and he would never speak to anybody unless they spoke to him first. He was bewitched, he was. But it began to wear off by and by, and it was only then he told us how it all happened – and now I have told you. These, then, are some of the things I have seen,' concluded Matthias.

'Have you never seen a brownie?' I asked.

'Yes, of course I have,' answered Matthias, speaking with the greatest conviction, 'when I was at home with my parents at Laskerud, where we had one in the house. I only saw him once. One fine moonlight evening after we youngsters had gone to bed, my father went out to take a turn round the yard, and saw a lad sitting on the barn-ridge, dangling his legs and looking up at the moon, just as if he did not see the old man. "You had better go in and get to bed now, Matthias," said my father, for he thought it was me; "and don't sit there and stare at the moon at this time of night!" But in the same moment the lad vanished, and when my father came in and asked for me, he found me a-bed, snoring hard.

'But it was about the time when I saw him myself, that I was going to tell you. It was just about a year after I had been confirmed, on a Saturday afternoon which had taken me to town with a cart-load of planks. I had had something to drink during the day, and as soon as I came home I lay down. Towards evening I got up and had something to eat – it wasn't much, because I still felt giddy and queer in my head – when my father said to me: "You had better give the horse his fodder before you go to bed again. I suppose the others are out running after the lasses."

'I went into the stable first to see to the horse, and found him neighing and waiting for his hay, so I went up into the hay-loft for an armful, but as I put out my hands I caught hold of something hairy, like the ears of a dog, and the next moment I saw two eyes, red as fire, glaring at me out of the darkness. I thought it could not be anything else but a dog, so I gave it a kick and sent it flying into the barn below, where I heard it fall with a heavy thud. When I had foddered the horse, I went into the barn and took the handle of an old rake to chase the dog out with. I looked and searched, but there was no dog or any trace of one, although there wasn't a hole big enough for a squirrel to escape through. I went up into the hay-loft and there was no dog there either, but just as I was going out I fell, as if someone had struck the legs from under me, and I rolled head over heels down the barn-ridge as I never had done before. When I got on my legs again there was the brownie standing in the door, screaming with laughter till his red cap shook.'

In this manner Matthias kept on telling about fairies, huldres and brownies, till we came to Kulrudsaas, whence we could see the wide plains of Upper Romerike, spread out before us and bathed in clear moonlight; to the north rose the Mistberg mountain in a bluish mist, with a few patches of snow here and there. Directly below me were the Heni and Gjerdrum churches. These were sufficient landmarks for me, and as I was well known in the district from having formerly shot over it, I bade my guide farewell, and was fortunate enough to reach my destination without being teased by the brownies, or tempted by the huldres.

❄

The Lad and the Devil

Once upon a time, there was a lad who went along a road cracking nuts. He happened to find one which was worm-eaten, and shortly afterwards he met the devil. 'Is it true,' said the lad, 'what they say, that the devil can make himself as small as he likes, and go through a pin-hole?' 'Yes, of course,' answered the devil. 'Well, let me see you do it; creep into this nut if you can,' said the lad. And the devil did it. But he had no sooner got through the worm-hole, than the lad put a small peg in the hole. 'I have got you safe now,' he said, and put the nut in his pocket.

When he had walked some distance he came to a smithy. He went in there and asked the smith if he would crack that nut for him. 'Yes, that's easily done,' said the smith, and took the smallest hammer he had, laid the nut on the anvil, and gave it a blow – but it didn't break. So he took a somewhat bigger hammer, but that wasn't heavy enough either; then he took a still bigger one, but no – the nut would not break. This made the smith angry, and he seized the big sledge-hammer. 'I shall soon make bits of you,' he said, and he gave the nut such a blow that it went into a thousand pieces, and sent half the roof of the smithy flying in the air. Such a crash! just as if the hut were tumbling together.

'I think the devil was in that nut,' said the smith.

'So he was,' said the lad.

✳

The Man who was Going to Mind the House

There was once upon a time a man who was always cross and surly, and he was always telling his wife that she didn't do enough work in the house. So one evening at hay-making time he came home and began to scold and swear all over the house. 'Dear me, don't get into such a temper,' said the wife; 'tomorrow we will try and change our work. I'll go with the mowers and mow the hay, and you can stop at home and mind the house.' Yes, the husband rather liked that, and he was quite willing for his part.

Early next morning the wife took a scythe on her shoulder and went out into the fields with the hay-mowers to mow while the man stayed to do the work in the house. He thought he would churn the butter first of all, but when he had churned a while, he became thirsty and went down into the cellar to draw some beer. While he was busy filling the jug, he heard that the pig had got into the room above. Away he ran up the cellar stairs, with the tap in his hand, just to see the pig didn't upset the churn, but when he saw that the pig had already knocked the churn over and stood there licking up the fine cream which was running over the floor, he got so furiously wild that he forgot the beer-barrel and turned round on the pig. He got hold of it in the doorway and gave it such a tremendous kick that it killed the poor pig on the spot. All at once he remembered the tap he had in his hand, but when he got back to the cellar, all the beer had run out of the barrel.

He then went into the larder, found cream enough to fill the churn again and commenced churning once more, for butter he would have by dinner-time. When he had churned some time he recollected that the cow, which they kept at home, hadn't been let out of the cow-house, and hadn't had a straw of hay or anything to drink, although it was late in the day. He thought it was too far to take the cow to the field where she generally grazed, so it struck him he would put her on the roof; the cottage had a turf-roof, and there was a splendid crop of grass growing there. The cottage lay close to a steep little hill, and if he placed a plank between this and the roof, he thought he could easily get the cow up there. But he could not leave the churn very well, because the baby was crawling about on the floor and he thought the child might easily upset it, so he took the churn with him on his back. He thought he had better water the cow, once she was on the roof, so he took a bucket to get some water from the well, but as he stooped down to pull the bucket up, all the cream ran out of the churn over his neck and down into the well. It would soon be dinner-time, and although he still hadn't got any butter, he thought he had better get on and boil the porridge.

When he had hung the pot of water over the fire, he began to feel afraid that the cow might fall off the roof and break her legs or her neck, so he went up on to the roof to tie her up. One end of the rope he tied round the neck of the cow, the other he let down the chimney and tied round his leg when he came down – for the water was boiling already and he must put the oatmeal in and begin to make the porridge. While he was stirring it, the cow fell off the roof and dragged the man up the chimney by the rope which was tied to his leg; there he stuck, and the cow hung outside against the wall between heaven and earth, for she could neither get up nor down.

The man's wife had waited in seven lengths and seven breadths for her husband to come and call the people home to dinner; but she saw no sign of him, so she thought at last she would wait no longer but go home. When she saw the cow hanging so awkwardly, she went at once and cut the rope with her scythe – and of course at the same moment her husband came down the chimney so that when she went inside she found him standing on his head in the porridge pot.

The Cormorants of Udröst

Bright, 'mid the skerries of the Western sea,
  An island rides upon the wave. Yet none
May know its beauty; for if mortal ship
  By chance should drift too near th'
  enchanted shore,
A curtain of dark mist enshrouds the isle.
  No eye can see its brightness, and no foot
May leave its print upon the golden fields.
  'Tis but in fancy he who dwells ashore
May picture, in the longings of his dreams,
  This fairy jewel of the Western sea.

When the fishermen in the north of Norway come to land, they often find straw stuck between the rudder and the stern-post, or grain in the stomach of the fish. It is then said that they have sailed over Udröst, or some of the other fairylands about which so many legends are told in the north. These fairylands are only seen by very pious people or by those who are gifted with second sight; when such people are in danger of their lives at sea, these fairylands appear where at other times no land is to be found. The supernatural people who live here have farms and keep cattle, own ships and fish, like other folk, but here the sun shines on greener pastures and richer cornfields than elsewhere in the north; and fortunate, indeed, is he who has landed on or even seen one of these sunny isles – 'he is a made man,' say the people in the north. An old ballad, in the style of Peder Dass, gives a full description of an island off Trænen in Helgeland, called Sandflæsen, with rich fisheries and abounding with game of all sorts; in the middle of the Vestford a large flat land with rich cornfields also appears, but it only rises high enough above the surface of the water to leave the ears of the corn dry; and outside Röst, off the southern point of the Lofoten islands, a similar fairyland with green hills and golden barley fields is spoken of, and it is called Udröst. The farmer on Udröst owns his fishing-smack just like any other farmer in the north; sometimes the fishermen see it under full sail, steering right down upon them, but just as they expect to be run down, it disappears.

On Værø, not far from Röst, lived once a poor fisherman, whose name was Isaac. All he possessed was a boat and a couple of goats, which his wife managed to keep alive on fish offal and the few stray wisps of grass to be found on the neighbouring cliffs; but he had a whole cottage full of hungry children. Even so Isaac seemed always to be satisfied with the lot Providence had ordained for him. His only complaint was that he could never be left in peace by his neighbour, who was a well-to-do man who fancied that he ought to have everything better than such riff-raff as Isaac. He wanted, therefore, to get rid of Isaac that he might have the harbour in front of Isaac's cottage.

One day when Isaac was fishing a good many miles out at sea, a thick, dark fog came upon him, and before long a tremendous gale broke loose and raged with such a fury that he had to throw all the fish overboard to lighten the boat and so save his life.

Still it was no easy task to keep the boat afloat; but he knew well how to handle his little craft, and how to steer her among the heavy seas, which every moment threatened

to swamp her. When he had been sailing at this rate for
five or six hours, he thought he ought soon to sight land
somewhere. But hour after hour passed and the storm
and the thick fog got worse and worse. Then it dawned
upon him that he must be steering right out to sea, or
that the wind had shifted; he soon became convinced that
he must have guessed right, for he sailed and sailed, but
saw no sign of land. All of a sudden he heard a terrible
screech ahead and he thought it must be the bogie
singing his dirge. He prayed for his wife and children, for
he knew now that his last hour had come. While he sat
thus and prayed he caught sight of something black; as he
came nearer he saw it was only three cormorants sitting
on a piece of drift-wood and the next moment he had
sailed past them. The time wore on and he began to feel
so thirsty and so hungry and so tired that he did not for
the life of him know what to do. He was sitting half
asleep, with the tiller in his hand, when all at once the
boat grated against the beach and ran aground. Isaac was
not long in getting his eyes open. The sun was breaking
through the fog and shone upon a splendid country; the
hills and the cliffs were green right to the top, with
meadows and cornfields on the slopes, and there was a
scent of flowers and grass such as he had never before
experienced.

'The Lord be praised,' said Isaac to himself. 'I am safe
now; this must be Udröst.' Straight before him was a
field of barley, with ears so large and full that he had
never seen their like, and a narrow path led through this
field to a green turf-roofed hut at its far side. On the roof
of the hut was a white goat with gilt horns, grazing; its
udder was as large as the largest cow's. Outside the hut
sat a little old man on a wooden stool, smoking a cutty-
pipe. He was dressed in blue, and had a full long beard
which reached down to his waist.

'Welcome to Udröst, Isaac!' said the old man.

'Thank you!' answered Isaac. 'You know me, then?'

'Perhaps I do,' said the man. 'You want to stop here tonight, I suppose?'

'Well, if I might I should like nothing better,' said Isaac.

'It's rather awkward with those sons of mine,' said the old man; 'they don't like the smell of Christians. Have you not met them?'

'No, I have met nothing but three cormorants sitting on a bit of drift-wood screeching.'

'Yes, those were my sons, those were,' said the old man, as he knocked the ashes out of his pipe. 'You had better go inside in the meantime. I suppose you are both hungry and thirsty?'

'Thanks for your offer, my friend,' said Isaac. But when the man opened the door, he found it was such a fine and grand place he was quite taken aback. He had never seen anything like it before. The table was covered with the most splendid dishes – sea perch and sour cream, venison and cod-liver stew with treacle and cheese, heaps of cakes, brandy, beer and mead – in fact, everything that was good. Isaac ate and drank as much as he was able, but still his plate never became empty, and although he drank a good deal, his glass was always full. The old man did not eat much, and he did not speak much either; but just as they were sitting, they heard a screech and a great noise outside. The old man went out, and soon came back with his three sons. Isaac felt just a little queer when they came in, but the old man must have been telling them to behave themselves, for they were kind and pleasant enough. They said he must follow their custom and sit down and drink with them, for Isaac was going to leave the table. He had done very well, he said, but he would join them if they wished, and they drank glass after glass of brandy, and now and then took a pull at the beer and the mead. They became good friends and got on very well together. Isaac must go fishing a trip or two with them, they said, so that he could have something to take home with him when he went away.

The first trip they made was in a terrible gale. One of the sons was steering, the other held the sheet, and the third son was midships, while Isaac bailed out the water with a big scoop until the perspiration ran down his back in big drops. They sailed as if they were stark mad; they never took in a reef in the sail, and when the seas filled the boat, they sailed her up on the back of a wave till she stood nearly on end and the water rushed out over her stern as out of a spout. Shortly the storm abated, and they commenced to fish. The fish were so thickly packed, that the lead could not reach the bottom and the young men from Udröst hauled in one fish after another. Isaac had plenty of bites too, but he had brought his own fishing tackle with him, and every time he got a fish as far as the gunwale it got off; he did not catch as much as the tail of one. When the boat was full, they sailed home to Udröst. The sons cut up the fish and cleaned them and hung them up across some poles to dry, but Isaac could only complain of his bad fortune to the old man, who promised him better luck next time and gave him a couple of fish-hooks. The next time they went out fishing Isaac caught as many fish as the others, and when they came ashore and hung up their catch, he had three long poles full for his share. Isaac soon began to feel homesick, and when he was leaving the old man made him a present of a new eight-oared boat, filled with bags of flour, canvas and other useful things, for which Isaac tendered his best thanks. The old man told him to come back again by the time the fishing smacks were about to start for their yearly trips to Bergen, where he was going himself with a cargo, and Isaac could go with him and sell his fish. Yes, Isaac would be pleased to do that, and asked what course he was to steer when he sailed for Udröst again.

'Straight after the cormorants, when they fly to sea,' said the old man. 'That's your right course, and a safe journey to you!'

But when Isaac had shoved off from the shore and turned round to give his friends a farewell wave, Udröst was not to be seen any more; he saw only the open sea far and near.

When the time came for the smacks to sail for Bergen, Isaac arrived again at Udröst. But such a smack as the old man had Isaac had never seen before; it was two cables long, and the mate, who stood forward on the lookout, could not shout loud enough to make himself heard by the man at the helm. They had therefore to station another man amidships close to the mast, and he had to sing out to the man at the helm, and even then he had to shout as loud as he could to make himself heard. Isaac's share of the cargo was stowed forward in the smack; he took the fish down off the poles himself, but he could not make out how it came to pass that as soon as he took the fish off the poles, they were full of new fish again; and when they sailed, there was just as much fish as when he came. When he came to Bergen, he sold his fish and got so much money that he bought a new smack, with cargo and everything that was wanted for a good outfit, just as the old man had advised him to do. Late in the evening, when he was getting ready to sail, the old man came on board to him and asked him not to forget those who had been his neighbours when he was lost at sea, and then he prophesied good luck for Isaac with his smack.

'Everything on board is sound and good, and you may be sure that all aloft will stand,' said he, meaning that there would always be one on board whom nobody could see, who at a pinch would put his back to the mast and steady it.

Isaac was always very successful after that time. He knew well where his good luck came from, and he never forgot to provide well for the man who kept watch on board when the smack was laid up for the winter. Every Christmas Eve there was such a glare of light from the smack that it could be seen afar off, and you could hear the sound of fiddles and music and laughter and merriment – and there was every indication that dancing was going on in the cabin.

❄

The Giant who had No Heart

There was once upon a time a king who had seven sons. He loved them all so much that he could never do without them all at once; one had always to be with him. When they were grown up, six of them set out to woo. But the father kept the youngest son at home, and for him the others were to bring back a princess to the palace. The king gave the six the finest clothes you ever set your eyes upon, and you could see the glitter of them a long way off; and each had his own horse, which cost many, many pieces of gold; and so they set out on their journey.

After having been to many royal palaces and seen all the princesses there, they came at last to a king who had six daughters; such lovely princesses they had never seen, and so each of them began wooing one of the six sisters; and when they had all made sure of their sweethearts, they set out for home again; but they quite forgot to bring a princess with them for Ashiepattle – who was the prince left at home – so busy were they making love to their sweethearts.

When they had journeyed a good bit of the way, they passed close to the side of a steep mountain, where there was a giant's castle. As soon as the giant saw them, he came out and turned them all, princes and princesses, into stone. Meanwhile the king waited and waited for his six sons, but no sons came. He was very sad, and said that he should never be glad again. 'Had you not been left to me,' he said to Ashiepattle, 'I should not care to live any longer. I am so sad because I have lost your brothers.'

'But I have been thinking to ask for leave to set out and find them, father,' said Ashiepattle.

'No, I cannot let you go,' said his father; 'I shall lose you as well.'

But Ashiepattle would go, and he begged and prayed till the king gave him permission. The king had no horse to give him but an old jade, for his six brothers and their men had taken all the other horses, but Ashiepattle did not mind that; he mounted the shabby old nag.

'Goodbye, father,' said he to the king, 'I shall come back, sure enough, and who knows but I shall have my six brothers with me as well,' and off he went.

Well, when he had gone a little way, he came to a raven lying in the road and flapping his wings, quite unable to get out of his way it was so famished.

'Oh, dear friend, give me something to eat, and I will help you in your utmost need,' said the raven.

'Very little food have I,' said the prince, 'and you don't look as if you could ever help me much, but a little I must give you, for I can see you need it badly.' So saying, he gave the raven some of the food he had with him.

When he had travelled some distance further, he came to a stream. There he saw a big salmon which had got ashore and was thrashing about trying to get back into the water again.

'Oh, dear friend! help me into the water,' said the salmon to the prince, 'and I will help you in your utmost need.'

'I don't suppose you could ever be much of a help to me,' said the prince, 'but it is a pity you should lie there and very likely perish.' So saying, he shoved the fish into the stream again.

He had travelled on a long, long way, when he met a wolf, which was so famished that he was only able to drag himself along the road.

'Dear friend, give me your horse to eat,' said the wolf. 'I am so hungry, I hear the wind whistling in my empty stomach. I have had nothing to eat for two years.'

'No,' said Ashiepattle. 'I can't do it; first I came to a raven which I had to give all my food to; then I came to a salmon which I had to help back into the water; and now you want to eat my horse. But that is impossible, for then I should have nothing to ride upon.'

'Be that as it may, my friend, you must help me,' said the wolf. 'You can ride on me instead; and, in return, I shall help you in your utmost need.'

'Well, the help you can give me will not be great; but I suppose you must have the horse, since you are so needy,' said the prince.

When the wolf had finished the horse, Ashiepattle took the bridle and put the bit in the wolf's mouth and the saddle on his back, and the wolf felt now so strong and well after what he had had to eat, that he set off with the prince as if he were no weight at all. Ashiepattle had never ridden so fast before.

'When we get a little bit further I will show you a giant's castle,' said the wolf, and, sure enough, in a little while they came there. 'See, here is the giant's castle,' said the wolf, 'and there you will see all your six brothers, whom the giant has turned into stone, and with them their six brides. Over yonder is the door of the castle, and you must go in there.'

'I dare not,' said the prince, 'the giant will kill me.'

'Not at all,' answered the wolf; 'when you go in there you will meet a princess. She will tell you what to do to make an end of the giant. Only do as she tells you.'

Well, Ashiepattle went into the castle, but to tell the

truth he felt rather afraid. When he got inside, he found the giant was out; but in a chamber sat the princess, just as the wolf had said. Such a lovely maiden Ashiepattle had never seen before.

'Good heavens! what has brought you here?' said the princess, as soon as she saw him. 'It's sure to be your death; no one can kill the giant who lives here, for he has no heart.'

'But as I am here, I might as well try my luck,' said Ashiepattle, 'and see if I can't release my brothers who are standing outside here, turned into stone. And I will try to save you as well.'

'Well, since you won't go, we must try and do the best we can,' said the princess. 'You must creep under the bed over there and listen well to what he says when I speak with him, and be sure to lie as quiet as you can.'

So Ashiepattle crept under the bed, and no sooner had he done so than the giant came home.

'Ugh, what a smell of Christian blood there is in here,' shouted the giant.

'Yes, a magpie flew over the house with a man's bone and let it fall down the chimney,' said the princess. 'I made haste to throw it out, but the smell is hard to get rid of.'

So the giant said no more about it, and when evening came, they went to bed. When they had lain a while, the princess said: 'There is one thing I wanted so very much to ask you about, if I only dared.'

'Well, what can that be?' asked the giant.

'I should so like to know where your heart is, since you don't carry it about you,' said the princess.

'Oh, that's a thing you needn't know anything about,' said the giant, 'but if you must know, it's under the stone slab in front of the door.'

'Ah, ha! we shall soon see if we can't find that,' said

Ashiepattle to himself, under the bed.

Next morning the giant got up very early and set out for the wood, but no sooner was he out of sight than Ashiepattle and the princess commenced looking for the heart under the door-slab, but although they dug and searched all they could, they could not find anything.

'He has made a fool of me this time,' said the princess; 'but I must try him again.'

So she picked all the prettiest flowers she could find and strewed them over the door-slab, which they put in its right place again. When the time came for the giant to return home, Ashiepattle crept under the bed, and he had scarcely got well under before the giant came in.

'Ugh, what a smell of Christian blood there is here,' screamed the giant.

'Yes, another magpie flew over the house and dropped a man's bone down the chimney,' said the princess. 'I made haste to clear it away, but I suppose the smell hasn't gone away yet.'

So the giant said no more about it, but in a little while he asked who it was that had been strewing flowers around the door-slab.

'Why, I, of course,' said the princess.

'And what's the meaning of it?' asked the giant.

'Well, you know, I am so fond of you,' said the princess, 'that I couldn't help doing it when I knew that your heart was lying under there.'

'Ah, indeed,' said the giant, 'but it isn't there after all.'

When they had gone to bed in the evening, the princess asked again where his heart was, because she was so very fond of him, she said, that she would so like to know.

'Oh, it's over in the cupboard on the wall there,' said the giant.

Ah, ha, thought both Ashiepattle and the princess, we will soon try to find it.

Next morning the giant was early out of bed, and made for the wood again; the moment he was gone Ashiepattle and the princess were looking in the cupboard for the heart, but they looked and searched and found no heart.

'Well, we must try once more,' said the princess. She hung flowers and garlands around the cupboard, and when the evening came Ashiepattle crept under the bed again.

Shortly the giant came in. 'Ugh, Ugh!' he roared, 'what a smell of Christian blood there is here.'

'Yes, yet another magpie flew past here just now, and dropped a man's bone down the chimney,' said the princess. 'I made haste to throw it out, but I suppose that's what you can still smell.'

When the giant heard this, he said no more about it; but as soon as he saw the cupboard decked out with flowers and garlands, he asked who it was that had done that. The princess told him that, of course, it was she.

'But what's the meaning of all this foolery?' asked the giant.

'Well, you know how fond I am of you,' said the princess; 'I couldn't help doing it when I knew your heart was there.'

'How can you be so foolish to believe it?' said the giant.

'Well, how can I help believing it when you say so?' answered the princess.

'Oh, you are a foolish creature,' said the giant, 'you can never go where my heart is!'

'Ah, well,' said the princess, 'but I should like to know for all that where it is.'

So the giant could not refuse to tell her any longer, and he said: 'Far, far away, in a lake, lies an island, on that island stands a church, in that church there is a well, in that well swims a duck, in that duck there is an egg and in the egg – well, there is my heart.'

Early next morning, almost before the dawn of day, the giant set out for the wood again.

'Well, I suppose I had better start as well,' said Ashiepattle. 'I wish I only knew the way!' He said farewell to the princess for the time being, and when he came out of the castle there was the wolf still waiting for him. He told the wolf what had happened inside, and that he was now planning to set out for the well in the church – if he only knew the way. The wolf asked him to jump on his back – for he would surely be able to find the way, he said – and away they went over hills and mountains, over fields and valleys, while the wind whistled about them. When they had travelled many, many days, they came at last to the lake. The prince did not know how he should get across it; but the wolf asked him only not to be afraid, and then he plunged into the water with the prince on his back and swam across to the island.

When they came to the church, they found the key for the church-door hanging high, high up on the steeple, and at first the young prince did not know how to get hold of it. 'You will have to call the raven,' said the wolf, which the prince did. The raven came at once and flew up for the key and with it the prince got into the church. When he came to the well, the duck was there sure enough. It was swimming about just as the giant had said. He commenced calling and calling, and at last he lured her up to him and caught her. But just as he was lifting her out of the water, the duck let the egg fall into the well and Ashiepattle didn't know how to retrieve it. 'You had better call the salmon,' said the wolf, which the prince did. The salmon came and fetched the egg from the bottom of the well.

Now that Ashiepattle had the egg at last, the wolf told him to squeeze it, and, as soon as he squeezed it, they heard the giant screaming. 'Squeeze it once more,' said the wolf, and when the prince did so, the giant screamed still more piteously, and prayed so nicely and gently for himself: he would do all the prince wished, if he only wouldn't squeeze his heart to pieces.

'Tell him, that if he will give you back again alive your six brothers and their brides, whom he turned into stone, you may spare his life,' said the wolf, and Ashiepattle did so.

Yes, the giant would do that at once and immediately he restored the six princes and the six princesses to life.

'Now, squeeze the egg to pieces,' said the wolf.

Ashiepattle squeezed it flat between his hands, and the giant burst.

So when Ashiepattle had got rid of the giant, he rode back again on his friend, the wolf, to the giant's castle, and there stood all his six brothers and their brides, all alive, and then Ashiepattle went into the castle for his own bride, and they all set out together for their home, the royal palace. The old king was pleased, I can tell you, when all his seven sons came back, each with his bride. 'But the loveliest of the princesses is Ashiepattle's bride after all,' said the king, 'and he shall sit at the top of the table with her.'

And then the wedding came off, and the king gave a grand feast which lasted for many a day, and if they have not done feasting by this, why they are still at it.

※

The Pancake

Once upon a time there was a good housewife, who had seven hungry children. One day she was busy frying pancakes for them, and this time she had used new milk in the making of them. One was lying in the pan, frizzling away – ah! so beautiful and thick, it was a pleasure to look at it. The children were standing round the fire, and the good man sat in the corner and looked on.

'Oh, give me a bit of pancake, mother – I am so hungry!' said one child.

'Ah, do! dear mother,' said the second.

'Ah, do! dear, good mother,' said the third.

'Ah, do! dear, good, kind mother,' said the fourth.

'Ah, do! dear, good, kind, nice mother,' said the fifth.

'Ah, do! dear, good, kind, nice, sweet mother,' said the sixth.

'Ah, do! dear, good, kind, nice, sweet, darling mother,' said the seventh. And thus they were all begging for pancakes, each one more prettily than the last, because they were so hungry, and such good little children.

'Yes, children dear, wait a bit till it turns itself,' she answered – she ought to have said 'till I turn it' – 'and then you shall all have pancakes, beautiful pancakes, made of new milk – only look how thick and happy it lies there.'

When the pancake heard this, it got frightened and made a sudden effort to turn itself in order to get out of the pan, but it fell back into the pan again, this time on its other side. When it had been fried a little on that side too, it felt a little stronger in the back, jumped out on to the floor and rolled away, like a wheel, right through the door and down the road.

'Hallo!' cried the good wife, and away she ran after it, with the frying-pan in one hand and the ladle in the other, as fast as she could, and the children behind her, while the good man came limping after, last of all.

'Halloo, won't you stop? Catch it, stop it! Halloo there!' they all screamed, the one louder than the other, trying to catch it on the run; but the pancake rolled and rolled, and before long, it was so far ahead that they could not see it, for the pancake was much smarter on its 'legs' than any of them.

When it had rolled a time, it met a man.

'Good-day, pancake!' said the man.

'Well met, Manny Panny,' said the pancake.

'Dear pancake,' said the man, 'don't roll so fast, but wait a bit and let me eat you.'

'Since I have run away from Goody Poody and her good man and seven squalling children, I must run away from you too, Manny Panny,' said the pancake, and rolled on till it met a hen.

'Good-day, pancake,' said the hen.

'Good-day, Henny Penny,' said the pancake.

'My dear pancake, don't roll so fast, but wait a bit and let me eat you,' said the hen.

'Since I have run away from Goody Poody and her good man and seven squalling children, and from Manny Panny, I must run away from you too, Henny Penny,' said the pancake, and rolled on like a wheel down the road. Then it met a cock.

'Good-day, pancake,' said the cock.

'Good-day, Cocky Locky,' said the pancake.

'My dear pancake, don't roll so fast, but wait a bit and let me eat you,' said the cock.

'Since I have run away from Goody Poody and her good man and seven squalling children, from Manny Panny and from Henny Penny, I must run away from you too, Cocky Locky,' said the pancake, and rolled and rolled on as fast as it could. When it had rolled a long way, it met a duck.

'Good-day, pancake,' said the duck.

'Good-day, Ducky Lucky,' said the pancake.

'My dear pancake, don't roll so fast, but wait a bit and let me eat you,' said the duck.

'Since I have run away from Goody Poody and her good man and seven squalling children, from Manny Panny, Henny Penny and Cocky Locky, I must run away from you too, Ducky Lucky,' said the pancake, and with that it fell to rolling and rolling as fast as ever it could. When it had rolled a long, long way, it met a goose.

'Good-day, pancake,' said the goose.

'Good-day, Goosey Poosey,' said the pancake.

'My dear pancake, don't roll so fast, but wait a bit and let me eat you,' said the goose.

'Since I have run away from Goody Poody and her good man and seven squalling children and Manny Panny and Henny Penny and Cocky Locky and Ducky Lucky, I must run away from you too, Goosey Poosey,' said the pancake, and away it rolled. When it had rolled on for a long, a very long time, it met a gander.

'Good-day, pancake,' said the gander.

'Good-day, Gander Pander,' said the pancake.

'My dear pancake, don't roll so fast, but wait a bit and let me eat you,' said the gander.

'Since I have run away from Goody Poody and her good man and seven squalling children, and from Manny Panny and Henny Penny and Cocky Locky and Ducky Lucky and Goosey Poosey, I must run away from you too, Gander Pander,' said the pancake, and rolled and rolled as fast as it could. When it had rolled on a long, long way, it met a pig.

'Good-day, pancake,' said the pig.

'Good-day, Piggy Wiggy,' said the pancake, and began to roll on faster than ever.

'Nay, wait a bit,' said the pig, 'you needn't be in such a hurry-scurry; we two can walk quietly together and keep each other company through the wood, because they say it isn't very safe.'

The pancake thought there might be something in this, and so they walked together through the wood; but when they had gone some distance, they came to a brook. The pig was so fat it wasn't much trouble for him to swim across, but the pancake couldn't get over.

'Sit on my snout,' said the pig, 'and I will ferry you over.'

The pancake did so.

'Ouf, Ouf,' grunted the pig, and swallowed the pancake in one gulp, and as the pancake couldn't get any farther – well, you see, we can't get any farther with this story, either.

A Day with the Capercaillies

Early in May – this was long before the game laws had
been hatched – we started on our way to Skjœrsjöhaug,
according to local tradition the place where we were
most likely to see the capercaillies at their play. There
were four of us – my friend the captain, myself, an old
sportsman from Sognedale, called Peter Sandaker, and a
smart boy, who had charge of two brace of hounds. We
were to try for a hare, as soon as our sport with the
capercaillies was over. Down in the valley spring had
fairly set in, but when we reached the top of the hill, we
found snow still lying on the ground and in deep drifts in
the hollows. The evening was still very warm, and the
birds in the woods were singing in praise of spring.
When we came near the Ask dairy, where we intended to
spend the night, we turned off towards Skjœrsjöhaug, a
hill well known to every sportsman who has roamed
through these woods. We made for this hill for the
purpose of finding out where the capercaillies went to
roost for the night. When we reached the top of the hill
we had a fine view before us. The setting sun cast his
golden beams across a cloudless sky. The landscape
before us was not of a friendly or inviting character; dark
forests stretched interminably over the hills which surrounded us on all sides as far as the eye could see; the
view was broken only by an ice-bound lake here and
there amid the extensive bogs.

Not long after the sun had gone down we heard a rushing sound which betrayed the flight of a heavy bird, flying to roost in a neighbouring tree.

'That was no old bird,' said the captain, with the air of an expert, when the bird remained silent after it had roosted.

Soon afterwards two other capercaillies came sweeping past and settled on their roost, likewise in silence, and the next moment we heard a fourth bird approaching, with a still heavier stroke and a still louder rush. This one, however commenced snapping its beak as soon as it had roosted.

'That fellow was not born yesterday. He is the cock of the walk here,' said Peter. 'I shouldn't wonder if it is our old friend himself.'

Three more birds came in, and as each took up his roosting place, the old bird repeated his challenge by snapping his beak at them. Two made no answer, but the third made the same sort of snapping sound in reply.

'He's a stranger,' exclaimed Peter, 'he does not know the old one; if he did, he would have held his tongue. He'll be sorry for it in the morning, believe me, when our old friend singles him out, for he is not one to be played with when he gets his temper up. I once saw what a dressing down he gave a silly chattering fool that had answered his challenge some time before.'

As he spoke, his open weather-beaten face assumed a curious grinning expression, which was heightened by the sardonic folds and wrinkles invariably called forth by the recollection of some mysterious story or another. According to the description our captain had given me of Peter Sandaker once when he had dropped behind on the march, he was particularly good at telling tales and stories about goblin-birds, *doppelgängers* and fairies, and had a special fancy for entering into the most minute detail when describing one or the other of the eighteen bears he had killed in his time. He was very silent, however, about all those bears malicious tongues reported he had missed, the number of which, according to the same good authority, exceeded the number he had shot.

'But what sort of a fellow is this big old bird, you are speaking about?' I asked.

'I'll tell you all about him,' the captain was quick to volunteer as we started on our way for the dairy. He was apparently afraid that this curt, ill-timed question of mine would, after the short acquaintance I had with Peter, create a suspicion in his mind and probably silence him altogether. 'I'll tell you about him,' continued the captain; 'there is an old capercaillie cock on this pairing ground, which has become the talk of the whole parish – a sort of a goblin-bird, in fact. The sportsmen about here call him the "bleater", for instead of sitting quiet on his branch and displaying, he often flies about between the tops of the fir trees, bleating like a goat. Not before this performance is over does he settle down to his ritual, which includes gobbling and snapping his beak. Well, that kind of behaviour, there's little sense in, and nobody can come within shot of him. He plays on us, however, still oftener, another trick, which is even worse: he sits quietly and displays; after a while he commences his gobbling, but when he ought to begin his snapping, he flies to another tree. If anybody by chance happens to hit him, the shot has no effect. Our friend Peter, here, has shot at him both with salt and silver, but although the feathers flew out, he didn't seem to take any more notice of the shot than if the charge had been a blank one. The next morning he gobbled away as fast as ever and out of tune as usual.'

'You might as well shoot at a stone,' said Peter, with

the decisive tone of one fully convinced. 'I came across him once,' he continued, 'down on the main road to Skaug; there he sat in the middle of the road with a lot of hens around him – I counted seven, and there were more round about in the wood, for I heard them clucking and calling behind every bush. The hens on the ground ran around him, stretched out their necks, trailed their wings along the ground and showed themselves off for him, but he sat on the ground and preened his feathers, and made himself as fine and haughty as a Spanish count. All at once he stuck his tail up and spread it out like a fan, swept the ground with his wings, and jumped right up in the air as high as this. Well, I didn't know it was that fellow, else I would have had a shot at him at once before he had time to make himself shot-proof; as it was, I thought it such great fun to watch him. But while he was in the middle of the display, another cock, a big one, though not quite as big as the old one, came sweeping down and wanted to join in. Then came the real fun! The old one stuck up his tail, and his beard stuck out like the teeth in a carding-comb; he snapped and grated his beak, till he set my teeth on edge – and the newcomer, he answered the challenge. He was a bold one to be sure. But then our old friend rushed at him, and when their beaks and wings met, the crash sounded all over the wood. The next moment they jumped up at each other and fought with their beaks, their wings and their claws, and they were so wicked that they nearly lost all sense and feeling, and I thought I could almost walk up and catch them both with my hands. But at last the old cock got hold of the other by the nape of the neck and beat him and knocked him about so savagely that I fancied I heard him squeak. I couldn't help pitying the poor bird, who was being lugged about by the top of his head in this way. The old one crushed him to the ground and kept him under him till he almost came sliding out over the hillside on top of him, close to where I was standing. Then I put up my gun in an instant. There was a report, and the strange bird lay dead on the spot, but the old one stuck to him and kept pulling at him; he did not even move his wings. Aha! I thought, if you are so sure of your hold, you shall soon be mine! I loaded again and was just going to take aim at him, when he gave himself a shake and flew straight up in the air. If he was further than ten steps from me, may I never in my life shoot a bird again.

'Another time I was up here and heard, just like tonight, where he went to roost in an old fir tree. I went out early in the morning long before there was a bird awake in the woods. And when he commenced his display, he did it properly this time. He played away till the tree shook; he did not forget the gobbling and snapping this time, nor did he stir from his place either. When he commenced his performance for the fourth time I had got within shot of him; he was sitting on one of the lower branches close to the trunk of the tree.

' "Now you are mine," thought I, for instead of a bullet I had loaded with a silver sixpence, which I had cut up for the purpose. But I made a mistake after all. I had no sooner fired than he flew straight away, as if nothing was the matter, although his feathers flew out in a cloud. No, the bullet isn't made yet that will kill that fellow.'

'Anyhow, Peter, we will have another try at him tomorrow,' said the captain with a somewhat malicious expression. 'We know where he roosts at any rate.'

'Well, if there were no other birds to be found in the woods, one might perhaps take the trouble to run after him,' answered Peter in a somewhat angry tone. 'But, dear me,' he added ironically, 'if the captain will go after him, good luck to him – only I don't intend to waste a grain of powder on him. I can only say,' he concluded with an air of simplicity, 'that such a display no one has ever seen or heard before. And such a bird! Why, it's the most remarkable bird you ever saw. He is not like other capercaillies at all – he is at least half as big again, and perhaps more.'

'Yes, you are right, he is a tough old one, scarcely worth powder and shot,' said the captain; 'his flesh must be as tough and bitter as the fir-twig he roosts on. I would, however, like to see someone put a bullet through him to bring an end to all these pranks he has so often played on us. I have been after him several times, without being able to get within shot of him during the display. Twice, however, I have had a shot at him, but both times from such a distance that there was but little chance of my hitting him. It is of course a most foolish thing to take a long shot twice in a capercaillie wood, as you know,' said the captain, appealing to me; 'but the last time I had no choice, because I heard that villainous Anders stalking the bird at the same time. He is really, as Peter says, a wonderful bird, this old capercaillie cock,' he continued, and gave me a wink, which clearly showed his intention of getting some more stories out of Peter. 'When we get to the dairy I shall tell you of an adventure I had with a hare – a goblin-hare it must have been – which was still more remarkable and wonderful than our capercaillie.'

We came soon to the deserted mountain dairy. The boy had gone on before us, while we went up the hill to listen to the capercaillies, with orders from the captain to air the room and to make a good fire in the hearth. As soon as we had put away our guns and game-bag and partaken of a good supper provided out of the captain's hamper, he commenced the story he had promised us about the goblin-hare, assuming at the same time a decorous air in speech and manner.

'When I was a lieutenant, I was one summer encamped on Thoten, where my regiment had to do their yearly drill. I had brought my hounds with me, as I intended to have some shooting. I was standing in the kitchen of my quarters one afternoon, getting ready for the evening's sport, when a peasant came in.

' "Are there any hares about here?" I asked. "Well, there are some left to be sure," answered the peasant. "On the Sukkestad Moor there is an old jack-hare, which many a hound and sportsman have been after, but he is not so easily killed, it appears." And the worthy peasant shook his head somewhat mysteriously.

' "Not easily killed? That's all nonsense. I suppose there isn't a hound worth having about here?" said I, and stroked my dogs, which were pulling at the couples and wanted to get out. "If my hounds here once start him I think there will be little difficulty in catching him."

' "Ah, maybe! Quite possible," said the peasant, and grinned rather incredulously.

'I started straight for the Sukkestad Moor and had scarcely let the hounds loose before they found scent and were in full cry. But there seemed to be little satisfaction got out of this run; the hare kept jinking and the hounds lost the scent time after time. I fired several times, but only made miss after miss. At last he settled in front of a clump of young fir trees about forty paces distant from me. I fired, and went quite confidently to pick him up; but when I came over to the pines there was no sign of any hare; I could see nothing but an old stick and a rag.

'The day after I was busy cleaning my rifle when the peasant came up to me, "Well, what about the hare, lieutenant?" he asked with a wink.

'I told him what had happened.

' "Many have been after him, as I told you, but you

must understand it's not an easy job to catch him," he repeated with a great deal of mystery. "I see you are cleaning your gun, sir, but I should say that's not of much use. It won't kill Puss any better for that."

' "But, goodness gracious, what can that hare be made of?" I asked "Do you mean to say that powder and shot have no effect on him?"

' "I think it is as you say," he answered. "I may as well tell you that the hare himself is possessed; the one which you saw yesterday is only his *doppelgänger*; he himself plays no pranks like that. But I'll give you a bit of advice! Take a blindworm – I'll find you one – and ram it into the barrel of your gun and then fire it; after that you may try what powder and shot will do."

'I did as he said. He got me a live blindworm, which we forced into the barrel of the gun; I fired it against the barn wall, and strange to say, there was nothing to be seen but a wet mark.

'Some days later I went up on the Sukkestad Moor. It was very early in the morning. The dogs were no sooner let loose, than the hare was afoot. This time there was no stopping or casting, but the hounds were soon in full cry, and after half an hour's run, the hare came dancing down the moor towards me. I put up my gun and fired; he dropped down dead on the spot. He was a big old rake, full of marks and scars, and he had only an ear and a half.'

'I have also heard about a similar hare,' said Peter, who had listened to the captain's story with great attention. 'He used to knock about here in Holleia, and they said he was nearly black. A good many were after him and had a shot at him, but they never had any luck. Then this rascally Anders came here. He shot it, for he must put his nose in everywhere, you know. It was he we saw the tracks of down by Rausand Hill. He is a scamp, he is, and it isn't difficult to find his tracks and signs of his reckless shooting, for he can never wait, like other folk, till the birds have had a good start.'

'I dare say,' said the captain, twirling his moustaches, 'that it isn't the first time he has trespassed on other people's territory. But tell me, was it he who shot that goblin-hare down by Christiania, which you told me about once?'

'Oh, that hare! No, that was a professional shot from those parts called Lars Brandte. You must know him, surely, since you are from Christiania?' said Peter, addressing himself to me.

No, I did not know him.

'What! you don't know him? Why, he lives in a small cottage under the hill just below Grefsen. I met him once in Halland, when he was out shooting with some swells from town. He is a queer fellow, but a good shot. He never misses his hare, and shoots on the wing just like the captain here. But about that hare the captain spoke of – he told me all about that and much more.

' "I was going out one day for old Simonsen in the marketplace," he said, "to try and get him some game. We had three hounds: one of them called Rap, over which the evil spirits had no power, because he was red, you must know; the other two both pretty decent hounds. Well, it was one morning early in the spring," said Lars, "that I started for Linderudsœter. I slipped Rap and he was soon in full cry and made the hillside ring. I posted myself near a place where they had been burning charcoal, and very soon the hare came running past, close to where I was standing. I missed, and away went the dogs again in full cry after the hare. Before long he came past the same place again and I missed again.

' " 'But how is all this?' said I to myself. 'Won't the other dogs acknowledge the scent too?' for by now it was only Rap who was after the hare. 'No, this can't be a real hare; but I must have another look at him.' Well, he came past for the third time, and I missed him again, sure enough. Both the other dogs were close by me, but they didn't take the slightest notice of him. But then I took a charm and put it in the gun," he said.'

'How!' I asked.

'You must tell him that, Peter,' said the captain.

'Well, Lars wouldn't tell me at first,' said Peter, 'but after I had given him a good dram and a roll of tobacco, he told me all about it.'

' "You take the bark of the mountain ash and put it round the gun's breech," said Lars, "and then you scrape three bits off a silver coin which has come down in the family – it must be one of the real good old coins, one that has been out in the wars; and then you scrape three parings off the nail of the little finger of your left hand; and then take three barleycorns – if you have not got these handy, take three breadcrumbs – and put them all above the shot, and then you might shoot the very devil with it," he said. "That's what I did the time I was telling you about, and when the hare came past the fourth time, he fell stone dead the moment I fired," he said. "He was a dry little beast, and he was so old that he was nearly black all over."

' "Well, I took him and hung him up by his hind legs to a gnarled birch to clean him, but would you believe me, he kept on bleeding as if he were a young cow, and the dogs were licking up the blood as it ran down the hill. I had to take him with me at last, but somehow I could not find my way, and the blood kept running off the hare all the time. I came back twice to that gnarled birch tree, and I thought it was rather odd, as I ought to know my way thereabouts as well as round my own parlour. But, of course, once you make a wrong start, you go wrong altogether. Well, thought I, I had better let the dogs find the way, and I followed them until, skirting some rocks, I came upon an old witch on the edge of a small birchwood. She wore a cloth on her head, a leather jacket and black skirt and she was leaning on a crutch-handled stick and looking just like a woman from the country.

' " 'I say, Lars,' said she, 'you have got many a hare on the moors here and I have wished you well, so you might have left alone that hare of mine! If you had not had that red dog of yours, you wouldn't have got him either.' "

' "I didn't say a word," said Lars, "but cut away over Mœrre Bog up to Bamsebraaten, where I let the dogs loose. They were soon in full cry, Rap being the first, and I stood and listened whether the other two were going to join in. I heard them all three, sure enough, and then I knew it must be a real hare; but when I heard them bearing off for the Linderudsœter again, I felt rather down in the mouth. They had an awful long run, but when they came round again, the hare came galloping like a young colt up to me – he was nearly as big as a small goat – and I shot him. Then I went southwards towards Alun Lake. There the dogs got a new scent and off they went in full cry in the direction of Linderudsœter again – drawn back there by another hare. At last they circled round so that I was able to shoot the hare, and then I had three in all. That'll do for today, my dear Lars, thought I, and so I went home and hung the hares up in Simonsen's cellar. But that little black thing bled for three days after, and filled the cellar nearly half full of blood." '

'You spoke just now about a goblin-hare who was seen here in Holleia; but are there not also some legends about all the gold and silver to be found in the mountains hereabouts? It would not be a bad thing to have some of that, would it, Peter?' said the captain, who was trying to get a story out of him again.

'Oh, what would you want with that?' said Peter, and

shook his head. 'You have enough, I should say, sir, and perhaps more than enough. It might be worth it for a poor fellow; but believe me, it isn't so easy to get hold of, I can tell you.'

'It seems very strange to me that you have never tried to get your hands on some,' continued the captain.

'Ah, but how should that have happened?' asked Peter. 'To scratch about in the hills, as old Joe Haugen did all over Holleia, is not a thing I should care for.'

'But there are other ways to find such riches,' said the captain mysteriously. 'What do you say to making friends with the fairies in the mountains? You have, by my faith, not been such an ill-looking lad in your youth, Peter! You could have made your fortune, sure enough.'

'Ha, ha, ha!' laughed Peter in a subdued tone, apparently pleased with the captain's allusion to his good looks. 'I have never believed in such beings, for I have never seen a troll or a huldre.'

'But there once lived a fairy over in Holleia,' said the captain.

'Oh, that's an old fairytale. I have heard people talk about it, to be sure, but I don't believe there's anything in it,' answered Peter.

'Yes, but you must know something about it for all that, since you have been knocking about on the moors here for so long. You must tell us what you know. My friend here is mad for such stories.'

'Ah, indeed! Well, I don't mind repeating these things but for my part I don't believe a word of them,' Peter assured us, and commenced.

'South of Holleia, there are two mountains – they call them the Big-peak and the Little-peak. There, where you are sitting, you can see a little of that very range of mountains! There are a great many old workings over there, and there is any amount of gold and silver in those mountains, in fact, they say there's no end to the riches there. But it is not an easy job to get at them, for an old witch lives in those peaks. She owns them all, and she broods on them like a dragon – that's what they say, anyhow. She is much richer than the King of Konigsberg. Indeed, once, when the miners had dug out a fearful lot of silver ore, the king went into the mine and said to the people: "Well, I cannot stand this much longer! If you go on at this rate I shall be a poor man. You will ruin me entirely. Why don't you go over to my sister Guri, in the Holleia Peaks? She is ten times richer than I." '

'Guri must be a sister to the Egeberg king, then?' I remarked.

'The Egeberg king! Who's he?' asked Peter. 'He is from Christiania, perhaps?'

I told him the legend of the Egeberg king, and how, in 1814, he had to move to his brother in Konigsberg, as he could not stand all the noise and mining going on in his mountain.

'Ah well, he must be a brother to the Guri I am speaking about,' agreed Peter in good faith. 'I also have heard tell of one who had to move because he couldn't stand the noise. But he lived in these parts. Whether he was the husband of this Guri, or somebody else, I don't know, but he was one of those who lived in the mountain here and had a lot of riches. But this is how it happened! Just about the time they were beginning to mine in the Skaugs moors, there lived a woman called Rönnau Skaugen, over by the brook between Sognedale and Tyristrand. One morning early, when she was standing by the brook rinsing some clothes, she saw such a lot of silver things in the water – plates, dishes, spoons, ladles and all sorts of fine things – lying at the bottom of the brook, glittering and shining in the sunshine. When she saw all these riches, she almost lost her senses: she ran straight home for a tub to take them away in. But when she came back they were all gone, every one of them. There wasn't as much as a silver sixpence left; there was only the clear water which glistened in the sun as it ran over the pebbles. Shortly afterwards they began working the copper mines in the same neighbourhood, and there was such a noise, firing and blasting, early and late, that there was no peace at any time. Late one evening when Rönnau had been down to the brook, she met a big man on a large black horse. He had a whole row of carts after him loaded with all sorts of household effects and furniture, and he also had some cows and sheep with him.

' "Good-evening, Rönnau," he said; "I am moving away."

' "So I see,'" she answered; "but why are you leaving?"

' "Oh, they are making such a noise in the mines here now, that I feel as if my poor head were going to pieces. I can't stand it any longer, so I am moving to my brother Tinn in Thelemarken. But I say, Rönnau," he asked suddenly, "why did you want all my silver things that time you saw them in the brook? If you had been satisfied with what you could have carried in your apron, you could have had that."

'Since that time,' added Peter, 'I have not heard of anybody who has seen anything of this kind in our neighbourhood, either because they have moved away from here or because they keep themselves at home. Such witchcraft has no power now to show itself, because the people don't believe in it any more.'

'Yes, there is more truth in that than you think, my dear friend,' said the captain; 'people who know more than both you and I, say the same. But for all that, you may still run the risk of coming across some of them.'

At the repeated requests of the captain, Peter continued to divert us during the night with legends, tales and stories about his sporting adventures. Now and then the captain would treat us to some of his own experiences on his hunting expeditions, which generally contained some sarcastic reference to one or another of the bears which Peter had missed, at which Peter always assumed a curious grinning smile and scratched his ear. Sometimes he would give me a sly wink with one of his eyes, which seemed to say, 'That was one for you, Peter Sandaker, put that in your pipe and smoke it!'

At midnight we lay down on a couple of benches in front of the fire and refreshed ourselves with a short snooze. When we awoke, Peter said it was time to make a start for the pairing-ground of the capercaillies. It was a cold, sharp morning; there was a thin crust on the snow, so that it crackled beneath our tread. The sky was, however, clear and blue, and a few white clouds which were quietly drifting towards us from the south, predicted an early end to the chilly night air. The moon stood low on the horizon, and instead of lighting us on our nocturnal expedition, it only threw a faint light on the distant hills and the tops of the trees, while it created that mysterious twilight between the tall fir trees which lengthens the shadows interminably, and calls forth ghostly figures between the trunks of the trees, and makes the forest so mysterious, so deep and awe-inspiring.

The robin alone with his soft morning song broke the silence which reigned in the forest.

'There's the bird singing who is the first to wake up in the morning,' said Peter. 'It won't be long now before the whole forest is alive and stirring; we had better hurry on a bit.'

'There's plenty of time, my dear Peter,' said the captain; 'the capercaillie performs best on the hill between here and the Löndals bog, and I don't think we shall have much of the display this morning; it is too cold.'

'We shall have it much warmer as the morning wears on,' answered Peter rather positively; 'there is a southerly draught in the air, and I think we shall have some fine play, as the nights have lately been so chilly. When the sun rises we shall have some splendid play. Only hear the woodcock, how he is roading; he expects fine weather. There is the snipe drumming also. We shall have it fine!' he added, with an air of conviction.

We heard the peculiar note of the woodcock, which resembles the repeated croaking of the frog, followed by a sharp hissing sound, somewhat like the noisy chirping of the wagtail, and by the faint light of the setting moon we saw one shadow after the other of these birds passing over the tops of the trees. We heard the unpleasant braying of the snipe, now near to us, now far off, now high up in the air, now right over our heads, now suddenly close to our ears, now on all sides – still without our ever being able to catch sight of the bird. But the shrill wild cry of the heron overpowered the cries of all the other birds, whom it seemed to terrify; they were silent the moment they heard it, and a silence followed which made the interruption doubly unpleasant. At this moment the woodlark commenced his morning song with his clear ringing notes, which in the darkness of the night reminded us of the bright approaching dawn, and formed a cheerful contrast to the ghostly flight and unpleasant notes of the nocturnal birds.

'There goes the capercaillie bell, as the Swedes call this merry little bird,' said the captain. 'As soon as he starts singing, the capercaillie commences its morning hymn in its roosting-place. Let us remain here a while; we are not far away from the birds that came to roost so late last night. By going nearer we might easily frighten them away.'

After having listened for a few minutes, we heard a

capercaillie calling a couple of hundred paces off.

'I almost think it is the fellow that came last and snapped his beak,' said Peter; 'I really wonder if he won't get a dressing down. The old one hasn't generally a short memory.'

The captain gave me the choice of going in the direction where we heard the bird calling, or of going more to the north where he expected the younger birds were roosting. I chose the first, and the captain went in a northerly direction. Peter and I quietly approached the capercaillie, and carefully avoided making any noise by treading on the snow or the dry crackling branches. Every time we heard the bird commence the first part of his love song we stopped for a moment, but as soon as he had done the gobble and began snapping his beak we advanced rapidly two or three paces each time. When he went on with the first strain again, and while he did the gobble, we remained of course motionless. When we, in this manner, had arrived within a distance of forty or fifty paces from the tree where he was sitting, we heard the flight of another bird, which settled down in the tree with a great noise. The sound of clashing beaks and wings soon told us that our old friend had paid the visit which Peter had predicted to the stranger, his rival, on the morning roost. During the fight, we ran forward a few paces, but a heavy, rushing flight betokened an easy victory, and the stranger flew away. All was now quiet for a time, but a hen was soon heard cackling, and immediately the old capercaillie cock commenced his courting ritual; he went through the first part and did his gobble, but as soon as we moved a foot to get nearer, he flew to another tree, where he commenced his deceitful play anew.

'I thought as much,' said Peter with some vexation. 'Now he is at it again! It's no use whatever to stalk him; one might as well try to stalk the clouds. No, let us go more to the north; there are more birds thereabouts, and I dare say there is at least one among them who dares open his beak, although they are all afraid of that beast there! I wish Old Nick had him.'

'Do you know where the old fellow plays at sunrise?' I asked.

'Yes, of course I do,' answered Peter; 'he plays in a fir tree on a small knoll, just below here in the bog; but it is very difficult to get a shot at him, because the tree is so very high.'

'We will go there,' said I; 'but since you think it advisable, we will first go a little to the north.'

We walked for some distance in this direction, but we did not hear a single bird call. Peter wondered very much what could have become of the birds, and came finally to the conclusion that the fight had frightened them away, or given them such a scare that they dared not open their beaks.

Just as the day was breaking we heard the report of a gun north of Sandtjærn Hill, where Peter told me the captain and he used to have bear-bait set. This place was not far away from his dairy on the mountains or from his home in Sognedale. Soon afterwards we heard another report, which, like its predecessor, Peter declared came from the captain's gun. While we were crossing the bog, on our way to the fir tree Peter had spoken of, and whither he apparently went with little inclination, he broke out afresh in lamentations over the bad sport we had had, and kept on talking to himself in disjointed sentences.

'Only a waste of powder – no, no, the captain is the right sort of man, he is – he has got one, perhaps two – that wasn't Anders' shot at all – that good-for-nothing gun of his – no, there is something like a report in the captain's.'

'Be comforted, Peter,' said I, 'perhaps we shall get the cock of the walk here after all.'

'You must know some queer trick or another then,' answered Peter; 'he is a sly, deep one, and he is shot-proof too, I can tell you.'

When we arrived at the knoll, after having crossed the frozen bog, I took – on account of the considerable distance from which the bird would have to be shot at, if he, as we supposed, would settle in the top of the fir tree – the shot out of my gun, and loaded again with a wire cartridge.

Peter watched this operation, shook his head, and expressed in the following words his want of confidence in it: 'And you think that will help?'

'We shall see,' I answered just as curtly.

The knoll on which we found ourselves appeared like a small island in the big bog. On its summit towered aloft the fir tree which has often been referred to, like a mighty mast, full of woodpeckers' holes. On the eastern side of the knoll was another fir tree, which must have been just as majestic at one time, but was now stooping forward over the bog; the storms had broken its top, and only a few of the lower, almost naked, branches were left, which, like some brawny giant's arms, stretched themselves out against the clear morning sky. The sun was rising; it gilt the hilltops and gradually threw its lustre over the dark pine forests on the mountain slopes. But the Skjœrsjö bog, which in a southerly direction extended so far that the forest at its far end could scarcely be distinguished in the blue hazy mist, was still in the deepest shade. The woodcock, the snipe and other nocturnal birds were all gone to rest; but the merry songsters of the wood now filled the air with their jubilee; the nutcracker began his monotonous clattering, the chaffinches and the wrens sang high in the sky, the black-

cock scolded and blustered loudly, the thrush sang his
mocking songs and libellous ditties about everybody, but
became occasionally a little sentimental and warbled
gently and bashfully some tender stanzas. On the opposite side of the bog a capercaillie was calling in the top of
a fir tree; the hens were making themselves agreeable,
and cackled and snuffled their hoarse nasal sounds, which
to the songbirds would be as unattractive as an old lady's
whisperings of girlish love and soft words would be to us.

In the meantime we were hidden in a close juniper
thicket on the little knoll, and expected the capercaillie
cock every moment; but our old friend tarried a long
time in his harem. At last, just as the sun was gilding the
top of the fir tree, he came flying with a heavy rushing
sound, and settled, not in the tall fir tree above us, but in
the crestless fir, which was leaning over the bog. He was
truly a splendid bird – a noble animal – as he sat there
against the sky on the naked branch, with his shining,
bright green breast glittering in the sunlight. A hen now
came flying and settled in the tree above our heads. At
once the cock began his display; he stuck out his beard,
trailed his wings down by his legs and made, with great
solemnity and wavelike motions of his neck, a few steps
forward on the branch, while he stuck up his tail and
spread it out like a big wheel. I was waiting with my
finger on the trigger for the decisive moment when he
would spread out his wings for flight and thereby give me
a much larger target at which I, at this long distance,
could make a surer shot. But, while the hen continued
her cackle, he had finished his first play and was com-
mencing the gobble of his second when a twig cracked
beneath my feet. The hen uttered a sharp warning cry
but our old friend was in such an ecstasy that he took no
notice of her well-meant warning and was finishing his
love-song when his faithful mistress flew straight at him,

apparently with the intention of pushing him off the branch. This recalled him to his senses, and he spread his wings out to take flight; but my gun was up, and the mighty bird fell head foremost down on the bog. It was an easy death; he only flapped his wings once or twice.

Peter ran and seized the bird. A look of surprise lighted up his face, which soon gave way to a pleased and admiring grin. He shook his head and said: 'I shouldn't have believed it, even if the captain had told me himself, for this is the right bird; I know him by his bill – such a yellow, crooked and thick beak has no other capercaillie hereabout. Look how green he is on the breast, and how his feathers shine! And such a big heavy one!' exclaimed Peter, as with almost childish joy, he weighed the bird in his hand. 'I don't think I am telling a lie when I say he weighs fifteen pounds. That was a shot! But the captain will be glad! Ho, ho, here we are!' he cried, and his cry was re-echoed from all the hills around. The captain soon made his appearance, followed by the boy and the hounds. The captain and the boy carried each a capercaillie.

Peter lifted our prize triumphantly aloft and shouted, while they yet were at some distance – 'It is the old rascal, captain!'

'What do you say?' cried the captain, and came running towards us. 'Is it really the old one? Now, that is a decent day's work, which deserves a glass. Long live all republics of birds! Perish all tyrants!' he exclaimed, as he took the bottle and silver goblet out of his bag and drank to us.

'Did I not say the captain would be pleased?' said Peter with a grin, as he winked with his eye and took a good sup of the goblet which was handed to him. 'There will be different sport about here now, when we have got rid of this devil of a bird.'

After having exchanged accounts about our sport, the hounds were let loose. They soon found scent, and away they went in full cry. The echo repeated their baying over and over again between the hills, and our hearts beat with rapture at this promising sound of fine sport in the early sunny morning.

The Greedy Youngster

Once upon a time there were five women who were in a field reaping corn. None of them had any children, but they were all wishing for a child. All at once they found a big goose egg, almost as big as a man's head.

'I saw it first,' said one. 'I saw it just as soon as you did,' shouted another. 'But I'll have it,' screamed the third, 'I saw it first of all.'

Thus they kept on quarrelling and fighting over the egg, and they were very near tearing each other's hair. But at last they agreed that it should belong to them all, and that they should sit on it as the geese do and hatch a gosling.

The first woman sat on it for eight days, taking it very comfortably and doing nothing at all, while the others had to work hard both for their own and her living.

One of the women began to make some insinuations to her about this.

'Well, I suppose you didn't come out of the egg either before you could chirp,' said the woman who was on the egg. 'But I think there is something in this egg, for I fancy I can hear someone inside grumbling every other moment for: "Herring and soup! Porridge and milk!" You can come and sit for eight days now, and then the others will take it in turns.'

When the fifth and last had sat for eight days, she heard plainly someone inside the egg screeching for 'Herring and soup! Porridge and milk!' And so she made a hole in the shell; but instead of a gosling, out came a baby – but it was awfully ugly, with a big head and a tiny little body. The first thing it screamed out for, as soon as it put its head outside the egg, was 'Herring and soup! Porridge and milk!' And so they called it 'the greedy youngster'.

Ugly as he was, they were fond of him at first; but before long he became so greedy that he ate up all the meat they had. When they boiled a dish of soup or a pot of porridge which they thought would be sufficient for all six, he finished it all by himself. So they would not have him any longer.

'I have not had a decent meal since this changeling crept out of the eggshell,' said one of them, and when the youngster heard that they were all of the same opinion, he said he was quite willing to go his way; if they did not want him, he was sure he did not want them, and with that he left the place.

After a long time he came to a farm where the fields were full of stones, and he went in and asked for a situation. They wanted a labourer on the farm, and the farmer put him to pick up stones from the field. Yes, the youngster went to work and picked up the stones, some of which were so big that they would make many cart-loads; but whether they were big or small, he put them all into his pocket. It did not take him long to finish that job, and he wanted to know what he should do next.

'You will have to get all the stones out of the field,' said the farmer, whereupon the youngster emptied his pockets and threw all the stones in a heap. Then the farmer saw that he had finished the work, and he thought he ought to look well after one who was so strong. 'You must come in and get something to eat,' he said. The youngster thought so too, and proceeded to eat unaided what was prepared both for master and servants; and still he was only half satisfied.

'He is the right sort of man for a labourer, but he is a terrible eater, to be sure,' thought the farmer. 'A man like him would eat a poor farmer out of house and home before anybody knew a word about it.' He had no more work for him he said; it was best for him to go to the king's palace.

The youngster set out for the palace, where he got a place at once. There was plenty of food and plenty of work. He was to be errand boy, and to help the girls to carry wood and water and do other odd jobs. So he asked what he was to do first.

'You had better chop some wood,' they said. Yes, he commenced to chop and cut wood till the splinters flew about him. It was not long before he had chopped up everything in the place, both firewood and timber, both rafters and beams, and when he was done, he came in and asked what he was to do now.

'You can finish chopping the wood,' they said.

'There is no more to chop,' he answered.

That could not be possible, thought the overseer, and had a look in the wood-shed. But yes, the youngster had chopped up everything; he had even cut up the timber and planks in the place. This was vexatious, the overseer said; and then he told the youngster that he should not taste food until he had gone into the forest and cut just as much timber as he had chopped up for firewood.

The youngster went to the forge and got the smith to help him make an axe of five hundredweight of iron, and then he set out for the forest and began to make a regular clearance, not only of the pine and the lofty fir trees, but of everything else which was to be found in the king's forests, and in the neighbours' as well. He did not stop to cut the branches or the tops off, but he left them lying there as if a hurricane had blown them down. He put a sizeable load on the sledge and put all the horses to it, but they could not even move it; so he took the horses by the heads to give the sledge a start, but he pulled so hard that the horses' heads came off. He then turned the horses out of the shafts and drew the load himself.

When he came to the palace, the king and his overseer were standing in the hall to give him a scolding for having destroyed the forest – the overseer had been there and seen what he had been doing. But when the king saw the youngster dragging half the forest after him, he got both angry and afraid; and he thought he had better be a little careful with him, since he was so strong.

'Well, you are a wonderful workman, to be sure,' said the king; 'but how much do you eat at a time, because I suppose you are hungry now?'

Oh, if he was to have a proper meal of porridge, it would take twelve barrels of meal to make it, replied the youngster; but when he had put that away, he could wait a while, of course, for his next meal.

It took some time to boil such a dish of porridge, and meantime he was to bring in a little firewood for the cook. He put a lot of wood on a sledge, but when he was coming through the door with it, he was a little rough and careless again. The frame got almost out of shape, and all the joists creaked; he was very near dragging down the whole palace. When the porridge was nearly ready, they sent him out to call the people home from the fields. He shouted so that the mountains and hills around rang with echoes, and when the people did not come quickly enough for him, he came to blows with them, and killed twelve of them.

'You have killed twelve men,' said the king; 'and you eat for many times twelve; but how many do you do the work of?'

'For many times twelve,' answered the youngster.

When he had finished his porridge, he was to go into

the barn to thresh. He took one of the rafters from the roof and made a flail out of it, and when the roof was about to fall in, he took a big pine tree with branches and all and put it up instead of the rafter. So he went on thrashing the grain and the straw and the hay all together. This was doing more damage than good, for the corn and the chaff flew about together, and a cloud of dust arose over the whole palace.

When he had nearly finished threshing, enemies came into the country, as a war was brewing. Thinking they would surely kill him, the king told the youngster that he should take men with him and go to meet the invaders.

No, he would not have any men with him to be cut to pieces; he would fight by himself, answered the youngster.

'So much the better,' thought the king; 'I shall get rid of him the sooner; but he must have a proper club.'

They sent for the smith; he forged a club which weighed a hundredweight. 'A very nice thing to crack nuts with,' said the youngster. So the smith made one of three hundredweight. 'It would do very well for hammering nails into boots,' was the reaction. Well, the smith could not make a bigger one with the men he had. So the youngster set out for the smithy himself, and made a club that weighed five tons, and it took a hundred men to turn it on the anvil. 'That one might do for lack of a better,' thought the youngster. Then he wanted a bag for his provisions and this they made out of fifteen ox hides; they filled it with food, and away he went down the hill with the bag on his back and the club on his shoulder.

When he came to within sight of the enemy, they sent a soldier to ask him if he was going to fight them.

'Yes; but wait a little till I have had something to eat,' said the youngster. He threw himself down on the grass and began to eat with the big bag of food in front of him. But the enemy would not wait, and commenced to fire at him at once so that bullets rained down on him.

'I don't mind these crowberries a bit,' said the young-ster, and went on eating harder than ever. Neither lead nor iron had any effect upon him, and the food-bag in front of him guarded him against the bullets as if it were a rampart.

So they commenced throwing bombshells and firing cannon at him. He only grinned a little every time he felt them.

'They don't hurt me a bit,' he said. But just then he got a bombshell right down his windpipe. 'Fie,' he shouted, and spat it out again; but then a chain-shot made its way into his butter-can, and another carried away the piece of food he held between his fingers.

That made him angry; he got up and took his big club and struck the ground with it, asking them if they wanted to take the food out of his mouth, and what they meant by blowing crowberries at him with those pea-shooters of theirs. He then struck the ground again till the hills and rocks rattled and shook, and sent the enemy flying in the air like chaff. This finished the war.

When he came home again, and asked for more work, the king was quite taken aback, for he thought he should have got rid of him in the war. He could think of nothing else but to send him on an errand to the devil.

'You had better go to the devil and ask him for my ground-rent,' he said. The youngster took his bag on his back and started at once. He was not long in getting there, but the devil was gone to court, and there was no one at home but his mother, and she said that she had never heard talk of any ground-rent. He had better call again another time.

'Yes, call again tomorrow is always the cry,' he said; but he was not going to be made a fool of, he told her. He was there, and there he would remain till he got the ground-rent. He had plenty of time to wait. But when he had finished all the food in his bag, the time hung heavy on his hands, and so he asked the old lady for the ground-rent again. She had better pay it now, he said.

No, she was going to do nothing of the sort, she said. Her words were as firm as the old fir tree just outside the gates, which was so big that fifteen men could scarcely span it.

But the youngster climbed right up into the top of it and twisted and turned it as if it was a willow, and then he asked her if she was going to pay the ground-rent now.

Yes, she dared not do anything else, and scraped together as much money as he could carry in his bag. He then set out for home with the ground-rent, but as soon as he was gone, the devil came home. When he heard that the youngster had gone off with his bag full of money, he first of all gave his mother a hiding, and then he started after him, thinking he would soon overtake him.

This was an easy matter, for he had nothing to carry, and now and then he used his wings; but the youngster had of course to keep to the ground with his heavy bag. Just as the devil was at his heels, he began to jump and run as fast as he could. He kept his club behind him to keep the devil off, and thus they went along, the youngster holding the handle and the devil trying to catch hold of the other end of it, till they came to a deep valley. There the youngster made a jump across from the top of one hill to the other, and the devil was in such a hurry to follow him that he ran his head against the club and fell down into the valley and broke his leg, and there he lay.

'There is the ground-rent,' said the youngster when he came to the palace, and threw the bag with the money to the king with such a crash that you could hear it all over the hall.

The king thanked him, and appeared to be well pleased,

and promised him good pay and leave of absence if he wished it, but the youngster wanted only more work.

'What shall I do now?' he said.

As soon as the king had had time to consider, he told him that he must go to the hill-troll, who had taken his grandfather's sword. The troll had a castle by the sea, where no one dared to go.

The youngster put some cart-loads of food into his bag and set out again. He travelled both long and far, over woods and hills and wild moors, till he came to the big mountains where the troll, who had taken the sword of the king's grandfather, was living.

But the troll seldom came out in the open air, and the mountain was well closed, and even the youngster was not man enough to get inside.

So he joined a gang of quarrymen who were living at a farm on top of the hill, and who were quarrying stones in the hills about there. They had never had such help before, for he broke and hammered away at the rocks till the mountain cracked, and big stones the size of a house rolled down the hill. But when he rested to get his dinner, for which he was going to have one of the cart-loads in his bag, he found it was all eaten up.

'I have generally a good appetite myself,' said the youngster; 'but the one who has been here can do a trifle more than I, for he has eaten all the bones as well.'

Thus the first day passed; and he fared no better the second. On the third day he set out to break stones again, taking with him the third load of food; but this time he lay down behind the bag and pretended to be asleep. All of a sudden, a troll with seven heads came out of the mountain and began to eat his food.

'It's all ready for me here, and I will eat,' said the troll.

'We will see about that,' said the youngster, jumping up and hitting the troll with his club so that the heads rolled down the hill.

Then he went into the mountain which the troll had come out of and in there stood a horse eating out of a barrel of glowing cinders, and behind it stood a barrel of oats.

'Why don't you eat out of the barrel of oats?' asked the youngster.

'Because I cannot turn round,' said the horse.

'But I will soon turn you round,' said the youngster.

'Rather cut my head off,' said the horse.

So he cut its head off, and the horse turned into a fine handsome fellow. He said he had been bewitched, and taken into the mountain and turned into a horse by the troll. He then helped the youngster to find the sword that the troll had hidden at the bottom of the bed in which the old mother of the troll lay asleep and snoring hard.

So they set out for home by water, but when they had got some distance out to sea the old mother came after them. As she could not overtake them, she lay down and began to drink the sea, and she drank till she dropped but she could not drink the sea dry, and so she burst.

When they came to land, the youngster sent word that the king should arrange to fetch the sword. He sent four horses, but no, they could not move it; he sent eight, and he sent twelve; but the sword remained where it was. They were not able to stir it from the spot. But the youngster took it and carried it up to the palace alone.

The king could not believe his eyes when he saw the youngster back again. He appeared, however, to be pleased to see him, and promised him land and riches. When the youngster wanted more work, the king told him he would like him to go to an enchanted castle he had, where no one dared to live, and stay there until he had built a bridge over the sound, so that people could get across to the castle.

If he was able to do this he would reward him handsomely, yes, he would even give him his daughter in marriage, said he.

'Well, I think I can do it,' said the youngster.

No one had ever got away alive; those who had got as far as the castle, lay there killed and torn to pieces as small as barley, and the king felt sure he would never see him again.

But the youngster started on his expedition; he took with him the bag of food, a crooked, twisted block of a fir tree, an axe, a wedge, some chips of the fir root and the small pauper boy from the palace.

When he came to the sound, he found the river full of ice and the current running as strong as in a waterfall but he thrust his legs straight in and waded till he got safe across.

When he had warmed himself and had something to eat, he began to drowse but was aroused by a terrible noise, as if someone were turning the castle upside down. The door burst wide open, and he saw nothing but a gaping jaw extending from the threshold up to the lintel.

'There is a mouthful for you,' said the youngster, and threw the pauper boy into the swallow; 'taste that! But let me see now who you are! Perhaps you are an old acquaintance?'

And so it was; it was the devil who was about again.

They began to play cards, for the devil wanted to try and win back some of the ground-rent which the youngster had got out of his mother by threats, when he was sent by the king to collect it; but the youngster was always the fortunate one, for he put a cross on the back of all the good cards, and when he had won all the money which the devil had upon him, the devil had to pay him out of the gold and silver which was in the castle.

Suddenly the fire went out, so they could not tell one

card from another.

'We must chop some wood now,' said the youngster, driving the axe into the fir block and forcing the wedge in; but the twisted, knotty block would not split, although the youngster worked as hard as he could with the axe.

'They say you are strong,' he said to the devil. 'Just spit on your hands, stick your claws in and tear away, and let me see what you are made of.'

The devil put both his fists into the split and pulled as hard as he could, whereupon the youngster suddenly struck the wedge out and the devil stuck fast in the block. To add insult to injury, the youngster let him have a taste of the butt end of his axe on his back. The devil begged and prayed so nicely to be let loose, but the youngster would not listen to anything of the kind unless he promised that he would never come there any more and create any disturbance. He also had to promise that he would build a bridge over the sound, so that people could pass over it at all times of the year, and that it would be ready when the ice was gone.

'They are very hard conditions,' said the devil, but there were no two ways about it – if he wanted to be set free, he would have to promise it. He bargained, however, that he should have the first soul that went across the bridge. That was to be the toll.

Yes, he could have that, said the youngster. So the devil was let loose, and he started home. But the youngster lay down to sleep, and slept till far into the day.

When the king came to see if he was cut and chopped into small pieces, he had to wade through all the money before he came to his bedside. There was money in heaps and in bags which reached far up the wall, and the youngster lay in bed asleep and snoring hard.

'Lord help me and my daughter,' said the king when he saw that the youngster was alive.

Well, all was good and well done, that no one could deny; but there was no hurry talking of the wedding before the bridge was ready. One day, however, the bridge stood ready, and the devil was there waiting for the toll which he had bargained for.

The youngster wanted the king to go with him and try the bridge, but the king was not enthusiastic. So he mounted a horse himself, and put the fat dairy-maid from the palace on the pommel in front of him – a girl who looked almost like a big fir block – and rode over the bridge, which thundered under the horse's feet.

'Where is the toll? Where have you got the soul?' cried the devil.

'Why, inside this fir-block,' said the youngster; 'if you want it you will have to spit on your hands and take it.'

'No, many thanks! if she does not come to me, I am sure I shan't take her,' said the devil. 'You got me once into a pinch, and I'll take care you don't get me into another,' and with that he flew straight home to his old mother, and since that time he has never been heard or seen thereabouts.

The youngster went home to the palace and asked for the reward the king had promised him. When he saw that the king wanted to get out of it, and would not stick to what he had promised, the youngster said it was best he got a good bag of food ready for him, and he would take his reward himself.

Yes, the king would see to that. When the bag was ready the youngster asked the king to come outside the door. The youngster then gave the king an almighty kick, which sent him flying up in the air. The bag he threw after him that he might not be without food, and if he has not come down again, he is floating about with his bag between heaven and earth to this very day.

✳

The Seven Fathers in the House

There was once upon a time a man who was travelling about, and he came at length to a big and fine farm; it was such a fine mansion that it might well have been a little palace. 'It would be a nice thing to get a night's rest here,' said the man to himself, when he came inside the gate. Close by an old man with grey hair and beard was chopping wood.

'Good-evening, father,' said the traveller; 'can I get lodgings here tonight?'

'I am not the father in the house,' said the old man. 'Go into the kitchen and speak to my father!'

The traveller went into the kitchen; there he met a man who was still older, and he was on his knees in front of the hearth, blowing into the fire. 'Good-evening, father; can I get lodgings here tonight?' asked the traveller.

'I am not the father in the house,' said the old man; 'But go in and speak to my father; he is in the parlour.'

So the traveller went into the parlour and spoke to an old man who was sitting by the table; he was much older than the other two, and he sat there with chattering teeth, shaking, and reading in a big book, almost like a little child. 'Good-evening, father; can you give me lodgings here tonight?' said the man.

'I am not the father in the house; but speak to my father over there, he who sits on the bench,' said the man who was sitting at the table with chattering teeth, and shaking and shivering.

So the traveller turned to the old man who was sitting on the bench; he was getting a pipe of tobacco ready; but he was so bent with age, and his hands shook so much, that he was scarcely able to hold the pipe. 'Good-evening, father,' said the traveller; 'can I get lodgings here tonight?'

'I am not the father in the house,' said the old, bent-up man; 'but speak to my father, who is in the bed over yonder.'

The traveller went to the bed, and there lay an old, old man, and the only thing about him that seemed to be alive was a pair of big eyes.

'Good-evening, father; can I get lodgings here to-night?' said the traveller.

'I am not the father in the house; but speak to my father, who lies in the cradle yonder,' said the man with the big eyes.

Yes, the traveller went to the cradle; lying there was a very old man, so shrivelled up, that he was not larger than a baby, and one could not have told that there was life in him if it had not been for a sound in his throat now and then.

'Good-evening, father; can I get lodgings here to-night?' said the man.

It took some time for the very old man to reply that, like the others, he was not the father in the house. 'But speak to my father; he is hanging up in the horn against the wall there.'

The traveller stared round the walls, and at last he caught sight of the horn; but when he looked to see if there was anyone in it, there was scarcely anything to be seen but a lump of some white substance, which had the appearance of a man's face. Then he was so frightened, that he cried aloud: 'Good-evening, father; will you give me lodgings here tonight?'

There was a sound like a little tom-tit's chirping; he was only just able to make out the words, 'Yes, my child.'

And now a table came in which was covered with the costliest dishes and with ale and brandy; and when he had eaten and drunk, in came a good bed with reindeer skins; and the traveller was very glad indeed that he at last had found the right father in the house.

❄

Brave Old Bruin

Once upon a time there was a farmer who went into the hills for a load of leaves for his cattle in the winter. He soon found a fine heap of leaves so backed the horse and sledge close to it, went to the other side and began to shovel them on to the sledge. But under the heap there was a bear, who had made his lair there for the winter, and when he felt someone stirring round about him, he made a jump and came right out on to the sledge. When the horse got wind of Bruin he was frightened and took off as if he were stealing both the bear and the sledge, so that away they went down the hill ten times as fast as they came up. Bruin has the reputation of being a brave fellow, but this time, to tell the truth, he felt somewhat fright-ened as he sat there on the sledge. He stuck to it as well as he could, but gave a timid look round now and then to see if there was any place where he could throw himself off with safety; but he was not used to sledge-driving, and he thought he had better not risk it.

When he had driven some distance he met a pedlar.

'Where is the sheriff off to today?' said the pedlar; 'he must have a long way and little time, since he is driving so fast.'

But Bruin did not say a word, for he had more than enough to do to hold on. In a little while he met a beggar-woman. She greeted him, nodded her head, and begged for a penny in God's name. Bruin said nothing, but stuck to the sledge, and away he went as fast as ever.

When he came a little further down the road he met Reynard the Fox.

'Hallo, are you out taking a drive?' shouted Reynard. 'Wait a bit; let me sit behind, and be your postboy!'

Bruin made no reply, but held on to the sledge, and the horse ran as fast as his legs would carry him.

'All right!' shouted Reynard after him, 'if you won't take me with you I tell you this, that although you drive like a travelling gent today, all in your furs, you'll hang tomorrow with your back bare.'

Bruin did not hear a word of what Reynard said; he never stopped a moment. But when the horse came into the farmyard, he galloped right through the stable door at such a speed, that he left both harness and sledge behind; and Bruin – why he knocked his skull against the top of the door, and there he lay, dead on the spot.

In the meantime the farmer went on turning over one layer of leaves after another, till he thought he had loaded his sledge; but when he came round to tie the rope round the load, he saw neither horse nor sledge. So he had to tramp along the road looking for his horse.

In a while he met the pedlar. 'Have you met a horse and sledge?' said the farmer to the pedlar.

'No,' said the pedlar, 'but I met the sheriff down the road. He was in such a hurry, he was surely going to serve a writ on someone.'

Shortly he met a beggar-woman. 'Have you seen a horse and sledge on the road?' he said to the beggar-woman.

'No,' said the beggar-woman, 'but I met the parson down below here; he was surely going to some sick person who was dying, for he travelled so fast, and he was driving in a common sledge.'

In a while the farmer met the fox. 'Have you seen a horse and sledge?' asked the farmer.

'Yes,' answered Reynard, 'but old Bruin sat on the sledge and drove just as if he had stolen both horse and turn-out.'

'Bad luck to him, the rascal!' said the farmer. 'I suppose he will drive my horse to death.'

'If he does, take and skin him and roast him on the cinders,' said Reynard; 'but if you should get your horse back again, you might give me a ride over the mountain one day; I have such a mind to try what it's like to have four legs before me.'

'What will you give for the lift?' asked the farmer.

'Oh, anything you like, wet or dry,' said the fox; 'you'll always get as much out of me as old Bruin, for he is generally a rough fellow to deal with, especially when he goes a-driving and sticks to the horse's back.'

'Well, yes. You shall have a lift over the mountain,' said the farmer, 'if you'll meet me here tomorrow about this time.'

He guessed that Reynard was going to make a fool of him and play some of his tricks upon him, so next day, having recovered his horse and sledge, he set off with a loaded gun. When Reynard came, thinking to get the drive promised him for nothing, the farmer shot him dead, and flayed him as he had the bear. And so he had both bear-skin and fox-skin.

※

Mother Bertha's Stories

Reynard had been ringed and shot; his funeral was celebrated at the bailiff's, and in the evening the festivities wound up with a dance. In consideration of the day's work, the acquired glory and the five miles' journey I had before me, we got permission to break up soon after eleven, and the bailiff offered me in the bargain a horse and sledge. It was an offer worthy of all honour; but as the road was twice as long as the way I had come on my snowshoes I preferred this direct route, and with the fox and the gun on my back, and the staff in my hand, I set out homewards. The snow was in splendid condition for my mode of travelling; there had been a little sunshine during the day and the chill of the evening had formed a light crust on the deep snow; the moon shone brightly, and the stars were twinkling in the sky.

What more could I desire? Away I went, down the hills, over the fields, through the woods and past the erect, silvery beech trees, the crowns of which formed lofty, sparkling domes of a white, glistening tissue, under which the owls sat relating their terrible stories in the peaceful night. The hare cried and complained of the terrible February cold and the disgusting chatter of the owls; the fox, out on love-adventures, abused his rivals and uttered scoffing screams and howls.

I kept on the side of the parish road for some distance until a person in a big fur coat and driving in a sledge came up with me. Seeing by the gun and the fox, which I carried on my back, that I was a sportsman, he entered into conversation with me. If I hurried down to the river, he said, I should be sure to fall in with a pack of wolves, for just as he was driving up the hill close to the sound, they had started up the river on the ice. I thanked him for the information, and made for the river, coming out at a point where a pine wood stretched itself down to the water's edge, and prevented a full view of the river. I saw no signs of the wolves. I shot, however, down the hill on my snowshoes, sweeping through the wood in the shadow of the pine trees with the protruding alder branches continually slapping me in the face. It was impossible for me to distinguish any object as I sped on with the swiftness of an arrow, and before I knew where I was I had run against the stump of a tree. I lay with my head buried in the snow, and with one of my snowshoes broken.

When I got on my feet, I felt such a pain in one of my legs that I could scarcely stand. I crept about on my knees for some time till I at last found my gun, which was buried in the snow. I had scarcely lain down in wait near the bank of the river, before the pack of wolves came leisurely along on the ice; there were five of them altogether. I waited with a sportsman's impatience; when they were about forty paces distant, I put my gun up and fired, first one barrel, which misfired, and then the other, which went off; but the bullet hit the tops of the pine trees on the other side of the river, and the wolves set off at full speed with their tails straight out behind them.

I rose rather annoyed; the pain in my leg had grown more intense, but with the help of my gun as a stick, I dragged myself out on to the river to see whereabouts I really was. To my great joy I saw a column of smoke ascending between the tops of the trees on the opposite bank, and I also discerned the roof of a cottage amid the pines. I knew the place now: it was Tuppenhaug, a small farm held by a tenant on the estate where I lived at that time. With great difficulty I crawled up the steep incline, which might have been a couple of hundred paces in length, and had the satisfaction of seeing the light from a big fire shining through the windows. I limped towards the door, raised the latch and entered the room, just as I was, covered all over with snow.

'Bless me, who can that be!' cried old Mother Bertha in a great fright, and dropped a leg of dried mutton which she had on her knee. She was sitting on a small stool in front of the fire, cutting herself some slices off the mutton.

'Good-evening, Bertha,' I said; 'don't be afraid! You know me, I think!'

'Ah, is it the student, who is out so late? I really was frightened; you looked so white, with all that snow on you, and it's so late,' answered old Bertha, and rose from her seat.

I told her of my mishap, and asked her to call one of the lads and send him up to the house for a horse and sledge.

'Well, it is, as I say, that the wolves take their revenge,' she muttered to herself. 'They wouldn't believe it when they chased and ringed them last year, and Peter broke his leg; now he knows that they take their revenge.

'Some of the neighbours have been carting timber from the river lately,' she continued, as she went over to the bed in the corner of the room, where the family lay sleeping and snoring in chorus, 'so there is a good road across the fields on the snow. Here, Little Ola, get up and go for a horse for the student! Do you hear, Ola!'

'Oh, yes!' said Little Ola through his nose, and began putting his clothes on. But he enjoyed a good sleep too well to be easily disturbed. Rubbing his eyes, gaping, gasping and asking silly questions, it was only when he had managed to extricate himself from the entangled bedclothes and specimens of humanity in the bed, and got his trousers and jacket on, that he could really understand what he was to do. The promise of a sixpence seemed, however, to impart some clearness to his comprehension and even dispel his fear at the thought of passing the birch tree on the road where Ole Askerud had hanged himself. While this was going on between the fair-haired Ola and old Bertha, I took a survey of the room and its contents – looms, spinning-wheels, chairs, brooms, buckets and half-finished axe-handles, the hens on their perch behind the door, the old musket under the roof, the long poles hanging from the rafters groaning under the weight of steaming stockings, and hundreds of other things, which I will not tire my readers by enumerating.

When the boy at last was gone, old Bertha seated herself down by the hearth. She was in her holiday dress, the one worn by old people in her native district, Hadeland, where she came from when she moved to Romerike – a blue jacket trimmed with braid, black kilted skirt and cap with tassels and bows. Her sharp unwavering eyes with their irregular pupils, her projecting chin, her broad nose, and her yellow complexion gave Bertha's face a strange, Oriental, almost witch-like appearance; and this was not to be wondered at, because she was considered the foremost wise woman for a good many miles around.

I wondered that she still was up, and I asked if she expected visitors, since she had her best clothes on.

'No, not that exactly,' she answered, 'but I have been up in Ullensogn to see to a woman who suffered from a wasting disease, and from that place I was fetched to a youngster who had the rickets. I had to read and melt lead over that child. I have only just returned home, although they drove me as far as the innkeeper's.'

'And if I recollect rightly, Bertha, you can cure sprains as well?' I asked, as seriously as possible.

'Oh yes, I think I can, sir, for our neighbour didn't get well before I came to her, although the doctor and Mother Kari, from the farm just below here, had been experimenting on her leg,' she said with a wicked expression; 'and if you think it will do any good,' she continued, with a suspicious look, 'I don't think it would hurt your foot to read over a little brandy and put that on it.'

'Yes, do so, Bertha, read over the brandy and try it; it's sure to do me good,' I said, hoping to become initiated into one or other of the mysteries of the art of healing by magic. Bertha fetched a square, bluish-looking flask and a glass with a wooden stem from her flower-painted cupboard, poured out the brandy, put the glass on the hearth by her side, unfastened my snowshoes and pulled my boot off. She then began making crosses over the brandy and whispering into it, but as she was rather deaf herself, she did not adjust her voice to my ear, and so I heard the whole formula:

> 'As I was riding through a gate,
> My black horse chanced to get a sprain,
> Flesh placed 'gainst flesh and blood
>   against blood
> Have made my black horse well again.'

Her voice now subsided to an inaudible whisper. The end of the verse consisted of a repetition of the word 'fie', which she hurled to the four corners of the world.

During the height of this incantation she had risen from her seat; now she sat down again by the hearth. The cold brandy, which she presently poured over my foot, had a pleasant cooling effect.

'I think it has already done me good, Bertha,' said I;

'but tell me, what was that you read over the brandy?'

'No, I dare not tell you that, for you might tell the parson and the doctor,' she said with a sly grin, which apparently meant that she did not care much for either of them; 'and I had to promise the one who taught it to me that I would not tell any human being except my own kin. I have sworn to it with such a frightful oath, that I hope I shall never utter anything so frightful again.'

'Well, there is no use asking you any more about that, Bertha,' said I, 'but I suppose it's no secret, who taught you the art? He must have been a regular sorcerer.'

'Yes, you are quite right there; he was a regular sorcerer – he was my mother's own brother,' she answered. 'He could read over and cure all sorts of ailments and sprains, stop bleeding, melt lead, and tell of stolen goods; and to tell the truth, he knew also a little about witchcraft, and could afflict people with evil. It was he who taught me! But wise as he was, he could not protect himself 'gainst witchcraft for all that!'

'How?' I asked, 'was he bewitched then? Was he possessed?'

'No, not exactly,' answered Bertha. 'But something happened to him, and afterwards he seemed to be quite another man for some time. He must have been spell-bound by the huldre. You don't think it's true, I suppose,' she said with a searching look; 'but it was my mother's brother, as I told you, and I have heard him tell it and swear to it over a hundred times.

'He lived at Knœ, in Hurdale, and he was often up in the mountain cutting wood and timber; and when he was working up there, he used to live there altogether; he built himself a hut of pine branches, and lighted a fire in front of it at night, and there he used to sleep. He and two others were once living thus in the forest. He had just felled a big tree, and sat resting himself on it, when a ball of wool came rolling down a bare part of the rock right before his feet. He thought it was very strange; he was afraid to pick up the ball. It would have been a good thing for him if he never had touched it.

'But he looked up the mountain, as he wanted to see where it came from, and on the top of a rock a lassie sat and knitted. She was so fair and so lovely that the air seemed to shine round her. "Bring me that ball of wool," she said. He did so, and remained standing near her and looking at her. He thought he never should tire of looking at her; she seemed so lovely to him. But he had to take his axe at last and begin cutting trees again.

'When he had been working away for some time, he looked up to see her but she had gone. He could not help thinking of her all day; it seemed very strange to him, and he did not know what to think about it. When the evening came, and he and his two comrades were going to bed, he wanted to lie between them for safety's sake; but there was not much help in that, I have to tell you, for during the night the huldre came and took him away with her. He had to go, whether he liked or not. So they came into the mountain, where he found everything so splendid that he had never seen anything so grand before, and he never could describe it properly. He was three days with the huldre. The third night he awoke and found himself in bed between his two comrades again. They thought he had been home for provisions, and he told them that he had. But he was not quite in his right senses afterwards; just as he was sitting down, he would jump up and run away; he was spellbound, I can tell you.

'A good while after that he was up in the forest busy splitting wood for fencing. He was driving a wedge into a big log, when, as he thought, his wife came up to him with his dinner. It was cream porridge, floating in butter. She brought it in a pail, which was so bright that it shone like silver. She sat down on the log, while he put his axe aside and seated himself on a stump near her; it was then he noticed that she had a cow's tail which hung down into the cleft in the log.

'Now you may easily suppose that he did not touch the porridge, but he sat joking and playing with the wedge, until it came out and the tail was nipped by the log; and at the same time he managed to write a sacred name on the pail.

'The huldre took to her heels then, you may be sure; she jumped up in such a hurry that the tail came right off and stuck in the log and she was gone – he did not see what became of her. The pail was only of bark, and there was nothing but dirt in it. Since that time he scarcely ever dared to go into the wood, for he was afraid she would have her revenge upon him.

'But four or five years after that, a horse of his ran away from the farm, and he had to go himself and look for it. All of a sudden, while he was walking through the forest, he found himself inside a hut with some people, but he never knew how he came there. An ugly old hag was walking about the room, tidying it up, and in a corner sat a child, who might be about four years old. The woman took the beer-tankard and went over to the child with it and said: "Go and give your father a drink!" He got so frightened that he took to his heels, and since then he has never seen or heard of her or the youngster; but he was always queer and confused after that.'

'Yes, but he must have been a fool,' I said; 'he couldn't have been very wise if he couldn't look after himself better. But that about the ball of wool was very amusing.'

Bertha agreed, but insisted he was the wisest man for many miles around. While we were sitting and chatting about this, I asked Bertha to bring me my game-bag, and when I had filled my pipe she gave me a splinter of wood to light it with and commenced a new story, which I had heard she knew.

'One summer, long, long ago, the Melbustad people sent their cattle up to their dairy in the Halland Hills. But before long the cattle began to be so restless that it was impossible to manage them. They set one young lass after the other to watch them, but there was no peace to be had till they got a young woman who had just been engaged. The cattle suddenly became quiet, and it was no trouble to look after them after that time. She was there all by herself with the exception of a dog. She was sitting in the dairy one afternoon, when her sweetheart, as she thought, came in and sat beside her and began speaking about their wedding. But she sat quite silent and made no answer, for she began to feel so strange. By and by more people came in, and they began to lay the table and put all sorts of dishes and silver plate on it. The bridesmaids brought in the bridal crown, the silver ornaments, and a fine wedding gown, which they put on her. They put the crown on her head, as was usual at that time, and on her fingers they put rings.

'She thought she knew the people who were there; they were farmers' wives, and some girls of her own age were there also. But the dog must have noticed that there was something wrong. He set off for Melbustad, and began whining and barking, and gave them no peace till they showed signs of going back with him.

'Her sweetheart took his rifle and set out for the dairy; when he came to the slope in front of it, he saw a number of saddled horses about the place. He stole up to the house and looked through the door, which was ajar, and he saw all the people who were sitting in the room. He soon guessed that it was all witchcraft, and so he fired his gun over the roof of the dairy. The next moment the door flew wide open, and a number of balls of wool, each one bigger than the other, came rolling out of the door between his legs. When he went in he found his sweetheart in her wedding-dress, and with her crown on; all she lacked was a ring on her little finger.'

' "But, good heavens, what does all this mean?" he asked, and looked round. All the silver plate was yet on the table, but all the fine dishes had turned to moss and mushrooms, dirt and toads, frogs and all such things.

' "What's the meaning of all this?" he repeated. "You are sitting here dressed like a bride."

' "How can you ask such a question?" said she. "You have been sitting here and talking to me about the wedding all the afternoon."

' "You are mistaken, I only came this minute," he said. "It must have been someone who had taken on my appearance."

'She then began to come back to her senses; but she was not quite herself for some time afterwards. She told him that she thought she had plainly seen him and their relations and neighbours amongst the people who were there. He took her home at once, and that there should come no more witchery to her, they were married there and then while she was still dressed in the finery of the fairies. The crown and the dress were hung up at Melbustad, and they say they are there to this day.'

'But I have heard that this happened in Valders, Bertha,' said I.

'No, this happened exactly as I told you in Halland,' she answered, 'but when I was at home, I heard someone from Valders speak of something which had taken place there, and which I'll now tell you about.'

'On one of the farms in Valders there was a girl called Barbro, and she was up at the dairy, sitting at her work, when she suddenly heard someone shouting from inside the hill: "King Haaken, King Haaken!"

' "Yes," answered King Haaken, till it sounded all over the hills.

' "King Haaken, my son, will you get married?" it cried again inside the hill.

' "Yes, that I will," said King Haaken, "if I can have Barbro in the dairy over yonder!"

' "Yes, yes, we'll see to that," Barbro heard the voice in the hill answer, and she got so frightened that she did not know what to do.

'Before long a lot of people came into the room, one after the other, carrying food and drink on silver dishes and in silver jugs, and a wedding dress with crown and brooches and other such finery. They commenced laying the table and some began dressing her for the wedding. She felt as if she could not resist them.

'This girl also had a sweetheart and he happened to be out shooting on the mountain. But suddenly such a fear came over him that he seemed as if he must go to the dairy. When he came in sight of the house, he saw a number of black horses with old-fashioned saddles and harness about, and he soon guessed what was going on. He stole round to a small window, and looking in, he saw the whole company; King Haaken was the bridegroom and the bride was ready dressed.

' "I don't think there is anything else to be done now except to turn her eyes," said one of the bridesmaids.

'The lad thought it was high time to put a stop to all this, and he took a silver button, which had come down to him, put it in his rifle and fired right at King Haaken so that he fell. But the wedding guests rushed out taking the body of King Haaken with them. The food had turned into moss and toads, which jumped away and hid themselves. The only things left were the wedding dress and a silver dish – and they are still to be seen at the farm.'

Mother Bertha told me many other stories till we

heard the noise of the sledge in the snow and the horses panting outside the door. I put some coins into Bertha's hand for her advice and attention, and in a quarter of an hour I was at home.

A bandage of vinegar and cold water soon put my foot right; but when Mother Bertha one day came into the kitchen and was appropriating to herself all the honour of my rapid cure by her art, the children could not restrain themselves. They shouted into her ears the incantation verse which I had taught them, and asked her if she believed that a drop of brandy and her nonsense could cure a sprain. This put her on her guard and although she told me many a wonderful story after that time I never succeeded with all my cunning and persuasion in bringing Bertha Tuppenhaug to lift a corner of that icy veil in which she shrouded the mysteries of her miraculous cures.

❄

The Smith and the Devil

Once upon a time, in those days when the saints used to
wander about on earth, two of them came to a smith. He
had made a bargain with the devil that he should belong
to him after seven years, if during that time he was to be
the master over all masters in his profession. Both he and
the devil had put their names to this contract. So the
smith wrote with great letters over the smithy door:
'Here lives the master over all masters.'

When the two saints saw this, they went in to the
smith, and the elder asked him: 'Who are you?'

'Read what is written over the door,' answered the
smith; 'but perhaps you cannot read writing, so you had
better wait till someone comes by who can help you.'

Before the saint could answer him a man came with his
horse, which he asked the smith to shoe for him.

'Will you let me shoe it?' asked the saint.

'You may try,' said the smith; 'you cannot do it so
badly that I won't be able to put it right again.'

The saint went out and took one leg off the horse and
put it in the fire on the forge and made the shoe red hot;
he then sharpened the points, clenched the nails, and put
the leg back in its place again. When he had done with
that leg, he did the same with the other fore-leg; when
he had restored that to its place, he took the hind legs,
first the right and then the left, put them in the fire,
made the shoes red hot, sharpened the points and

clenched the nails, and then he put them on the horse again. The smith stood and looked on all the while. 'You are not such a bad smith after all,' he said.

'Ah, you think so,' said the saint.

Just then the smith's mother came across to the smithy and asked him to come home and eat his dinner; she was very old, and had a crooked back and big wrinkles in her face, and she was scarcely able to walk.

'Take notice of what you now will see,' said the saint. He took the woman, put her in the fire, and forged a young, lovely maiden out of her.

'I say what I said before,' said the smith, 'you are not at all a bad smith. You will find over my door: "Here lives the master over all masters," but for all that, I now see that one learns as long as one lives' – and with that he went home and ate his dinner.

As soon as he came back to the smithy, a man came riding up who wanted to have his horse shod.

'I shall soon do that for you,' said the smith; 'I have just learned a new way to shoe horses, and a very good one it is when the days are short.' With that, he commenced cutting and hacking away at the horse's legs till he got them all off – 'for I don't see the use of going forwards and backwards with one at a time,' he said – and put them in the fire as he had seen the saint do. He put plenty of coals on, and let his boy work the bellows smartly; but it went as one might expect – the legs were burnt up, and the smith had to pay for the horse. This was not exactly to his liking, but at that moment a poor old woman, who went about begging, came past, and he thought if one thing does not succeed another may. So he took the old woman and put her in the fire, and although she cried and begged for her life, it was of no use. 'You don't know what is good for you, although you are so old,' said the smith; 'I will make a young woman of you in half a minute, and I shan't charge as much as a penny for the job.'

He fared no better with the poor old woman than with the horse's legs. Just then the saints came round again to him. 'That was ill done,' said the one saint.

'Oh, I don't think there are many who will be asking after her,' answered the smith; 'but it is a great shame that the devil doesn't hold to what is written over the door.'

'If you might have three wishes from me,' said the saint, 'what would you wish for yourself?'

'Try me,' answered the smith, 'and you will get to know.'

The saint then gave him three wishes.

'First of all, I wish that when I ask anybody to climb up into the pear-tree just outside the smithy, he will sit there till I myself ask him to come down again,' said the smith. 'Secondly, I wish that anyone I ask to sit down in the armchair in the smithy there, remain in it till I myself ask him to get up; and, last of all, I wish that if I ask anybody to creep into the steel-ring purse which I have in my pocket, he will remain there till I give him leave to creep out again.'

'You have wished like a foolish man,' said the other saint. 'First of all you should have wished for leave to get into paradise.'

'I dared not ask for that,' said the smith, and bade the saints farewell.

Well, days came and days passed and, when the time was up, the devil came to fetch the smith according to the agreement.

'Are you ready now?' he said, as he put his nose in at the door of the smithy.

'Well, yes; but I want to finish the head of this nail first,' said the smith; 'just climb up into the pear tree and take a pear. You must be both hungry and thirsty after your journey.'

The devil thanked him for the kind offer, and climbed up into the tree.

'Now that I think of it,' said the smith, 'I don't think I shall get this head finished for the next four years, for this iron is so terribly hard. You can't come down in that time, but you may sit there and rest yourself.' The devil begged and prayed that he might have leave to come down again, but all in vain. At last he offered to promise that he would not come back till the four years were out, whereupon the smith said, 'Well, on that condition, you may come down.'

When the time was up, the devil came again to fetch the smith.

'You are ready now, I suppose?' he said. 'I think you have had time to finish the head of that nail by now '

'Yes, I have finished the head, of course,' answered the smith; 'but still you have come a trifle too early, because I have not sharpened the point yet; such hard iron I have never in my life worked at before. While I hammer down the point of the nail, you might as well sit down in my armchair and rest yourself, for I suppose you are pretty tired.'

The devil thanked him for his kindness, and sat down in the armchair; but no sooner had he sat down for a good rest than the smith told him that, taking everything into consideration, he could not get the point properly sharpened in less than four years. The devil at first begged very prettily to be let out of the chair, but after a time he grew angry and began to threaten. The smith excused himself the best way he could, but said it was all the fault of the iron, for it was really so terribly hard. At least the devil had the consolation of being able to sit very comfortably in the armchair knowing that in four years' time the smith would let him out exactly to the minute. There was no other help for it, the devil had to promise that he would not come to fetch the smith till the four years were out. When he did so the smith said: 'Well, on that condition you may go,' and away the devil went as fast as he could.

In four years' time the devil came again to fetch the smith.

'You are ready now, of course?' said the devil, as he put his nose in at the door of the smithy.

'Ready, quite ready,' answered the smith; 'we can start when you like. But there is one thing,' he continued, 'which I have been meaning to ask you for a long time. Is it true, what they say, that the devil can make himself as small as he likes?'

'Yes, of course,' answered the devil.

'Ah, perhaps you could do me the favour to creep into this steel-ring purse and see if there are any holes at the bottom,' said the smith; 'I am so afraid I shall lose my money for the journey.'

'Oh, yes, with pleasure,' said the devil, and made himself small and crept into the purse. But he had scarcely got inside when the smith closed the purse.

'It is safe and sound everywhere,' said the devil inside the purse.

'I am glad to hear you say that,' answered the smith; 'but it is better to be prudent beforehand than wise afterwards. I think I will weld the joints a little better together, just for safety's sake you know,' and with that he put the purse in the fire and made it red hot.

'Oh dear! oh dear!' cried the devil. 'Are you mad? Don't you know I am inside the purse?'

'Yes, but I can't help you,' said the smith. 'There's an old saying, that one must "strike while the iron is hot",' and so he took his big sledge-hammer, put the purse on the anvil, and hammered away as hard as he could.

'Oh dear! oh dear! oh dear!' screamed the devil inside the purse. 'Dear friend, do let me out and I shall never come back again.'

'Well, I think the joints are pretty well welded together now,' said the smith, 'so you may come out again.' With this he opened the purse, and the devil rushed away in such a hurry that he did not even look behind him.

Sometime after this, the smith began thinking that he had perhaps done a foolish thing by making the devil his enemy. 'For suppose the saints above won't have me,' he said, 'I may run the risk of being homeless altogether, since I have fallen out with the old man down below.' He thought it would be as well to try and get into one of the two places at once, better early than late; and so he took his sledge-hammer on his shoulder and started. When he had gone some distance, he came to a place where the road divided into two – one leading to paradise and the other to the devil.

Just at this point he overtook a tailor, who was hurrying along with his smoothing-iron in his hand

'Good-day,' said the smith, 'where are you off to?'

'To paradise, if I can get in there,' answered the tailor; 'and you?'

'Well, I shan't have the pleasure of your company for long then,' answered the smith; 'I have made up my mind to try the other place first, because I happen to know the old man a little already.'

So they bade one another farewell, and each went his way. But the smith was a strong, powerful man, and he walked much faster than the tailor, so it did not take him long to get to his destination. He told the gatekeeper to go and tell his master that there was someone outside who wished to speak with him.

'Go and ask who he is,' said the devil to the gatekeeper, who went out and asked the smith.

'Give your master my compliments, and tell him that it is the smith who has that purse which he knows of,' said the smith; 'and just ask him kindly to let me in at once, for I was working in the smithy till dinner-time, and have walked all this way since.'

When the devil heard this, he ordered the gatekeeper to lock all the nine locks on the gate – 'and put on an extra padlock as well,' said the devil, 'for if he comes inside, he will upset the place altogether.'

'Well, there is no shelter to be got here, I see,' said the smith, when he heard them locking the gate more securely; 'I had better try my luck in paradise.'

And with that he turned round and went back till he reached the crossroads. There he followed the road which the tailor had taken. As he was rather angry at having had to walk all the way to the devil's and back for nothing, he hurried on as fast as he could and reached the gate of paradise just as St Peter opened it a little to let the thin-skinned tailor slip in. The smith was still six or seven paces from the gate. 'I think it's best to make haste now,' said the smith. He took the sledge-hammer and hurled it into the opening of the door just as the tailor got inside. If the smith didn't get in through the opening there and then, I don't know what has become of him since.

＊

The Three Billy-Goats who went up into the Hills to get Fat

There were once upon a time three billy-goats, who were going up into the hills to get fat. On the way there was a bridge over a torrent which they had to cross. Under the bridge lived a big, ugly troll, with eyes as big as saucers, and a nose as long as a rake-handle.

First to cross was the youngest billy-goat. Trip trap, trip trap, went the bridge.

'Who is that tripping over my bridge?' shouted the troll.

'Oh! it's only the smallest billy-goat; I'm going up into the hills to get fat,' said the goat; he had a very small voice.

'I'm coming to take you!' said the troll.

'Oh no! please don't take me, for I am so little. Wait a while till the next billy-goat comes; he is much bigger.'

'Very well!' said the troll.

In a little while came the next billy-goat. Trip trap, trip trap, trip trap went the bridge.

'Who is that tripping over my bridge?' shouted the troll.

'Oh, it's only the second billy-goat; I'm going up into the hills to get fat,' said the goat; he hadn't such a small voice as the first one.

'I'm coming to take you!' said the troll.

'Oh no! please don't take me. Wait till the big billy-goat comes; he is much bigger.'

'Very well then!' said the troll.

Just then came the big billy-goat. Trip trap, trip trap, trip trap went the bridge. He was so heavy that the bridge creaked and groaned under him.

'Who is that tramping over my bridge?' shouted the troll.

'It's the big billy-goat!' said the goat; he had an awful hoarse voice.

'I'm coming to take you,' screamed the troll.

> 'Come on, and blinded you shall reel
>   From my two spears, whose points are steel.
> Like grain between two granite stones
>   I'll crush your marrow and your bones!'

said the big billy-goat, and flew straight at the troll and poked his eyes out, crushed him, bones and all, to pieces, and pushed him out into the torrent. Then he went with the others up into the hills.

There the billy-goats got so fat that they were scarcely able to walk home again, and if the fat hasn't gone off them, they are still as fat as ever. And snip, snap, snout, my tale is out.

Peter Gynt

In the olden days there lived in Kyam a hunter, whose name was Peter Gynt, and who was always roaming about in the mountains after bears and elks, for in those days there were more forests on the mountains than there are now, and consequently plenty of wild beasts. One evening late in the autumn, long after the cattle had left the mountains, Peter set out on one of his usual expeditions. All the dairy-maids had also gone away, except the three girls at the Vala dairy. When Peter came up towards Hovring, where he intended to stay for the night in a deserted dairy, it was so dark that he could scarcely see an arm's length before him. The dogs began barking violently, and it was altogether very dismal and unpleasant. All of a sudden he ran against something and, when he put his hand out, he felt it was cold and slippery and very big. As he didn't think he had gone off the road, he had no idea what this something could be, but unpleasant it was at any rate.

'Who is it?' asked Peter, for he could now feel it was moving.

'Oh, it's Humpy,' was the answer.

Peter was no wiser for this, but walked on one side for some distance, thinking in this way to slip past the mysterious presence. But he ran against something again, and when he put his hand out he felt it was very big, cold and slippery.

'Who is it?' asked Peter Gynt

'Oh, it's Humpy,' was the answer again.

'Well, you'll have to let me pass, whether you are Humpy or not,' said Peter, for he guessed now that he was walking round in a ring, and that the monster had circled itself round the dairy. Just then the monster shifted itself a little, and Peter got past and soon found the house. When he came inside he found it was no lighter in there than outside. He was feeling his way about along the wall to put his gun away and hang his bag up, but when he felt again something cold, big and slippery.

'Who is it?' shouted Peter

'Oh, it's the big Humpy,' was the answer.

Whenever he put his hands out or tried to get past he ran against the monster. 'It's not very pleasant to be here, that's for sure,' thought Peter, 'since this Humpy is both outside and inside, but I'll see if I can't shunt this intruder out of my way.'

So he took his gun and went outside, feeling his way carefully, till he found what he thought was the head of the monster; he felt sure it was a monster troll.

'What are you, and who are you?' asked Peter.

'Oh, I am the big Humpy from Ethedale,' said the troll. Peter did not lose a moment, but fired three shots right into the troll's head.

'Fire another,' said the troll. But Peter knew better; if he had fired another shot, the bullet would have rebounded against himself.

Both Peter and the dogs then commenced dragging the troll out of the house, so that they might come inside and make themselves comfortable. Whilst he was so employed he heard jeers and laughter in the hills round about.

'Peter dragged a bit, but the doggies dragged more,' said a voice.

Next morning he went out stalking. When he came in between the hills, he saw a lassie who was calling some sheep up a hillside. But when he came up to the place, she was gone and the sheep too, and he saw nothing but a pack of bears.

'Well, I never saw bears in a pack before,' said Peter to himself. When he went nearer, they had all disappeared, except one.

> 'Look after your pig,
> For Peter Gynt is out
> With his gun so big,'

shouted a voice over in the hill

'Ah, he can't hurt my pig; he hasn't washed himself today,' said another voice in the hill. Peter washed his hands with some water he had with him. He fired, and shot the bear. Then he heard more jeers and laughter in the hill.

'You should have looked after your pig!' cried a voice.

'I forgot he carried water with him,' answered another.

Peter skinned the bear and buried the carcase. On his way home he met a fox.

'Look at my lamb! How fat it is,' said a voice in a hill.

'Look at Peter, he is lifting that gun of his,' said another voice, just as Peter put his gun up and shot the fox. He skinned the fox, and took the skin with him. When he came to the dairy, he put the head of the fox and the head of the bear on the wall outside the house, both with their jaws wide open. Then he lighted a fire and put a pot on to boil some soup, but the chimney smoked so terribly that he could scarcely keep his eyes open and had therefore to open a small window. Some time after a troll came and poked his nose in; the nose was so long that it reached across the room to the fireplace.

'Here is a proper nose, if you like,' said the troll.

'And here is proper soup! You never tasted the like,' and with that Peter poured the boiling soup over the troll's nose.

The troll ran away wailing and weeping, but in all the hills around they were jeering and laughing, and the voices shouted. 'Nosey stew! Nosey stew!'

It was now quiet for some time. Presently Peter heard a great noise and bustle outside the house. He looked out, and saw a mighty carriage drawn by bears. They were carting away the big monster into the mountain. Suddenly a bucket of water was thrown down the chimney, the fire was put out and Peter sat all in the dark. Then a laughing and chuckling commenced in all corners of the room, and a voice said: 'Now Peter is no better off than the girls at Vala.'

So Peter made the fire again, shut up the dairy, and set off for the Vala dairy, taking the dogs with him. When he had gone some distance he saw such a glare of light in the direction of the dairy that it seemed to him the house must be on fire. Just then he came across some wolves. Some of these he shot, and some his dogs killed. But when he came to the dairy it was all dark there; there was no sign of any fire. There were three strangers in the room amusing themselves with the dairy-maids, and one outside the door. They were four hill-trolls, and their names were Gust, Tron, Tjöstol and Rolf. Gust was standing outside keeping watch, while the others were inside courting the girls. Peter fired at Gust, but missed him. Nevertheless the troll ran away frightened, and when Peter came inside he found the trolls flirting with the girls more outrageously than ever. Two of the girls were terribly frightened and were saying their prayers, but the third, who was called Mad Kari, wasn't a bit afraid. They might stay there for all she cared; she would like to see what sort of fellows they were.

But when the trolls found that Peter was in the room they began whining and told Rolf to get a light. And then the dogs rushed at Tjöstol and knocked him over on his back into the burning embers of the fire so that sparks flew about him.

'Did you see any of my snakes about, Peter?' asked Tron – 'snakes' was what he called the wolves.

'I'll send you the same way as the snakes,' said Peter, and fired a shot at him, and then he killed Tjöstol with the butt-end of his rifle. Rolf had fled up the chimney.

So when he had cleared all the trolls out, the girls packed up their things, and Peter accompanied them home. They dared not stay any longer up on the hills.

Shortly before Christmas, Peter set out again on another expedition. He had heard of a farm on Dovrefell which was invaded by such a number of trolls every Christmas Eve that the people on the farm had had to move out and seek shelter with their neighbours. He was anxious to go there, for he had a great fancy to come across the trolls again. He dressed himself in some old ragged clothes, and took his tame white bear with him, as well as an awl, some pitch and some twine. When he came to the farm he went in and asked for lodgings.

'God help us!' said the farmer; 'we can't give you any lodgings. We have to clear out of the house ourselves soon and look for lodgings, for every Christmas Eve we have the trolls here.'

But Peter said he thought he would be able to clear the trolls out – he had done such a thing before – and so he got leave to stay and was given a pig's skin into the bargain. The bear lay down behind the fireplace, and Peter took out his awl and pitch and twine, and began making a big, big shoe, which it took the whole pig's skin to make. He put a strong rope in for laces, that he might pull the shoe tightly together, and, finally, he armed himself with a couple of handspikes.

Shortly he heard the trolls coming. They had a fiddler with them, and some began dancing, while others fell to eating the Christmas fare on the table – fried bacon and some fried frogs and toads and other nasty things which they had brought with them. During this some of the trolls found the shoe Peter had made. They thought it must belong to a very big foot. They all wanted to try it on at once, so each put a foot into it; thereupon Peter made haste and tightened the rope, took one of the handspikes and fastened the rope round it and got them at last securely tied up in the shoe.

Just then the bear put his nose out from behind the fireplace, where he was lying, and smelt something frying.

'Will you have a sausage, pussy?' said one of the trolls, and threw a hot frog right into the bear's jaw.

'Scratch them, pussy!' said Peter.

The bear got so angry that he rushed at the trolls and scratched them all over, while Peter took the other handspike and hammered away at them as if he wanted to beat their brains out. The trolls had to clear out at last, but Peter stayed and enjoyed himself with all the Christmas fare the whole week. After that the trolls were not heard of there for many years.

Some years afterwards, about Christmastime, the farmer was out in the forest cutting wood for the holidays, when a troll came up to him and shouted,

'Have you got that big pussy of yours, yet?'

'Oh, yes, she is at home behind the fireplace,' said the farmer; 'and she has got seven kittens all bigger and larger than herself.'

'We'll never come to you any more, then,' said the troll.

❄

Legends of the Mill

When the world goes against me, and it is very seldom it forgets to do so whenever there is an opportunity, I have always felt a relief in taking walks in the open air as an alleviation of my portion of troubles and anxieties. What there was the matter with me on this occasion I cannot now remember, but what I clearly recollect is that one summer afternoon some years ago I took my fishing-rod and strolled through the fields on the eastern side of the Akers river, on my way to the outlet of the Maridale lake.

The bright air, the scent of the new-mown hay, the fragrance of the flowers, the singing of the birds, the walk and the fresh breezes from the river, greatly revived my spirits. When I came to the bridge by the outlet, the sun was sinking behind the ridge of the hills, at one moment lighting up the evening clouds with all his lustre, that they for a brief time might rejoice in their borrowed splendour and reflect themselves in the clear waters of the lake, and then for another brief moment breaking through the clouds and sending forth a ray, which formed golden paths in the dark pine-forests of the farther shore. After the hot day the evening breeze carried a refreshing fragrance from the pine trees, and the distant expiring notes of the cuckoo's evening song disposed the mind to sadness.

My eyes followed mechanically the drifting flies as they floated down the river with the stream. But look! there rose a silvery fish; the line ran whizzing off the reel, and when I stopped it the rod was bent into a hoop; it must be a trout of about two pounds! There was now no time for going into raptures about the fragrance of the pine trees or the cuckoo's notes; I wanted all my presence of mind to land the fish. The current was strong and the fish fought bravely, and as I had no landing-net I had to pay out more line and wind in again twice or thrice before I could bring him with the current into a small bay, where he was successfully landed and found to be a fine purple-spotted fish of the size I had supposed.

I went on trying for fish along the western bank down the river, but only small trout rose at my flies, and a score was the total catch.

When I came to the saw-mill at Brække, the sky was overcast, it was already growing dark; above the level of the north-western horizon there appeared a last streak of light, which threw a subdued glimmer on the tranquil surface of the mill-pond. I went out on the timber boom and made a few casts but with little success. Not a breath of air was stirring, the winds seemed to have gone to rest. My flies alone disturbed the placid waters.

A half-grown lad, who was standing behind me on the bank, advised me to 'trawl with bait' – drag a cluster of worms fastened to the hook over the surface of the water in jerks – and offered to find the bait for me. I took his advice, and the trial succeeded beyond expectation; a trout of a pound weight rose to the bait and was, not without some difficulty, landed on the inconvenient spot where I was standing. But with this the day's sport seemed to be over; no fish ruffled the tranquil pond, the bats alone, which shot backwards and forwards in the air, produced sometimes, when they pounced down after the insects, trembling ripples which quivered over the bright surface of the water.

Before me was the saw-mill, its interior lit by a blazing fire on the open hearth. The mill was in full working order, but its wheels, its saws and levers, no longer appeared to be guided or directed by any human will or hand; it seemed to be a mere toy under the invisible power and subject to the every whim of the mill goblin. Soon, however, human forms became visible. One of these went out on the timber raft lying in the mill-pond, and with an immense pitchfork guided the logs into the channel towards the mill, setting the whole raft rocking with a wave-like motion; another rushed hurriedly about with an axe in his hand, shaping and squaring the huge logs, while the loose chips and bits of bark rushed into the roaring eddies below. From inside the mill there came a whizzing, whirring and clashing sound, and now and then a bright saw-blade flashed in the air, as if in combat with the spirits of the night, to cut the stumps and uneven ends off the logs.

Some cold gusts of a northerly wind coming down the course of the river made me feel that I was wet and tired, and I decided therefore to go into the saw-mill to get a little rest by the fire. I called to the boy, who was still standing on the bank, to take the fish-basket, which I had left behind, and follow me over the barrier; the slippery logs of which this was composed were rocking up and down, and were engulfed in the water at every step I took.

By the hearth in the mill sat an old grey-bearded peasant, with a red cap down over his ears, whose presence I did not at first discern as the shadow of the hearth hid him from me. When he heard that I wished to rest and warm myself, he at once prepared a seat for me on a block by the fire.

'That's a splendid fish,' said the old man as he took the last trout I had caught in his hand; 'and it's one of the golden ones too! It weighs almost two pounds You have caught it in the mill-pond here, I suppose?'

On my assenting to this, the old man, who appeared to be an ardent fisherman, told me of the large trout he had caught in the neighbourhood thirty years ago, when he came here from Gudbrandsdale, and made the most heartrending complaints of the decrease of fish and the increase of sawdust, echoing the sentiments of Sir Humphry Davy.

'The fish are becoming more and more scarce,' he said in a voice that penetrated clearly to me through the noise of the mill. 'Such a trout as that, small as it is, is a rare thing to catch now, but the sawdust increases year by year. You cannot wonder that the fish doesn't go into the river, for if he opens his mouth to get a mouthful of clear water, he gets his gills choked with sawdust and shavings. Drat that sawdust, although I shouldn't forget it is the mill that feeds me and mine, but I get so wild when I think of the big fellows I have landed here in days gone by.'

The boy had in the meantime arrived with the basket, but he seemed to be ill at ease amid the noise and commotion which prevailed in the mill. He stepped cautiously over the boards and in his face was depicted fear and anxiety at the rush of the water between the wheels underneath the floor where he was standing.

'This is an awful place to be in,' he said. 'I wish I was safe at home again.'

'Don't you belong to these parts?' I asked.

'Where do you come from?' asked the old man.

'Oh, I come from the Old Town,' answered the lad, who all the time kept himself as close to me as possible. 'I have been over to the clerk at Brække with a letter for the bailiff; and I am so afraid to go home alone in the dark.'

'You ought to be ashamed of yourself, such a big lad as

you are,' said the old man, but added in a comforting tone, 'The moon will be up shortly, and perhaps you may go in company with this stranger here.'

I promised the lad my company as far as the Beier bridge, which seemed to reassure him somewhat. In the meantime the saw was stopped and two of the men began filing and sharpening the blades, which produced such a piercing sound that it went through bone and marrow. It is very often heard at night through the rush of the waters as far as the town below. It seemed to have a very unpleasant effect upon the nerves of the frightened lad.

'Ugh! I dared not stay here a night for all the world!' he said, and stared around him, as if he expected to see a mill-goblin rise through the floor, or a brownie in every corner.

'Well, I have been here many a night,' said the old man, 'and little reward have I had for it.'

'My mother has told me that there is witchcraft and all sorts of evil spirits in these mills,' remarked the lad, apprehensively.

'I can't say I have seen anything,' said the old man. 'The water has, to be sure, been shut off and turned on at times, when I have had a little nap in the mill during the night, and I have heard noises in the back-shed, but I have never seen anything. Folks don't believe in such beings nowadays,' he continued, with an inquiring look towards me, 'and therefore they daren't show themselves. Folks are too sensible and too well read in our days.'

'You are perhaps right there,' I said, for I could perceive there was a meaning in his look, and I preferred that he should tell me some old stories rather than I should dispute his doubts or question his belief that civilisation was a terror to brownies and other supernatural beings. 'You are right to some extent in what you say. In the olden days people had a stronger belief in all kinds of witchery; now they pretend not to believe in it, that they may be looked upon as sensible and educated people, as you say. But far up in the country, in the mountain districts, we still often hear of fairies having been seen, of their spiriting people away into the mountains, and suchlike. Now, I'll tell you a story,' I continued, that I might give him some encouragement to start one; 'I'll tell you a story, which took place somewhere, but where and when I cannot exactly remember.

'There was a man who had a flour-mill, close to a waterfall, and there was a mill-goblin in that mill. Whether the man used to give him Christmas cakes and beer, as they do in some places, I don't know, but I should think he didn't, for every time he went to grind his corn the goblin got hold of the tub-wheel and stopped the mill, and he couldn't get any corn ground. The man knew very well it was the goblin who had his hand in this and one evening when he went to the mill, he took a big pot full of pitch-tar with him and put it on the fire. He turned the water on to the wheel and the mill went for a while, but suddenly it stopped, as he expected it would. He seized a long pole and struck at the mill-goblin round about the wheel, but all in vain. At last he opened the door which led out to the wheel, and there stood the mill-goblin in the door, gaping. His jaw was so big that it reached from the threshold up to the lintel.

' "Have you ever seen such a jaw?" said the goblin.

'The man ran for the pot and pitched the boiling tar into the gaping jaw, and said, "Have you ever felt anything so hot?"

'The goblin uttered a terrible shriek, and let go the wheel. He has never been seen or heard there after that time, nor has the mill been stopped since.'

'Yes,' said the boy, who had listened to my story with

a mixture of fear and curiosity; 'I have heard my grandmother tell that story, and she used also to tell another about a mill-goblin somewhere up in the country, where no one could get anything ground at the mill, it was so bewitched. But one evening came a beggar-woman, who badly wanted to get a little corn ground, and she asked if she could not get leave to stay there for the night and do it.

' "Oh, dear no!" said the owner of the mill. "You can't stay there at night; neither you nor the mill would have any peace for the goblin." But the beggar-woman wanted very badly to get her corn ground, for she had not a spoonful of meal to make either soup or porridge for the children at home. Well, at last she got leave to go into the mill and grind her corn at night. When she came there, she made a fire on the hearth, where a big pot of tar was hanging. She started the mill, and sat down by the hearth with her knitting. In a while a girl came into the mill and said "Good-evening" to her.

' "Good-evening," answered the beggar-woman, and went on with her knitting.

'Very soon the strange girl began raking the fire out over the hearth, but the beggar-woman raked it together again.

' "What's your name?" said the fairy, as you already will have guessed that is what the strange girl was.

' "My name is Self!" answered the beggar-woman.

'The girl thought that was a strange name, and once more began raking the fire about. This made the beggar-woman angry, and she began scolding and raking the fire together again. They had been thus employed for some time, when the beggar-woman, seizing an opportunity, upset the boiling tar over the girl, who began screaming and screeching. As she ran out of the mill, she cried: ' "Father, father, Self has burnt me!"

' "If you have burnt yourself, you have only yourself to blame," said a voice in the hill.'

'It was a good thing for the woman it didn't fare worse with her,' said the old man with the grey beard; 'she might have been burnt, both she and the mill, for where I come from I heard tell of something similar, which happened there long ago. There was a farmer who had a mill that was burnt down two Whitsun-nights in succession. The third year he had a tailor staying with him before Whitsuntide, making new clothes for the holidays.

' "I wonder if anything will happen to the mill this year?" said the farmer. "Perhaps it will burn tonight too!"

' "No fear of that," said the tailor; "give me the key and I'll look after the mill."

'The farmer was well pleased with that, and when the evening came the tailor got the key and went down into the mill. It was almost empty, as it had only just been rebuilt. He sat down in the middle of the floor, took his chalk out and marked a large ring around him, and round about this he wrote the Lord's Prayer, and then he did not feel afraid even if Old Nick himself should come.

'Towards midnight the door suddenly flew open, and in rushed such a number of black cats that the whole room swarmed with them. They were not long in getting a pot on the fire, and then they put more and more wood on, till the pot, which was full of pitch-tar, began to boil and sputter.

' "Ho, ho!" said the tailor to himself, "that's the way you do it, eh?" and no sooner had he spoken, than one of the cats put her paw behind the pot and was about to upset it.

' "Psht! cat! You'll burn yourself," said the tailor.

' " 'Psht! cat! You'll burn yourself!' says the tailor to me," said the cat to the other cats, and away they ran from the fire, and began jumping and dancing round the ring; but very soon the cat stole over to the fire again with the intention of upsetting the pot.

' "Psht! cat! You'll burn yourself! cried the tailor, and frightened it away from the fire.

' " 'Psht! cat! You'll burn yourself!' says the tailor to me," said the cat to the other cats; and they all began to dance and jump about, but the next moment they tried again to upset the pot.

' "Psht! cat! You'll burn yourself!" shouted the tailor so loudly that he frightened them away. They scampered away over the floor, the one over the other, and began jumping and dancing as before.

'They then formed a circle outside the ring and took to dancing round it, quicker and quicker, till the tailor thought the mill was going round too. The cats glared at him with such big, terrible eyes, as if they were going to eat him.

'But while they were in the middle of the dance, the cat which had been trying to upset the pot put her paw inside the ring as if she wanted to get hold of the tailor. But when he saw this he loosened his sheath-knife and held it ready. The moment the cat thrust her paw inside the ring again, the tailor was quick as lightning and chopped the paw off. The cats set up a terrible howl and away they rushed through the door as fast as they could.

'But the tailor laid himself down in the ring and slept till the sun shone far into the mill. Then he rose, locked up the mill, and went up to the farm.

'When he came in both the farmer and his wife were still in bed, for it was Whit Sunday morning.

' "Good-morning," said the tailor, and shook hands with the farmer.

' "Good-morning," said the farmer, who, as you may guess, was both glad and surprised to see the tailor safe back again.

' "Good-morning, mother," said the tailor, and offered the farmer's wife his hand.

' "Good-morning," said the wife; but she was so pale, and looked so queer and confused, and kept her right hand under the bedclothes. At last she offered the tailor her left hand. The tailor then guessed how matters stood, but what he said to the husband, and how it fared with the wife after that, I never heard.'

'The farmer's wife must have been a witch then?' asked the lad, who had been listening intently.

'Yes, of course she was,' said the old man.

We could scarcely hear each other's voices any longer; the saw was again hard at work and making a terrible noise. The moon had now risen. I felt refreshed after the short rest, and bade the old man farewell and started for town in company with the scared lad, following the footpath below the Grefsen hill. A white mist floated over the course of the river and the marshes in the valley below. Above the smoky veil over the town rose Akerhus Fort, with its towers standing out in sharp relief against the mirror of the fjord, beyond where the Nœs point loomed as a black shadow.

The sky was almost cloudless. Scarcely any draught could be noticed in the air. The light of the moon was blended with the gleaming of the summer night and softened the outlines of the landscape in the foreground, directly before us. But the distant fjord lay bathed in the bright and beaming moonlight, while the Asker and Bœrum hills loomed high up in the sky and formed the distant frame of the picture.

Refreshed by their cooling bath of evening dew, the violets and other nocturnal flowers emitted a pleasant fragrance over the fields, but from the bogs and the rivulets came up now and then damp, penetrating gusts, that sent an icy chill through me.

'Ugh! how it makes one shudder,' cried my companion on such occasions. He believed that these gusts were the breath of passing spirits of the night, and thought he saw a witch or cat with glowing eyes in every bush which the wind put in motion.

❄

The Lad and the North Wind

Once upon a time there was an old woman who had a son, and as she was very weak and feeble, she sent her son across the yard to the storehouse to fetch the meal for the porridge for dinner. But when he got outside on the steps, the North Wind came rushing past, took the meal out of his bowl, and away it flew through the air.

The lad went back to the storehouse to fetch more, but when he came out on the steps the North Wind came whistling past again, and away went the meal; and when the lad went back the third time for the meal the North Wind played him the same trick over again. The lad got angry at this, and thought it wasn't right of the North Wind to behave in this manner, so he made up his mind to give the North Wind a call, and ask him for his meal.

Well, the lad started off, but it was a long way, and he walked and walked. However he came at last to the North Wind.

'Good-day,' said the lad, 'and thanks for calling to see me yesterday.'

'Good-day,' answered the North Wind – his voice was hoarse and gruff – 'no thanks required. What do you want?'

'Oh,' said the lad, 'I was only going to ask you to be good enough to let me have back that meal you took from me on the steps, because we haven't much, and if you are going on in this way, and take what little we have, we shall starve.'

'I haven't got any meal,' said the North Wind, 'but since you are so hard up, you shall have a tablecloth which will provide you with everything you wish if you only say, "Cloth, spread yourself and serve up all kinds of fine dishes!" '

The lad was well satisfied with this. But as the way was so long that he couldn't get home that night, he went into a roadside inn, and when they were going to have supper, he put the cloth on a table which stood in the corner and said, 'Cloth, spread yourself and serve up all kinds of fine dishes.'

He had scarcely said these words before the cloth did as it was told, and all in the room thought it was a very nice thing to have, but no one liked it better than the innkeeper's wife. She thought that would be the very thing for her. It would save her such a lot of trouble in frying and boiling, laying the cloth, and putting the things on the table, and so on.

So in the middle of the night, when all were asleep, she took the cloth from the lad, and put another one in its stead, just like the one he had got from the North Wind, but her cloth couldn't, of course, serve up as much as an oatmeal cake.

When the lad awoke, he took the cloth and set out on his journey, and that day he got back to his mother. 'Well,' he said, 'I have been to the North Wind, I have! He is a decent fellow, I think, because he gave me this cloth, and I have only to say, "Cloth, spread yourself, and serve up all kinds of fine dishes," and then I get the best of everything I want to eat and drink.'

'Ah, indeed! I dare say,' said the mother, 'but I won't believe it, till I see it.' So the lad lost no time but took a table, laid the cloth on it, and said, 'Cloth, spread yourself and serve up all kinds of fine dishes,' but the cloth didn't serve up so much as a dry crust.

'Ah, well!' said the lad, 'there's no help for it, I must go to the North Wind again,' and away he went. Towards evening, he came to where the North Wind lived.

'Good-evening,' said the lad.

'Good-evening,' said the North Wind.

'I want my rights for the meal you took from us,' said the lad, 'for that cloth you gave me is not good for anything.'

'I haven't any meal,' said the North Wind, 'but here is a goat for you, which makes only golden ducats, if you only say, "Goat of mine, make money!" '

That pleased the lad, but as it was too late to get home that day, he went into the same inn where he had been before. But before he called for anything, he wanted to try the goat and see if it was true what the North Wind had said about it, and sure enough the goat made only golden ducats.

But when the innkeeper saw what kind of goat the lad had, he thought this was a goat worth having, so when the lad had fallen asleep, he took another goat which couldn't make any golden ducats, and put that in its place.

Next morning the lad started off home, and when he came in to his mother, he said, 'The North Wind is a good fellow, after all. This time he has given me a goat that makes only golden ducats, if I only say, "Goat of mine, make money!" '

'Ah, to be sure!' said his mother, 'that's all rubbish – I won't believe it till I see it.'

'Goat of mine, make money!' cried the lad, but not a shilling could the goat make.

So the lad went back again to the North Wind, and said that the goat wasn't worth anything, and he wasn't going to be done out of his meal, not he!

'Well,' said the North Wind, 'I have nothing else to give you but that old stick over there in the corner; but it is a good stick, and if you only say, "Stick of mine, lay on," it lays on, till you say, "Stick of mine, leave off." '

But it was a long way home, and the lad went into the old inn where he had slept before; and as he pretty well guessed how he had lost the cloth and the goat, he lay down at once on the bench and began snoring as if he were asleep.

The innkeeper, who thought that the stick must be good for something also, looked for a stick like the one the lad had, and was going to change the sticks while the lad was snoring away, but just as the innkeeper was going to take the stick, the lad cried out, 'Stick of mine, lay on,' and the stick commenced beating the poor innkeeper, till he jumped over chairs and tables, shouting and yelling: 'Oh dear! oh dear! Tell the stick to leave off, or else it will kill me; you shall have both your cloth and your goat back again!'

When the lad thought that the innkeeper had had enough, he said, 'Stick of mine, leave off.' Then he took his cloth and put it in his pocket and, with the stick in his hand and leading the goat by a string, he started off home. And now, thought the lad, he had been very well paid for the meal he had lost.

Ashiepattle and the King's Hares

There was once upon a time a man who gave up his farm to his eldest son and heir, but he had still three sons, and they were called Peter, Paul and Ashiepattle. They stayed at home and would do no work of any kind, for they had had too good a time of it in their young days, and now they thought they were above everything and nothing was good enough for them.

At last Peter got to hear that the king wanted a youngster to watch his hares, and so he told his father that he would go and try for this situation, which he thought would just suit him, for he would serve no less a man than the king, he said. His father thought that the work would be far from suitable for him, for he who would watch hares ought to be light and smart and no lazybones, and when the hares began to run and fly about he would find it a very different dance from hanging about the house all day doing nothing. Well, there was no help for it, Peter would try it and go he must; so he took his bag on his back and trudged down the hill. When he had gone a good long distance, he met an old woman who stood fixed with her nose in a big block, and when he saw how she pulled and tugged to get loose he began laughing with all his might.

'Don't stand there and grin,' said the woman, 'but come and help an old woman; I was going to chop up a little wood but got my nose stuck in this block and have been standing and tugging and pulling away, and have not tasted a mouthful of food for a hundred years,' she said.

But Peter only laughed more and more; he thought it was great fun, and said that since she had been standing thus a hundred years, she might hold out for another hundred years.

When he came to the king's palace, he got the job of looking after the hares at once. It was not at all a bad job; he was to have good food and good wages, and the princess into the bargain; but if even one of the king's hares was lost, they were to cut three red stripes out of his back, and throw him into the snake-pit.

As long as Peter was in the fields near the palace, he managed to keep all the hares in one flock, but as the day wore on and they went into the woods, the hares began to scamper and fly about in all directions. Peter ran after them as fast as his legs would carry him but soon he had only one of the hares left; by the time this too was gone, he was very near burst with running. And so he saw no more of the hares.

Towards evening he began strolling homewards; when he came to the gate, he stopped to see whether they would reappear, but no hares came. Inside the palace yard the king was waiting for him with his knife ready, and cut three red stripes out of his back, put pepper and salt into them and cast him into the snake-pit.

After some time Paul wanted to go to the king's palace and watch the king's hares. His father told him what he had said to his elder brother and more besides, but there was no help for it, he must and would go. It fared, however, no better with him than with Peter. The old woman stood there and tugged and pulled away at her nose, which was still stuck in the block, but Paul only laughed and thought it was great fun, and left her standing there. He got the position at once, there was no difficulty about that; but the hares ran away from him amongst the hills, although he ran and rushed about after them till he blew and panted like a sheepdog in the sunshine. When he came back to the palace in the evening without the hares, the king was waiting on the steps with the knife in his hand and cut three broad red stripes out of his back, put pepper and salt into them and sent him off to the snake-pit.

Well, when some time had passed, Ashiepattle wanted to set out for the king's palace and watch his hares. He told his father and said it would just suit him to run about the fields and woods amongst the strawberry hills after a flock of hares, and now and then lie down and take a nap on some sunny hill.

The old man felt sure the boy could find more suitable work to do, but although he may not fare better, at least he could not fare worse than his brothers. He that would watch the king's hares, he reminded him, must not drag himself along as if he were a lazybones with soles of lead to his boots, or like a fly on a tar-brush, for when the hares began to scamper about on the hillsides it would be a very different dance from lying at home and catching fleas with mittens on. He that wanted to get away from that work with a whole back would have to be smart and light on his legs; in fact he would have to fly about faster than a piece of dried skin or a bird's wing.

Well, that might be, said Ashiepattle, but for all that he would go to the palace and serve the king; he couldn't think of serving any man less than a king. He would look after the hares, he said; they couldn't be much worse than the goat and the calf he had to mind at home. So Ashiepattle took his bag on his back and trudged down the hill.

When he had gone a good bit of the way, he began to feel very hungry, and it was just then that he came up to the old woman, who was standing with her nose in the block, still tugging and pulling away at it to get loose.

'Good-day, old mother,' said Ashiepattle; 'are you standing there sharpening your nose, you poor old soul?'

'I haven't heard anybody call me mother for a hundred years,' said the old woman; 'come and help me out of this, and give me something to eat; I haven't had food in my mouth all this time. I'll be as good as a mother to you, if you do!'

Well yes, he thought, she must certainly want both meat and drink.

So he took the axe and split the block for her, and when she got her nose out of the cleft he sat down to eat and share his food with her; but the old woman had a splendid appetite, as you may guess, and finished the best part of it.

When they had done, she gave Ashiepattle a whistle, and told him how to use it. If he blew into the one end of it, everything which he wished far away would be scattered to all sides, but if he blew into the other end all would come together again; and if the whistle were lost or was taken from him, he had only to wish for it and it would come back to him. That is something like a whistle, thought Ashiepattle.

When he came to the king's palace, he was taken into service at once, as they made little or no difficulty about that. He was to have both food and wages, and if he could look after the king's hares, so none were lost, he should have the princess as well; but if any got away, if it only were one of the youngest hares, they would cut three red stripes out of his back; and the king seemed to be so sure of the outcome he went and sharpened his knife there and then.

'Well, it's a small matter to look after these hares,' thought Ashiepattle at first, for when they were let out they were as tame as a flock of sheep, and as long as they were in the fields about the palace they were all in a flock and followed him; but when they came into the woods it was close upon noon, and the sun shone at his best, and off went the hares scampering away to the hills.

'Hallo!' cried Ashiepattle, and blew into the one end of the whistle; 'off you go!' and away the hares ran to all sides; not one was to be seen. But when he came to a clearing in the woods, where they had been burning charcoal, he took his whistle and blew into the other end of it, and before he could say a word there were the hares, all in a row, just as if they had been a regiment of soldiers on a parade ground. Well, that is something like a whistle, thought Ashiepattle; and so he went to take a nap over on a sunny hillside, while the hares scampered about and looked after themselves till the evening came. He then blew them together again, and came back to the palace with them just like a flock of sheep.

The king and the queen and the princess too stood in the door and wondered what sort of a youngster this was, who could look after the hares so well and bring them home with him again. The king counted them backwards and forwards, pointing to each with his finger, but no, not so much as one of the young hares was missing.

'That is something like a lad,' said the princess.

The next day he set out again for the wood with the hares, but as he lay and took a rest amongst the strawberries, the housemaid from the palace came up to him. They had sent her after him to find out how it was that he managed to look after the king's hares so well.

He took out his whistle and showed it to her; he blew into the one end of it and away flew the hares like the wind all over the hills, and when he blew into the other end, they came scampering back and stood in a row before him.

'What a pretty whistle,' said the housemaid; she would willingly give a hundred golden crowns for it, if he would sell it.

'Well, yes,' said Ashiepattle, 'it is something like a whistle.' It was not to be bought for money, he said, but if she would give him a kiss for every golden crown she offered, she should have it.

Yes, that she would willingly; she would not even mind giving him two kisses for every golden crown and thank him for it besides.

So she got the whistle, but when she came back to the palace, the whistle was gone, for Ashiepattle had wished for it back again; and when the evening set in, he came home with his hares just like any flock of sheep. For all the king counted and pointed and reckoned, he could not find as much as a hair of them missing.

The third day when he was out with the hares, they sent the princess after him to try and get the whistle from him. She made herself as blithesome as a lark, and at last she offered him two hundred golden crowns if he would sell her the whistle, and tell her how to get it home.

'Well, yes, it is something like a whistle,' said Ashiepattle; and it was not for sale, he said; but for all that he would let her have it, if she would give him two hundred golden crowns and a kiss for each golden crown into the bargain. On those terms she could have the whistle, but as to getting it home, that was her problem.

'That is a very high price for a hare-whistle,' thought the princess, and she was rather shy about giving him the kisses, but since they were out in the wood, where no one could see or hear them, she would not mind giving him the kisses; for the whistle she must and would have, she said.

When Ashiepattle had got what he was to have, she got the whistle and set off for home holding it tight and fingering it all the way; but when she came to the palace and was about to show it to the king it slipped out of her fingers.

The next day the queen determined to go herself and try to get the whistle from him; she thought she would be sure to bring it back with her.

She was rather close-fisted in money matters and offered him only fifty golden crowns, but she had to raise her price when Ashiepattle said that it was something like a whistle, and that was really no bid at all for it, but for her sake he wouldn't mind selling it to her, if she would give him three hundred golden crowns and a smacking kiss for each golden crown into the bargain. He got that, and much more, for she was not so stingy in that respect.

When she had got the whistle, she tied it up well and put it in a safe place; but she fared no better than the others, for when she went to pull the whistle out it was gone, and in the evening Ashiepattle came home driving the king's hares before him like a tame flock of sheep as usual.

'This is all stuff and nonsense,' said the king; 'I shall have to go myself, if we are to get this confounded whistle from him. I see no other way out of it.'

So when Ashiepattle next day had got into the wood with the hares, the king set out after him, and found him on the same sunny hillside where the womenfolk had met him and made their bargains with him.

Well, the king and Ashiepattle became good friends and got on very well together, and Ashiepattle showed him the whistle and blew both in the one end and the other. The king thought it was a funny whistle, and would buy it by all means, even if he had to pay a thousand golden crowns for it.

'Yes, it is something like a whistle,' said Ashiepattle, and it was not to be had for money. 'But do you see that white horse down yonder?' he said, and pointed over to the wood.

'Yes, that's my own mare, Snowflake,' said the king.

Ashiepattle knew that himself without anybody telling him. 'Well, if you will give me a thousand golden crowns and will kiss that white mare a thousand times down in the bog behind that big fir tree you shall have the whistle.'

'Is it not to be had at any other price?' said the king.

'No, it is not,' said Ashiepattle.

'But I suppose I may put my silk handkerchief between?' said the king.

Yes, he was allowed to do that. Thus the king got the whistle, and put it into his purse, and this he put into his pocket and buttoned it well up. Then he set off on his way home.

But when he came to the palace, and was going to pull out the whistle, he was no better off than the womenfolk; he had not the whistle any more than they. Ashiepattle came home driving the flock of hares and there was not a hare missing.

The king was in a great rage at the way in which Ashiepattle had made a fool of them all. There was no question about it, Ashiepattle must lose his life. The queen said the same; it was best to punish such a scamp right off.

But Ashiepattle thought it was neither right nor fair, for he had done nothing but what they had told him to do, and besides, he had only tried to save his back and life as well as he could.

So the king said he would pardon him if he could tell so many lies that they filled the large brewing-vat and flowed over. If he could do that he might keep his life.

Well, that would be neither a long nor a difficult piece of work, said Ashiepattle; he thought he could master that job. So he began telling them how he had fared from the very first; he told them about the old woman with her nose in the block, about the whistle he had got, and about the housemaid who came to him and wanted to buy it for a hundred golden crowns, and about all the kisses she had to give him into the bargain. Then he told them of the princess, how she came to him, and how much she had to kiss him to get the whistle, when there was nobody to see or hear – 'I must get on with these lies if the vat is to be full,' said Ashiepattle to himself – and about the queen, how stingy she was with the money but so liberal with kisses, that one could hear the smacks all over the wood – 'I must really get on with my lies if the vat is to be full,' said Ashiepattle.

'Well, I think it's pretty full,' said the queen.

'Not at all,' said the king.

At last Ashiepattle began to tell about the king, who came to him, and about the white mare down in the bog, and how the king wanted the whistle so much he agreed to . . . 'I beg your majesty's pardon, but I must put more lies together if the vat is to be full – '

'Stop, lad, stop! It is full!' cried the king. 'Don't you see the vat is flowing over?'

So the king and queen thought they could not do any better than give him the princess and half the kingdom; there was no help for it

'That was something like a whistle,' said Ashiepattle.

Mackerel Trolling

I have grown up by the sea – from my earliest childhood I have wandered about between the skerries, the breakers and the cliffs. There are smart sailors in my native place, and no wonder for they begin early. No sooner have the children learnt to walk than first thing in the morning with nothing on but their shirt, they must climb up on the nearest rock or knoll to have a look at the weather or the sea; if the weather is calm, they put their finger into their mouths and hold it up in the air to feel if there is any air stirring, and whence it comes. As soon as they can handle an oar they are out in boats, and before long they are playing with the dangers of the sea among the breakers. In my youth I used often to go to sea with a pilot from those parts, one of the finest seamen I have known. The happy times I spent with him belong to my dearest memories of the past. Free and happy as a bird I flew over the billows; in the pilot's light yawl we cruised about among the skerries shooting ducks, eider-ducks and seals; in his deck-boat we steered out far to sea, trolling for mackerel, and when he got a ship to pilot in, I sailed the boat home, sometimes alone, sometimes in company with the pilot's boy. Since that time I have always yearned for a sailor's life and the open sea. But instead of losing myself in extolling the glories of a sailor's life I will give you an account of a trip we made together when I, some years ago, was on a visit at home.

We were to spend some days by the outermost skerries. We had the deck-boat, and its crew consisted of Rasmus Olsen (this was the name of my old friend), the pilot's boy, and myself.

One morning in the early grey of the dawn we stood out to sea to troll for mackerel. There was a light breeze off the land; it was scarcely strong enough to lift the heavy fog which lay over the skerries and the naked cliffs, from which the scared sea-gulls flew and hovered around us with their hoarse cry; the sea-swallows uttered their ringing 'tree, tree', and the oyster-catchers their mocking 'click, click', which has caused so many an unsuccessful sportsman to smile. A hazy, close atmosphere hung over the leaden sea; an auk, a guillemot, an eider-duck or a tumbling porpoise now and then enlivened the scene.

Rasmus sat in the after-hatch at the helm, while the boy was now forward, now aft, as circumstances required. Rasmus was a tall, powerful man, with a weatherbeaten, furrowed face and a good-natured expression. In his grey intelligent eye lay an earnest searching look, which told that he was used to encountering dangers and looking deeper into things than the smile about his mouth and jesting words would denote. As he sat there with a sou'wester down over his ears and in a long pilot coat, his figure appeared in the misty morning air to assume quite supernatural proportions, and you might almost imagine that you had one of the old Vikings before you – the Vikings, however, did not smoke tobacco, which Rasmus Olsen did, and that to a considerable extent.

'There isn't wind enough to capsize a tea-cup in a gutter,' said Rasmus, and shifted his chew of tobacco with a little black chalk pipe, while he looked around him on all sides. 'Last night, at sunset, there were plenty of the most respectable wind clouds, but now there isn't a capful.'

The pilot-boy, who was on the look-out forward, and was keeping the boat from falling off by using the starboard oar as the current went in a westerly direction, answered that he thought it 'went a little easier forward'.

'No fear!' answered Rasmus; 'it isn't as if it were sundown. We shan't get any wind before evening, my boy, but maybe we shall have more than we want for the mackerel.'

The breeze, however, soon grew stronger, and we were able to keep our course without the assistance of the oars, and we slipped now at a smart pace out to sea. The fog disappeared gradually, disclosing the blue line of the coast and the far outlying naked skerries, while before us lay the ocean in its interminable extent, blushing in the morning sun. The land wind still blew strongly, but the higher the sun rose, the stronger grew the sea breeze. The rising fog lay like a white sheet over the land. We had by this time a stiff mackerel breeze, and we were soon in the midst of the mackerel shoals.

The lines were ordered out, and the fish, one after another, took the bait till the whole line trembled; amid violent sprawling and struggling these silvery children of the sea were hauled in. But our joy was, as usual, not of a very long duration. Later in the forenoon the gale increased more and more; the seas set in, and the waves grew bigger and bigger; at last the fishing-line stood straight out behind, and the stone weights jumped along the tops of the billows, while the seas – notwithstanding the guiding hand of the pilot sought to avoid them – broke over our little nutshell, and sent the spray high above mast and sail. We pulled in the lines and gave up the fishing. The pilot-boy sat in the main hatch dangling his legs and looking round in all directions from old habit. Now and then he slipped down into the hold and looked at his watch, which he had shut up in a large, red-painted sea-chest.

'Yes, that chest and that watch,' said Rasmus, with a smile and a wink, 'I should think he is fond of them – and quite right, too – if it hadn't been for them, he would now have been at the bottom of the sea among the pebbles.'

I asked him for an explanation and he began: 'It was late in October last year; we had terrible weather, and it was with the greatest difficulty I could keep at sea. The lad was with me, in the boat. I bore down upon a Dutchman at last, and hailed him. I came safe on board, but I felt anything but easy about the boat and the boy. Even as I looked I saw a sea strike the boat aft, which sent it forward and under, and the next moment he was gone. We could not have given him any help because the lad was too far away.

'I prayed by myself, and thought I should never see him again but the first soul I met when I came home was the boy; he had got back long before me. He pulled out his watch and showed it to me and said, "I have saved the watch, captain, and it goes too." The Lord be praised, I thought, that you are saved!

'Yes, you rascal,' he said to the lad, who sat grinning at him, and swinging his legs backwards and forwards, 'he who is born to be hanged will never be drowned. How was the boy saved? Well, a brig came sailing past at the time. Suddenly the crew heard a cry and one of them ran forward, but he saw nothing; they never thought it came from the water, but all at once they heard the cry right under the bow, and when the captain himself came forward and looked over the ship's side, there sat the boy on the sea-chest, holding his watch in the one hand high above the seas. There was only just sufficient time for the captain to give the man at the helm a sign or they would have gone clean over him. They hove to, threw him a rope and pulled him up.'

In the afternoon the wind fell and we began fishing again. We caught a few fish, whiling away the time with all sorts of stories.

'Ah, well, well,' said Rasmus, and shook his head as he lit a fresh pipe, 'there is something brewing over there to the south. The wind we had was only an early puff! You'll see we shall have our full allowance! Even the fish know it; they don't rise to the bait any more and the birds are scared – hear how they wheeze and cry as they seek the land. There will be the right sort of weather for witches and suchlike tonight. But see! if that porpoise doesn't tumble himself so close to us that I might spit upon him . . . ' he was going to say more, but at that moment I fired – I had put up my gun and aimed at the porpoise which was gambolling about in the sea close to us. Being hit, he lashed the water so violently with his tail that he sent a shower of spray over us as high as the mast of our boat, and made us all wet through.

'That witch will not send us any bad weather, anyhow,' I said, when I saw the water coloured red from his blood. Soon after he appeared again, blowing very hard, but the next moment he turned over; Rasmus was not slow in putting the boat-hook in him and hauling him into the boat with my assistance. He was much pleased at the prospect of the oil he would get from him, turned the heavy creature from one side to the other, fondled him like a baby, and assured me he was a 'stunning, fat sea-cub', which should be welcomed at home for boot-grease and lamp-oil.

While we thus were joking about trolls and witches who cause gales and bad weather, a very remarkable witch-story came to my mind, which I believed I had heard Rasmus tell me in my childhood, but my recollection of it was so faint, that I was not sure whether I had heard it or dreamt it. I asked Rasmus if he had not told me such a story about three witches.

'Ah, that one!' he answered, and laughed; 'that's one of the sort we call skipper's yarns nowadays, but in the olden days they believed them like gospel. Old grandfather told it me when I was a small boy, but whether it was his grandfather or great-grandfather who was the cabin-boy I do not recollect. Anyhow, thus runs the tale.

'He had been sailing with a particular skipper as boy the whole summer, but when they were going out on a trip in the autumn, he got a sullen fit and would not join the ship. The skipper rather liked him, for although he was a young hand, he was very handy, and knew his work well, being a big and strong lad, and was not frightened to bend his back over a rope; he was almost as useful as an able seaman, and he was always in a merry, lively humour, and kept up the spirits of all on board, so the skipper did not like the idea of losing him. But the lad had no mind to spend the autumn nights on salt water; he would, however, stay on board till the cargo was in and they were ready to sail. One Sunday, when the crew had liberty ashore, and the skipper was gone to see a timber-dealer about some planks and firewood for deck-cargo – something on his own account I suppose – the boy was to keep on board and look after the vessel. But I must not forget to tell you that the lad was born on a Sunday, and had found a card with the four of clubs; therefore he was a seer, that is to say, he could see the supernatural people, but they could not see him.

'We are going to have a nasty night,' Rasmus interrupted himself, as he rose from his seat and held his hand up to protect his eyes against the ray of sunlight which now fell across the bright billows, so as to be able to see clearly in a southerly direction. 'See how it's working up; we shall have thunder and lightning. Best to go about in time; there isn't a breath of air now! We are lying here in still water and drift about like a bag of hay; but we must take in a reef before it is on us. Come on, Jack.'

While they were taking in the reef, I took the helm and watched the weather. It was now clear and perfectly calm. The wind had gone down, but our boat was rocking with the swell. Far to the south, above the horizon, stood a dark bank of cloud; we saw it first like a narrow streak melting into sky and sea, but gradually it had risen like a wall or a curtain, on which a border of heavy, yellow, torn and twisted thunder-cloud soon appeared. At some moments the curtain grew thinner; it appeared as if someone was walking behind it with a light. No flash was seen, but we heard a distant faint rumble, which we at first believed was occasioned by the sea.

'Well,' said Rasmus, when he had lighted his pipe and taken the helm again, 'the boy was, as I said, a seer, and all at once, as he sat forward in the forecastle, he heard someone speaking in the hold. He peeped through a crevice and saw three coal-black ravens sitting on a cross-beam and talking about their husbands, whom they were all tired of and whom they wished at the bottom of the sea. It was easy to understand that they were witches who had turned themselves into ravens.

' "But are you sure that nobody hears us?" asked one of the ravens. The boy knew by the voice that it was the skipper's wife.

' "No of course not," said the other two, who were the wives of the first and second mates, "there is not a living soul on board."

' "Well, then I'll tell you; I know a good way to get rid of them," said the skipper's wife, and jumped closer to the other two; "we will make ourselves into three heavy seas, and strike the vessel and sink it with all hands."

'Yes, the others thought that was a capital way, and they remained some time, and talked about the time and place.

' "But I suppose no one hears us?" said the skipper's wife again.

' "Well, you know that," answered the other two.

' "You see, there is a remedy they could use against us which, if it were used, would be a serious thing for us and would cost our lives."

' "What is that, sister,' said one of the mates' wives.

' "But are you sure that no one hears us? I thought I saw some smoke from the forecastle.'

' "You know there isn't anyone! We have looked into every corner. They forgot to put out the fire in the stove, that's the reason it smokes," said the mates' wives. "Let's hear about the remedy!"

' "If they buy three cords of birch logs," said the witch, " – but they must be exact measure and no bargaining about the price – and if they throw overboard the one cord of logs, piece by piece, when the first sea comes, and the second cord, piece by piece, when the second sea comes, and the third cord, piece by piece, when the third sea comes, then it's all over with us."

' "Yes, that's true, sister, then it's all over with us, then it's all over with us!" said the mates' wives; "but nobody knows it." They screeched and laughed aloud, and then they flew up through the main hatch, and screeched and gobbled like ravens.

'When they were ready to sail, the lad would not for the life of him go on the ship for all the skipper talked to him and promised him; there was no help for it, he would on no account go in the ship. At last they asked him if he was afraid, since it was getting so late in the autumn, and was it that he would rather sit in the chimney-corner behind his mother's petticoats.

' "No," said the lad, he was not afraid; he thought they never had seen any sign of his being afraid, or using tricks as the land crabs might do, and he would prove it to them, for now he would go with them in the ship, but on the condition that they bought three cords of birch logs, exactly measured, and that he was to have the command of the ship, as if he was the skipper, on a certain day. The skipper asked the meaning of this nonsense, and if he had ever heard of a boy taking the command of a vessel? The lad answered that might be and it was all the same to him; if they would not buy three cords of birch logs, and obey him, as if he was the captain for one day only – of which he would tell them beforehand – he would not set his foot on board any more, and still less would he dirty his hands in pitch and tar on board that ship.

'The skipper thought it was a very strange idea, and that he was a strange lad altogether, but he agreed at last, because he had set his heart on having the boy with him, and I suppose he thought he could easily manage him when they got out to sea. The mate was of the same opinion. "Oh! never mind! Let him take the command! If we go to seaward we'll have to give him a hand!' said the mate. So the birch logs were bought and correctly measured, and no bargaining was made about the price, and then they sailed.

'When the day arrived that the boy was to be skipper, the weather was calm and fine, but he called all men to reef sails, so the ship had scarcely any sail on her. It was just about the time when the middle watch was over and the morning watch was called. Both skipper and crew smiled and said: "It's easy to see who has command of the ship now; why not full the sails altogether?"

' "Not yet," said the lad, "but very shortly." Suddenly a squall burst on them, so violent that they thought the ship would have capsized. If they had not reefed the sails there was no doubt they would have foundered when the first squall struck the ship. The lad ordered them to throw out the first cord of birch logs, but piece by piece, only one at a time, never two, and they must not touch the other two cords of wood.

'The crew was very smart in carrying out his orders now, and they did not laugh any more at him, but threw the birch logs overboard, piece by piece. When the last piece went over the side they heard a moaning as from one who is in the last pangs of death, and the next moment the squall was over.

' "The Lord be praised!" said the crew.

' "Well, I must say that you have saved both ship and cargo, and I'll report it to the owners – and stand by it,' said the skipper.

' "Oh yes, that's all very well, but we haven't done with it yet," said the lad, "we shall have it worse directly," and he ordered them to furl every sail but the mizen.

'The second squall came still stronger than the first, and the crew were in a great fright. Just as it was blowing at its hardest the lad told them to throw the other cord of logs overboard, which they did; they threw piece by piece, and took good care not to touch the third cord. When the last log went over the side they heard a deep groaning and wind went down.

' "We have one bout left now, and that will be the worst," said the boy, and ordered every man to his post, while the ship only went under bare poles. The last squall was worse than both the preceding ones; the ship gave a lurch and they thought it would never right itself again; the seas washed over deck and gunwale. But the lad ordered them to throw overboard the last cord of logs, piece by piece, not two at a time. When the last log went over the side they heard the moaning of one who dies a hard death, and when the wind had gone down the sea was coloured with blood as far as they could see.

'When all was over the captain and the mates said

they would write to their wives.

' "You may as well leave that alone," said the lad. "You haven't got any wives any more!"

' "What nonsense is that, you young whelp? Have we no wives?" said the captain.

' "Have you finished them off, perhaps?" said the first mate.

' "Oh dear no, we have all had a hand in that," answered the boy; and then he told them what he had heard and seen the Sunday he was on board keeping watch, when the crew had liberty ashore, and the skipper went to see the timber-dealer.

'When they came home they heard that their wives had disappeared the day before the storm, and they had never been seen or heard of since.'

During this and other stories which Rasmus related, the evening had set in. The storm was approaching slowly, and gradually covered the sky like a dark curtain; some of the flashes of lightning struck the sea, others wound themselves like snakes in a horizontal direction across the sky and formed flaming fringes round the rich folds of clouds in the curtain. At other times the flashes made the whole curtain transparent like a veil. Still the storm was at some distance; the thunder rumbled faintly, and the sea rolled as far as we could see in long bright waves, but they appeared as if coloured by blood or wine, for the sun was setting in red clouds, the colour of which was reflected in the sea.

It was apparent that we could not escape the storm; the seas increased, the current carried us towards land, and only now and then a gust of wind filled our sail. By the last glimmer of the day we saw on the distant ridge of the horizon a black streak approaching us, the nearer it came the plainer appeared the white fringe of foam which came driving on before it. The storm and the dark night were upon us. Like an arrow the boat sped on, and before long we were by the outside skerries, where the sea-birds, disturbed at the constant flashes of lightning and claps of thunder, wheezed and screamed and flew about in swarms like white clouds. But their screams sounded faint amongst the breakers. The islands and skerries afforded us some shelter from the heavy seas, but further on towards the shore, where the waves broke upon it, they grew again, and by the light of the flashes of lightning we saw along the whole coast high foaming breakers, the roaring of which thundered in our ears. Rasmus kept a sharp look-out in this darkness, which appeared almost impenetrable; I could not distinguish anything but the broad white fringe of foam, which we were approaching with an alarming speed. Shortly I discerned a small dark point, for which we steered, and in a few moments we passed among the surf and breakers through the narrow sound by the Ullenhead, and reached in safety the peaceful harbour, where the high cliffs sheltered against storm and sea.

Peik

There was once upon a time a man and a woman; they had a son and a daughter who were twins, so like each other that you could not tell the one from the other, except by their clothes.

The boy they called Peik. He was of little use on the farm while the parents lived, for he did not care for anything else but playing tricks upon people, and he was so full of tricks and pranks, that no one was left in peace by him. But when the parents died he grew worse and worse – he would not do anything; he only did his best to make an end of what there was left after them, and to quarrel with everybody.

The sister worked and toiled all she could, but it was of little help and so she told him how wrong it was that he would not do anything useful, and asked him: 'What do you think we shall live upon, when you have finished everything?'

'Oh, I'll go and play a trick upon somebody,' said Peik.

'Yes, you are always ready and willing when you are bent upon that,' said his sister.

'Well, I'll try my best,' said Peik.

So when he had made an end of everything, and there was nothing more in the house, he set out on his journey, and walked and walked till he came to the king's palace.

The king was standing at the door, and when he saw the lad he said: 'Where are you off to today, Peik?'

'Oh, I am off to see if I cannot play a trick upon somebody,' said Peik.

'Can't you play a trick upon me, then?' said the king.

'No, I don't think I can, because I have left my trickery-sticks at home,' said Peik.

'Can't you go and fetch them?' said the king; 'I should like to see, if you are such a clever trickster as folks make you out to be.'

'I am not able to walk so far now,' said Peik.

'I'll lend you a horse and saddle,' said the king.

'I don't think I am able to ride either,' said Peik.

'We'll lift you up,' said the king, 'and I'm sure you'll be able to stick on to the horse.'

Well, Peik rubbed and scratched his head, as if he were going to pull all his hair off, but he let himself be lifted astride the horse at last; there he sat, and swung backwards and forwards and sideways as long as the king could see him, and the king laughed till the tears came into his eyes, for he had never seen such a sorry horseman before. But as soon as Peik came into the wood behind the hill, where the king could see him no longer, he sat straight and steady as if he was nailed to the horse and started off as if he had stolen both horse and bridle, and when he came to the town he sold them both.

In the meantime the king walked up and down and waited for Peik. He longed to see him coming back with his trickery-sticks; he could not help laughing when he called to mind how pitiable he looked, as he sat rolling to and fro on the horse like a hay bag which didn't know which side to fall off on; but hours went and hours came – and no Peik appeared. So the king guessed at last that he had been played a trick and had been done out of his horse and saddle, even though Peik did not have his trickery-sticks with him. Beside himself with rage, the king made up his mind to take Peik's life. But Peik got to know he was on his way and told his sister to put the porridge-pot on the fire with some water in it. Just before the king came in he took the pot off the fire and put it on the chopping-block and began making the porridge on the block.

The king wondered at this, and was so taken up with the wonderful pot that he forgot what he had come there for.

'What do you want for that pot?' said he.

'I can't spare it very well,' said Peik.

'Why can't you spare it?' said the king; 'I'll make it worth your while to sell it.'

'Well, it saves me both money and trouble, chopping and carrying,' said Peik.

'Never mind, I'll give you a hundred golden crowns for it,' said the king; 'you did me out of horse and saddle the other day, and the bridle too, but I'll let bygones be bygones, if I get the pot.'

'Well, I suppose you must have it then,' said Peik.

When the king came back to the palace he sent out invitations to a great feast, and the meat was to be boiled in the new pot, which was put in the middle of the floor.

The guests thought the king was out of his mind, and went about nudging each other and laughing at him. But he walked round the pot and cackled and chuckled to himself, saying all the time, 'All right, all right! wait a bit! it will boil directly'; but there was no sign of any boiling.

So the king guessed that Peik had been playing a trick upon him again, and he set out once again to kill him.

When the king came to his place Peik was standing by the barn.

'Wouldn't it boil?' he said.

'No, it would not,' said the king; 'but now you shall suffer for it,' and he was about to draw out his knife.

'I believe you there,' said Peik, 'for you did not have the block.'

'I shouldn't wonder if you are telling a lie again,' said the king.

'It's all for the want of the block,' said Peik; 'the pot won't boil without it.'

Well, what was he going to have for it?

'It is worth three hundred golden crowns at least, but for you I'll let it go for two,' said Peik.

So the king got the block, and set off for home. He invited guests again to a feast and put the pot on the block in the middle of the room. The guests thought the king was gone sheer mad, and went about making game of him. He cackled and chuckled round the pot, saying all the time, 'Wait a bit, it will boil soon – it will boil directly'; but there was no more chance of its boiling on the block than on the floor.

So the king guessed that he had been tricked by Peik that time as well. He tore his hair, and would not rest till Peik was dead; he would not spare him this time, whether he had got anything to say for himself or not.

But Peik was prepared to receive him again. He killed a sheep and took the bladder and filled it with the blood of the slaughtered animal. He then put the bladder in his sister's bosom and told her what she should say when the king came.

'Where is Peik?' shouted the king. He was in such a rage that his voice trembled.

'He is so poorly, that he is not able to move,' answered the sister, 'and so he thought he would try and get some sleep.'

'You must wake him up!' said the king.

No, she dared not do it; he was so hasty.

'Well, I am still more hasty,' said the king; 'and if you don't wake him I'll – ' and with that he put his hand to his side for his knife.

No, no, she would rather wake him; but Peik turned

round in his bed in great rage, pulled out his knife and stabbed her in the bosom, but the knife hit only the bladder; a stream of blood gushed out, and she fell down on the floor as if she were dead.

'What a villain you are, Peik,' said the king, 'you have stabbed your own sister and that while the king stands by and looks on.'

'Oh, there isn't much danger, as long as I have got breath in my nostrils,' said Peik, and he took a ram's horn and when he had blown a wedding march on it he put the horn to his sister's nostrils and blew life into her again and she rose up as if nothing had been the matter with her.

'Why, bless me, Peik! Can you kill people and blow life into them again?' said the king.

'Well, yes, what would become of me if I couldn't?' said Peik. 'You see, I am so hasty, and I can't help killing everyone who comes near me and annoys me.'

'I am also very hasty,' said the king, 'and I must have that horn; I'll give you a hundred golden crowns for it, and I'll forgive you besides for doing me out of the horse and cheating me on that pot and block business, and all the rest.'

Peik could not very well spare the horn, but for his sake he would part with it, and so the king got it, and set out home as fast as he could.

He had no sooner come home before he must try the horn. He began quarrelling and scolding the queen and his eldest daughter, and they scolded him back, but before they knew a word about it he pulled out his knife and stabbed them both, so they fell down stone dead, and all who were in the room ran out; they were so afraid.

The king walked up and down the floor for some time and kept on saying there was no danger so long as there was breath in his nostrils, and a great deal more nonsense which had flowed out of Peik's mouth. He then took the horn and began blowing, but although he blew all he could that day and the day after as well, he could not blow life into the bodies; they were dead, and dead they remained, both the queen and his daughter, and so he had to bury them, and to give them a grand funeral into the bargain.

When this was done the king set out to settle with Peik and to take his life, but Peik had everything prepared, for he knew the king was coming, and he said to his sister: 'You must change clothes with me and be off! You may take all we have with you.'

Yes, she changed clothes with him, packed up their things, and started off as fast as she could, while Peik sat all by himself in his sister's clothes.

'Where is that Peik?' said the king, as he came in a great rage through the door.

'He's gone away,' said he who sat in the sister's clothes.

'Well, had he been at home now he wouldn't have had long to live,' said the king; 'it's no use sparing the life of such a scamp.'

'He knew your majesty was coming to punish him for having played so many tricks upon you, and so he ran away and left me behind here both without food or money,' said Peik, trying to appear like a shy bashful maiden.

'Come along with me to the palace, and you shall get enough to live on; there is little use in sitting in the cottage here and starving,' said the king.

Yes, he would willingly do that, and so the king took him and let him learn everything, and kept him as one of his own daughters; in fact the king felt now as if he had all his three daughters again, for Peik stitched and sewed and sang and played with them, and was in their company early and late.

Some time afterwards a prince came to the palace to

woo one of the princesses.

'Yes, I have three daughters,' said the king; 'you have only to say which one you will have.'

So the prince got leave to go up in their bower and get acquainted with them. In the end he liked Peik best, and threw a silk handkerchief into his lap, and so they began getting everything ready for the wedding, and shortly the prince's relations arrived at the palace, and the wedding festivities commenced in earnest, with feasting and drinking; but on the wedding day, as night was coming on, Peik dared not remain any longer, and he stole out of the palace and ran across the fields; and there was no bride to be found.

And worse remains to be told, for the two princesses were suddenly taken ill, and all the guests had to break up and take their departure just as they were in the middle of all the fun and feasting.

The king was both enraged and sorrowful at these misfortunes, and began to wonder what could really be the cause of them.

So he mounted his horse and rode out, for he thought it was so lonely to stay alone by himself at home; but when he came out in the fields he saw Peik sitting there on a stone, playing a Jew's harp,

'Hallo! are you sitting there, Peik?' asked the king.

'Of course I am,' said Peik, 'I can't sit in two places at once.'

'Well, you have played such vile tricks on me time after time,' said the king, 'that you will have to come with me and get your deserts.'

'Well, I suppose there's no help for it,' said Peik, 'so I may as well jump into it as creep into it.'

When they came to the palace the king gave orders to get ready a barrel, which Peik was to be put in, and when it was ready they carted it up on a high mountain, where he was to lie in the barrel for three days to think on all that he had done, before they rolled the barrel down the mountain into the sea.

On the third day a rich man came past as Peik lay in the barrel singing –

> 'To paradise, to paradise I am bound,
>   Safe in my barrel as it turns round and round.'

When the man heard this, he asked Peik what he would take to let him take his place.

'I ought to be well paid for that,' said Peik, 'for its not everyday one gets the chance to go straight to paradise.'

The man was willing to give him all he possessed, and so he knocked out the bottom of the barrel and crept into it instead of Peik.

In the evening the king came to roll the barrel down the mountain.

'A safe journey to you!' said the king; he thought it was Peik who was in it. 'You'll roll faster into the sea than if you were drawn by the swiftest reindeer, and now there will be an end both to you and your tricks.'

Before the barrel was half way down the mountain there wasn't a whole stave or bit of it left, nor of the man who was inside. But when the king came home to the palace, Peik was there before him. He sat on the steps and played upon the Jew's harp.

'What! are you sitting here, Peik?' said the king.

'Of course I am,' said Peik. 'I suppose I may have lodgings and shelter for all my horses, my cattle and my money.'

'Where did I roll you to, that you got all these riches?' asked the king.

'Oh, you rolled me into the sea,' said Peik, 'and when I came to the bottom there was more than enough to take, both of horses and cattle, of gold and goods. Livestock went about in flocks, and the gold lay in heaps as big as houses.'

'What will you take to roll me the same way?' asked the king.

'Oh, that shan't cost you much,' said Peik. 'Since you didn't take anything off me, I won't take anything off you either.'

So he put the king into a barrel and rolled him down the mountain; and when he thus had got the king out of the way, he went home to the palace and married the youngest princess and had a grand wedding. Afterwards he ruled the land and kingdom well and wisely, but he left off playing tricks upon people and he was never spoken of as Peik any more, but as His Royal Majesty the King!

※

Foolish Men and Scolding Wives

There were once upon a time two women, who were always quarrelling, as women will do, and one day when they had nothing else to quarrel about, they began arguing about their husbands, as to who was the most foolish.

The longer they argued the more angry they got, and at last they were very near to pulling each other's hair, for as everyone knows, it is easier to begin a quarrel than to end it, and it's a bad look-out if sense is wanting in such a predicament.

One of them said there was nothing she could not get her husband to believe, for he was as stupid as the trolls, and believed anything. The other said that there was nothing so silly that she could not get her husband to do it, if she only said it ought to be done, for he was so foolish and stupid that you could not easily find his like.

'Well, let us see who can make the bigger fool of our husbands, and then we'll see which one is the most stupid,' they said one day, and to this they both agreed.

When the husband of the first of these women came home from the wood, his wife said: 'Goodness gracious, what ails you? You must be ill, you look as if you were dying.'

'Want of something to eat and drink is all that ails me,' said the husband.

'But gracious goodness!' screeched the woman, 'you

are looking worse and worse every minute! You look like a corpse! You must go to bed! Dear, oh dear, you can never last long.' And in this way she went on, till she got her husband to believe that he was on the point of dying, and she got him to go to bed, folded his hands, and closed his eyes; next she laid him out and put him into a coffin, and that he might not be smothered while he was there, she had some holes made in the boards, so he could both breathe and look out.

The other woman took a pair of carding-combs and began to card, but she had no wool upon them. The man happened to come in and see this foolish operation. 'There is little help in a spinning-wheel without yarn, but carding-combs without wool is the height of woman's nonsense,' said her husband.

'Without wool?' said the woman, 'why I have wool! But you don't see it, for it is of a very fine sort, I can tell you.' When she had done the carding she brought out her spinning-wheel and began spinning.

'But this is foolish work,' said the man; 'you are sitting there spinning and spoiling your wheel all the time, since you have got nothing on it.'

'Nothing on it?' said the woman. 'No the thread is so fine, that it wants better eyes than yours to see it.'

When she was ready with the spinning she took the yarn off the wheel and set up her loom and began weaving the cloth. She then took it off her loom, pressed it and cut it out, and sewed new clothes of it for her husband; and when they were ready she hung them up in the loft of the storehouse. The husband could see neither the cloth nor the clothes, but he had got the belief into his head that the cloth was so fine that he could not see it, and so he only said, 'Well yes, if it is so fine, it's very fine indeed.'

But one day his wife said to him: 'You must go to the

funeral today; our neighbour, who died last week, is going to be buried, and so you had better use your new clothes.'

Yes, he would go to the funeral, and she helped him to put the clothes on, for they were so fine that he might easily tear them to pieces if he put them on himself.

When he came to his neighbour's farm the funeral feast had already begun, and the guests had been drinking hard; their grief did not increase much, as you can imagine, when they saw the last arrival in his new clothes. But great indeed was their consternation when they set out for the churchyard and the dead man himself peeped out through the holes in his coffin and burst out laughing at the sight. The coffin positively shook.

Then the wife of the husband who believed himself dead but was alive, and the wife of the husband who believed himself clothed but was naked, agreed that it was impossible to tell which husband was the bigger fool. And this was the first time they had ever agreed about anything.

❄

The Parson and the Clerk

Once upon a time there was a parson, who was such a bully, that he screamed out a long way off, when anybody came driving towards him on the main road: 'Out of the way, out of the way! Here comes the parson himself!'

One day, when he was driving along and carrying on in this way, he met the king. 'Out of my way, out of my way!' he shouted, ever so far off. But the king drove straight on and took no notice of him, so that the parson had to pull his horse to one side. When the king came alongside him, he said: 'Tomorrow, you will have to appear at the palace, and if you cannot answer the three questions which I will ask you, you shall lose both your gown and your collar, for your pride's sake.'

That was something different to what the parson was used to. He could bawl and shout and carry on terribly, but to bother his brains with problems and answers was out of the question. So he went to the clerk, who they said had a much smarter tongue than he did, and he told the clerk he had no mind to go, 'for a fool can ask more than ten wise men can answer', and so he got the clerk to go instead.

Well, the clerk set out and came to the palace dressed in the parson's gown and collar. The king received him at the door with crown and sceptre, and was so fine that he glittered a long way off.

'Oh, you are here, are you?' asked the king. Yes, he was

there, sure enough. 'Now, tell me first,' said the king, 'how far is it from east to west?'

'Why, a day's journey,' said the clerk.

'How do you make that out?' asked the king.

'Well, don't you see, the sun rises in the east and sets in the west, and he does it easily enough in a day,' said the clerk.

'Very well,' said the king; 'but tell me now, what you think I am worth, as I stand here before you.'

'Well, our Lord was valued at thirty silver pieces, and I suppose I cannot put you higher than twenty-nine,' said the clerk.

'So, so!' said the king, 'since you are so very clever at everything, tell me what it is I am thinking about just now?'

'Why, you are surely thinking it is the parson who stands here before you; but so help me, if you don't think wrong, for I am the clerk.'

'Be off with you – go home, and you be the parson and let him be clerk,' said the king, and so it was.

The Giant and Johannes Blessom

Above Vaage parsonage rises a hill or small mountain, crowned with tall and majestic pine trees. It is called the Jutulsberg, or the 'giant's mountain', by the Vaage people. It is very steep and full of deep dark crevices. By a freak of nature a formation of the rocks, somewhat resembling a large gateway, can be seen in one of its most bare and weatherbeaten sides. If you stand on the bridge over the wild Finne river, or on the farther side of the fields, and look up at the gate above the overhanging garlands and luxuriant foliage of the weeping birch which grows out of the fissures in the rock, and if, in addition, you call your imagination to your assistance, the formation takes on the appearance of a double gateway, which at the top is joined in a gothic arch.

Old, white-stemmed birch trees stand as pillars at its sides, but their lofty crowns do not reach up to where the arch begins. If the gateway extended into the mountain the length of a church, you could put Vaage church with roof and spire into it. It is not an ordinary door or gate, it is the entrance to the giant's castle – the 'giant's gate' it is called – and under it the biggest troll with fifteen heads can comfortably pass without bending his neck.

If anyone in the olden days, when there was more intercourse between human beings and trolls, wanted to borrow anything from the giant, or to speak with him on other business, it was customary to throw a stone at the gate and say: 'Open, Jutul!'

One afternoon, a couple of years ago, I came on a visit to the parsonage. The family had gone up to their mountain dairy and there was no one at home but an old peasant, who, on being requested to show me the way, went with me up to the giant's gate. We knocked, but no one came to open it. It was not to be wondered at that the giant would not receive us, or that he at his advanced age so seldom received visitors, for, to judge by the numerous marks of stones on the gate, he must have been exceedingly troubled with visitors.

'One of the last who saw him,' said my companion, 'was Johannes Blessom, the parson's neighbour. But I should think he wished he never had seen him,' he added.

'This Johannes Blessom was once down in Copenhagen about a lawsuit – for there was no justice to be had here in the country in those days, and if anyone wished for "fair play" there was no help for it but to travel down there. His father, who also had a lawsuit, did the same thing before him. Well, it was a Christmas Eve, and Johannes had finished his business with the grand folks and was ready to start for home; he walked along the streets in a gloomy mood, for he was longing to be at home up in the far north, and knew there was no way of getting home till long after Christmas. Suddenly a person, who by his dress appeared to be a peasant from his own parish of Vaage, passed him in a great hurry. He was a big, tall man, with large shiny buttons as big as silver dollars on his white jacket. Johannes thought he knew him, but he walked past him so quickly that he did not get a good sight of his face.

' "You are in a great hurry," Johannes called after him

' "Yes, I have to make haste," answered the stranger; "I have to be at Vaage tonight!"

' "I wish I could get there as well," said Johannes.

' "Well, you can stand behind on my sledge," said the stranger, "for I have a horse who does the mile in twelve strides."

'Johannes thanked him for the offer, went with him to the stable and off they started. Johannes was only just able to stick on to the sledge, for away they went like the wind through the air. He could neither see earth nor sky.

'At one place they stopped to rest. Johannes could not tell where it was, but just as they were starting again he saw a skull on a pole. When they had travelled some distance Johannes began to feel cold.

' "Ugh! I forgot one of my mittens where we rested," said he; "my fingers are freezing!"

' "You'll have to stand it, Johannes Blessom," said the stranger, "it isn't far to Vaage now. Where we rested was half-way."

'The stranger stopped just before they came to the bridge over the Finne river to put Johannes down.

' "You are not far from home, now," said he, "and you must promise me not to look behind you if you hear any rumble or see any light around you."

'Johannes promised this and thanked him for the lift. The stranger proceeded on his way over the Finne bridge, and Johannes walked up the hillside to his farm. But all of a sudden he heard a rumble in the giant's mountain, and the road in front of him was suddenly lighted up – he could have seen to pick up a needle. He forgot what he had promised, and turned his head to see what it was. The gate in the mountain was wide open and there came a light from it as from many thousand candles. Right in the middle of the gate he saw the giant himself – it was the stranger he had been driving with. But from that day, Johannes Blessom's head was all on one side, and so it remained as long as he lived.'

✳

The Box with the Funny Thing in It

Once upon a time there was a little boy, who was walking along a road. When he had gone some distance he found a box. 'There must be something funny in that box,' he said to himself; but although he twisted and turned it he was not able to get it open.

When he had walked some distance farther he found a little key. He was tired, and sat down by the roadside. He thought it would be great fun to see if the key fitted the box, for there was a little keyhole in it. He took the little key out of his pocket; he blew first into the pipe of the key, and then he blew into the keyhole; he put the key into the keyhole and turned it round: 'Click,' said the lock, and when he tried the lid the box opened.

But can you guess what there was in the box? Why, it was a calf's tail, and if the calf's tail had been longer this tale would have been longer too.

❄

The Widow's Son

There was once a poor, very poor widow, who had an only son. She pulled through with the boy till he was confirmed, but then she told him that she could not feed him any longer; he would have to go out and earn his own bread.

The lad wandered out into the world, and when he had walked a day or so he met a stranger.

'Where are you going to?' asked the man.

'I'm going out into the world to try and get some work,' said the lad.

'Will you come into my service?' asked the man.

'Well, why not! just as well with you as with anybody else,' answered the lad.

'You will find it a very good place,' said the man; 'you are only going to keep me company and do nothing else besides.'

So the lad went with him home, and he got plenty of food and drink, and had little or nothing to do. But on the other hand he never saw a living soul come near the man.

So one day the man said to him: 'I'm going away for eight days, and during that time you will be here all alone, but you must not go into any of these four rooms here. If you do I will take your life when I come back.'

'No', said the lad, 'I will not go into any of the rooms.'

But when the man had been away three or four days the lad could not help going into one of the rooms. He looked round, but saw nothing but a shelf over the door, on which lay a briar twig. Well, this is surely something to forbid my seeing, thought the boy.

When the eight days were gone the man returned. 'You haven't been into any of the rooms, I hope?' said he.

'No, not at all,' said the lad.

'Well, we shall soon see,' said the man, and with that he went into the room where the lad had been. 'But I find you have been there after all,' said the man, 'and now you shall lose your life.'

The lad cried and begged for himself till he got off with his life; but he got a good thrashing. When that was over they were as good friends as ever.

Some time afterwards the man went away again; he was going to stay away for a fortnight this time, but first he told the lad that he must not put a foot in any of the rooms where he had not already been; he might, however, go into that room where he had been.

Well, it happened just as the last time, only that the lad waited eight days before he went into the second room. In this room he saw nothing but a shelf over the door, and a piece of rock and a water-jug on it. Well, that's certainly something to be afraid of, thought the lad again.

When the man came back he asked the lad if he had been into any of the rooms. No, not likely, the lad had not! 'We shall soon see,' said the man, but when he saw that the lad had been into one of the rooms after all, he said: 'I shall spare you no longer now; you will lose your life this time!'

But the lad cried and begged for himself again, and he got off with a good thrashing again, but this time he got as much as he could possibly stand. When he had got over the effects of the thrashing he led the same comfortable life as before, and he and the man were the best of friends again.

Some time after the man had to go on a journey again, and this time he should be away for three weeks, and so he said to the lad that if he went into the third room during his absence, he would not have the slightest chance of escaping with his life.

When fourteen days had gone the lad could not help himself and he stole into the third room; he saw nothing in there except a trap-door in the floor. When he lifted it up and looked down into the room below he saw a big copper kettle which stood there and boiled and bubbled; but he saw no fire under it.

It would be great fun to feel if it is hot, thought the boy, and put his finger into the kettle, but when he pulled it out again it was gilded all over. The boy scraped and washed it, but the gilding would not come off, so he tied a rag, round it, and when the man came home and asked what was the matter with his finger the lad said that he had cut himself very badly. But the man tore off the rag and saw immediately what really ailed the finger.

He was at first going to kill the lad; but as he began crying and praying for himself again, he gave him another sound thrashing instead, this time so severe that he had to keep to his bed for three days; and then the man took a jar down from the wall, and rubbed the lad with some of its contents and he was as well as ever again.

Before long the man went away again, and was not coming back for a month. But he told the lad that if he went into the fourth room he must not expect to have any hope of escaping with his life.

For two or three weeks the lad managed to resist the temptation, but then he couldn't help himself any longer – he must and would go into that room, and so he did. There stood a big black horse in a box by himself, with a manger of glowing cinders at his head and a truss of hay at his tail. The lad thought this was altogether wrong, so he changed them about and put the truss of hay at the horse's head.

So the horse said: 'Since you have such a good heart that you let me have something to eat, I will save you from the troll, for that's what the man is that you are with. But now you must go up into the room just above here and take a suit of armour out of those hanging there! And mind you do not take any of the bright ones, but the most rusty you see. Take that one! And sword and saddle you must look out for yourself in the same way.'

The lad did as he was told, but it was very heavy work to carry it all at once. When he came back the horse told him to take all his clothes off and jump into the kettle which stood and boiled in the room below, and to make sure he had a good dip there.

'I shall be an awful sight then,' thought the lad, but he did as the horse had told him. When he had finished his bath he became handsome and smart, and as red and white as blood and milk, and much stronger than before.

'Do you feel any different?' asked the horse.

'Yes,' said the lad.

'See if you can lift me,' said the horse.

Oh, yes, he could do that; and the sword, why, he swung it about his head as if it were nothing at all.

'Now, put the saddle on me,' said the horse, 'and put the suit of armour on you, and then don't forget the briar twig, the piece of rock, the water-jug and the jar of ointment, and then we'll be off.'

The lad had no sooner got on the horse than off they went at such a rate that he couldn't tell how fast they travelled. When he had been riding for some time the horse said to him: 'I think I hear a rumbling of something. Just look round; can you see anything?'

'Yes, there are a great, great many coming after us; at least a score,' said the lad.

'Well, that's the troll,' said the horse; 'he is coming after us with his imps.'

They rode on for a while, until they who were coming after them were close upon them. 'Now throw your briar twig over your shoulder,' said the horse, 'but throw it a good distance behind me!' The lad did so, and suddenly a big, close briar-wood grew up behind them. So the lad rode a long, long way, while the troll had to go home and fetch something to hew his way through the wood.

But in a while the horse said again, 'Look behind! Can you see anything now?'

'Yes, a great many,' said the lad; 'as many as would fill a church.'

'Ah ha! that's the troll – he has taken more with him this time. Throw the piece of rock you have, but throw it far behind me!'

As soon as the lad had done what the horse had said, a great steep mountain rose behind him, and so the troll had to go home and fetch something to mine his way through the mountain, and while the troll was doing this the lad rode again some distance on his way. But before long the horse asked him to look behind him again, and then the lad saw a crowd like a big army in bright armour, which glistened in the sun. 'Ah ha!' said the horse, 'that's the troll – now he has got all his imps with him. Take the water-jug and throw all the water out behind you, but mind you do not spill any of it on me!'

The lad did as he was told, but for all the care he took, he happened to spill a drop on the horse's flank. Well, the water he threw behind him became a great lake, but on account of the drop he spilled on the horse he found himself far out in the water; but the horse swam safely to land with him. When the troll and his imps came to the lake they lay down to drink it dry, and they drank till they burst. 'Now we have got rid of them,' said the horse.

So when they had travelled a long, long time, they came to a green plain in a wood. 'Now you must take off your whole suit of armour and only put your own ragged clothes on,' said the horse, 'and then take off my saddle and let me go; but hang all the things inside this big hollow lime tree here. You must then make yourself a wig of pine-moss and go up to the king's palace, which is close by; there you must ask for service. Whenever you want me, only come and shake the bridle, and I'll come to you.'

Yes, the lad did as the horse had told him, and when he put the wig of moss on his head he became so ugly and pale and miserable-looking that no one would know him again. He then went to the palace and asked if he could get some work in the kitchen and carry water and wood for the cook; but the cook asked: 'Why do you wear that ugly wig? Take it off you! I won't have such a fright in here.'

'I can't do that,' answered the lad, 'I am not all right in my head.'

'Do you think I will have you here near the food, if that's the case?' said the cook; 'go down to the coachman; you are better suited for cleaning out the stable.'

But when the coachman asked him to take off his wig and got the same answer he would not have him either. 'You had better go to the gardener,' he said; 'you are more fit for digging in the garden.' Yes, the gardener would take him, and gave him leave to stay with him, but none of the other servants would sleep with him, so he had to sleep by himself under the steps of the summer-house. It stood on posts, and a high staircase led up to it; under this he put some moss for a bed, and there he lay as well as he could.

When he had been some time at the palace, it happened one morning, just as the sun was rising, that the lad had taken off his wig of moss and was washing himself; he then looked so handsome that it was a pleasure to look at him.

The princess saw the lad from her window, and she thought that she never had seen anyone so handsome. She asked the gardener why the lad slept out there under the steps.

'Oh, none of his fellow-servants will sleep with him,' said the gardener.

'Let him come up and lie outside the door of my chamber,' said the princess, 'and then I suppose they will not think themselves too good to sleep in the same room as he.'

The gardener told the lad of it. 'Do you think I should do that?' said the lad; 'they would say that I was running after the princess.'

'Yes, you are very likely to be suspected of that,' said the gardener, 'you are so good-looking!'

'Well, if she orders it so, I suppose I must go,' said the lad.

When he was going upstairs in the evening he tramped and stamped so terribly that they had to tell him to walk more softly, that the king should not get to know it. So he lay down by the door and began to snore.

The princess then said to her maid: 'Just go quietly to him and pull off his wig.' The maid was just going to snatch it off his head, when he took hold of it with both his hands and said that she should not have it; and with that he lay down again and began snoring. The princess gave the maid a sign again, and this time she snatched the wig off him, and there lay the lad so lovely and red and white, just as the princess had seen him in the morning sun. After that the lad slept every night outside the princess's chamber.

But before long the king got to hear that the gardener's boy lay outside the princess's chamber every night, and he was so enraged at this that he almost took the lad's life. He calmed himself a little, however, and threw him into the prison tower instead. He shut up his daughter in her chamber, and told her she should not have leave to go out day or night. She cried and pleaded for herself and the lad, but all to no purpose. The king only got more vexed at it.

In a while a war broke out in the land, and the king had to take up arms against another king, who wanted to take the kingdom from him. When the lad heard this he asked the warder to go to the king and ask for a suit of armour and a sword and permission to go to the war. All laughed when the warder delivered his message, and they asked the king to give him some old rusty suit, that they might have the fun of seeing this poor wretch going to fight in the war. So the lad got permission and an old, wretched horse into the bargain, who jogged along on three legs and dragged the fourth after him.

So they all set out to meet the enemy; but they had not got far from the palace before the lad got stuck in a bog with his nag. There he sat and kicked away and cried: 'Gee up, gee up!' to his nag. All amused themselves at this sight, and laughed and made game of the lad as they rode past.

But no sooner were they out of sight than the lad ran to the lime tree, put on his suit of armour, and shook the bridle. The horse appeared at once, and said: 'You do your best, and I will do mine!' When the lad came up the battle had already begun, and the king was in a bad plight; but the lad rushed into the thick of the fight and put the enemy to flight. The king and his people wondered much who it could be who had come to help them; but no one came so near him as to be able to talk to him, and when the battle was over he was gone. When they rode home, they found the lad still stuck in the bog, kicking away at his three-legged nag, and they began laughing again. 'Just look! there sits that fool still!' they said.

The next day when they set out again, the lad was still sitting there; they laughed again and made game of him, but no sooner had they ridden past him than the lad ran to the lime tree, and all happened just as on the first day. Everyone wondered who this strange warrior could be that had helped the king. No one, of course, guessed it could be the lad.

When they were on their way home that night and saw the lad still sitting there on his horse, they jeered at him again, and one of them shot an arrow at him and hit him in the leg. He began to cry and wail so pitiably, that the king threw his pocket-handkerchief to him to tie round the wound.

The third morning when they set out, they found the lad still on his nag in the bog. 'Gee up, gee up,' he was shouting to his horse.

'I am afraid he will be sitting there till he starves to death,' said one of the king's soldiers, as they rode past him, and they laughed at him till they were nearly falling off their horses. But when they were gone, he ran again to the lime tree, and came up to the battle in the very nick of time. That day he killed the king of the enemy, and so the war was all over.

After the battle, the king happened to discover his handkerchief, which the strange warrior had tied round his leg, and he had no difficulty then in guessing who he was. They received him with great jubilation, and brought him with them to the palace, and the princess, who saw him from her window, became so animated, that no one could believe it, and she exclaimed joyfully: 'There comes my love.'

He then took the pot of ointment and rubbed himself

on the leg, and afterwards he rubbed all the wounded, so that all were well there and then.

So he married the princess, but on the very day the wedding took place, he went down into the stable to his horse, who was standing there quite sullen and dejected; his ears hung down, and he would not eat anything. When the young king – for he was now made king, and had got half the kingdom – spoke to him and asked what was the matter, the horse said: 'I have now helped you through, and I do not care to live any longer. You must take the sword and cut my head off.'

'No, I will do nothing of the sort,' said the young king; 'you shall have everything you want and do no more work.'

'Well, if you don't do as I tell you,' said the horse, 'you had better look out for your life, which is in my hands entirely!'

So the king had to do what was asked of him, but when he lifted the sword and was about to strike, he felt so grieved that he had to turn his face away, because he could not see the blow; but no sooner had he cut the head off, than the loveliest prince stood on the spot where the horse had stood.

'Where in all the world did you come from?' asked the king.

'It was I who was the horse,' answered the prince. 'At one time I was king in the land where the king came from that you killed in the battle yesterday. It was he who turned me into a horse and sold me to the troll. But now that he is killed, I shall get my kingdom back again, and you and I will be neighbouring kings; but we will never make war on one another.'

And no more they did; they were friends as long as they lived, and they used to go and visit each other very often.

❄

East of the Sun and West of the Moon

There was once a poor tenant who had many children, but very little food or clothes to give them. They were all pretty children, but the prettiest was the youngest daughter, who was so lovely that there was almost too much of her loveliness.

So one Thursday evening, late in the autumn, when there was terrible weather and it was dreadfully dark out of doors, and it rained and blew as well till the wall creaked, they were all sitting by the hearth busy with something or other. All at once someone knocked three times on the window-pane. The good man went to see what was the matter outside; and there he found a great big white bear.

'Good-evening!' said the white bear.

'Good-evening!' said the man.

'Will you give me your youngest daughter, and I will make you as rich as you now are poor,' said the bear.

Yes; the man thought it would be very nice to be so rich, but he must speak with his daughter first; so he went in and told her that a great white bear was outside, who promised that he would make them rich if he could only have her. She said 'No,' and would not agree to any such arrangement; so the man went out and arranged with the white bear that he should come again next Thursday evening for an answer.

In the intervening days they talked her round, and told

her of all the riches they would come into possession of, and how fine she herself would have it in her new home; so at last she gave in to their entreaties and began washing and mending her few rags and made herself look as well as she could, and was at last ready for the journey. Her baggage, of course, was not much to speak of.

The following Thursday evening the white bear came to fetch her; she got up on his back with her bundle, and away they went. When they had gone some distance the white bear said: 'Are you afraid?' – No, she wasn't afraid. 'Well, only hold tight to my coat and there's no danger,' said the bear.

And so she rode far, far away, and they came at last to a big mountain. The white bear knocked at it and a gate was opened, and they came into a castle where there were a great many rooms all lit up and gleaming with silver and gold, and amongst these was a great hall, where a table stood ready laid; in fact, all was so grand and splendid that you would not believe it unless you saw it. The white bear gave her a silver bell, which she was to ring whenever there was anything she wanted, and her wishes would be attended to at once.

Well, when she had eaten, it was getting late in the evening and she was very sleepy after the journey, so she thought she would like to go to bed. She rang the bell and scarcely had she touched it before she was in a room where she found the most beautiful bed anyone could wish for, with silken pillows and curtains and gold fringes; everything else in the room was made of gold and silver. But when she had gone to bed and put out the light, she heard someone coming into the room and sitting down in the big armchair beside the bed. It was the white bear, who at night could throw off his shape, and she could hear by his snoring as he sat in the chair that he was now in the shape of a man; but she never saw him, because he always came after she had put out the light, and in the morning before the day dawned he was gone.

Well, for a while everything went on happily, but then she began to be silent and sorrowful, for she went about all day alone, and no wonder she longed to be at home with her parents and her sisters and brothers again. When the white bear asked what ailed her, she said she was so lonely there, she walked about all alone, and longed for her home and her parents and brothers and sisters, and that was the reason she was so sad.

'But you may visit them, if you like,' said the white bear, 'if you will only promise me one thing. You must never talk alone with your mother, but only when there are others in the room. She will take you by the hand and try to lead you into a room to speak with you all by yourself; but you must not do this by any means, or you will make us both unhappy, and bring misfortune upon us.'

One Sunday the white bear came and told her that they were now going to see her parents. Away they went, she sitting on his back, and they travelled far and long; at last they came to a grand white farmhouse, where her sisters and brothers were running about. Everything was so pretty that it was a pleasure to see it.

'Your parents are living here,' said the bear; 'but mind you don't forget what I have said, or you will make us both unhappy.' No, she would not forget it.

When he had delivered her at the door, the bear turned round and went away. There was such a joy when she came into her parents that there was no end to it. They said they did not know how to thank her fully for what she had done for them. They had everything they wanted, and everybody asked after her and wanted to know how she was getting on, and where she was living. She said that she was very comfortable and had everything she wished for; but what she otherwise answered I don't know, but I believe they did not get much out of her.

But one day after dinner it happened exactly as the white bear had said; her mother wanted to speak with her alone in her chamber. But she recollected what the bear had told her, and would not go with her. 'What we have got to talk about, we can do at some other time,' she said. But somehow or other her mother talked her round at last, and so she had to tell her everything. She told her how a man came into her room every night as soon as she had put out the light, and how she never saw him, for he was always gone before the day dawned. She was sorrowful at this, for she thought she would so like to see him, and in the daytime she walked about there all alone and felt very lonely and sad.

'Oh, dear me!' said her mother, 'it may be a troll for all we know! But I will tell you how you can get a sight of him. You shall have a piece of a candle from me, and this you must take with you home in your bosom. When he is asleep, light that candle, but take care not to drop any of the tallow on him.'

Yes, she took the candle and hid it in her bosom, and in the evening the white bear came and fetched her.

When they had gone some distance of the way the bear asked her if everything hadn't happened as he had said. Yes, she couldn't deny that. – 'Well, if you have listened to your mother's advice you will make us both unhappy, and all will be over between us,' said the bear. – No, that she hadn't!

When they got home and she had gone to bed, the same thing occurred as before. Someone came into the room and sat in the armchair by her bedside, but in the middle of the night when she heard that he was asleep, she got up and struck a light, lit the candle and let the light fall on him. She then saw that he was the loveliest prince anyone could wish to see, and she fell at once in love with him; she thought that if she could not kiss him there and then she would not be able to live. And so she did, but she dropped three hot drops of tallow on him and he woke up.

'What have you done?' he said, 'you have now made us both unhappy for ever, for if you had only held out one year I should have been saved. I have a stepmother who has bewitched me, and I am now a white bear by day and a man by night. But now all is over between us, and I must leave you and go back to where she lives in a castle which lies east of the sun and west of the moon. In this castle there is a princess with a nose two yards long, and now I must marry her.'

She wept and cried, but there was no help for it; he must go and leave her. So she asked him if she might not go with him.

No that was impossible!

'But if you will tell me the way, I will try and find you,' she said. 'I suppose I may have leave to do that!'

Yes, she could do that, he said, but there was no road to that place; it lay east of the sun and west of the moon, and she could never find her way there.

Next morning when she awoke, both the prince and the castle were gone; she lay in a little green clearing deep in a dark thick forest, and by her side lay the same bundle of old rags which she had brought with her from home. When she had rubbed the sleep out of her eyes and wept till she was tired, she set out on her way and walked for many, many a day, till she at last came to a big mountain.

Close to it an old woman sat and played with a golden apple. She asked her if she knew the way to the prince who lived with his stepmother in a castle that lay east of the sun and west of the moon, and who was going to marry a princess with a nose two yards long.

'How do you know him?' asked the old woman, 'perhaps it was you who should have had him?'

Yes, it was she.

'Ah indeed! So it was you?' said the woman. 'Well, all I know is that he lives in the castle which lies east of the sun and west of the moon and thither you will come late or never, but I will lend you my horse, and on him you can ride to my neighbour, an old friend of mine; perhaps she can tell you more. When you have got there, just give my horse a blow with your whip under the left ear and ask him to go home again; and you had better take this golden apple with you.'

So she got up on the horse and rode a long, long time till she at last came to a mountain, where an old woman was sitting with a golden carding-comb. She asked her if she knew the way to the castle which lay east of the sun and west of the moon. She answered like the first old woman, that she didn't know anything about it, but it was sure to be east of the sun and west of the moon, 'and thither you will come, early or late, but I will lend you my horse as far as my neighbour; perhaps she can tell you. When you have got there, just give my horse a blow under the left ear and ask him to go home again.' And the old woman gave her the golden carding-comb, which might come in useful she said.

The young girl got up on the horse and rode for a long, long weary time and came at last to a large mountain, where an old woman was sitting and spinning on a golden spinning-wheel. She asked her if she knew the way to the prince, and where the castle was that lay east of the sun and west of the moon. And so came the same question: 'Perhaps it is you who should have had the prince?' – Yes, it was. But the old woman knew the way no better than the other two. It was east of the sun and west of the moon – she knew that – 'and thither you will come, early or late,' she said, 'but I will lend you my horse, and then I think you had better ride to the East Wind and ask him. Perhaps he knows those parts and can blow you there. When you have got there, just touch the horse under the ear and he'll go home again.' And so she gave her the golden spinning-wheel. 'You might find a use for it,' said the old woman.

She rode on many days for a long weary time before she got to the East Wind, but after a long time she did catch up with him and asked him if he could tell her the way to the prince, who lived east of the sun and west of the moon. Yes, he had heard tell of that prince, said the East Wind, and of the castle too, but he didn't know the way thither, for he had never blown so far. 'But if you like I'll go with you to my brother, the West Wind. Perhaps he may know it, for he is much stronger. Just get up on my back and I'll carry you thither.'

Yes, she did so, and away they went at a great speed. When they got to the West Wind, they went into him, and the East Wind told him that his companion was the one who should have had the prince who lived in the castle, which lay east of the sun and west of the moon; she was now on her way to find him again, and so he had gone with her to hear if the West Wind knew where that castle was.

'No, I have never blown so far,' said the West Wind, 'but if you like I'll go with you to the South Wind, for he is much stronger than any of us, and he has been far and wide; perhaps he may tell you. You had better sit up on my back and I'll carry you thither.'

Well, she got on his back, and off they started for the South Wind; they weren't long on the way, I can tell you! When they got there, the West Wind asked his brother if he could tell him the way to that castle which lay east of the sun and west of the moon. His companion was the

one who should have had the prince who lived there –
'Oh, indeed!' said the South Wind, 'is she the one? Well,
I have been to many a nook and corner in my time, but as
far as that I have never blown. But if you like, I'll go with
you to my brother, the North Wind; he is the oldest and
strongest of all of us, and if he doesn't know where it is
you will never be able to find anyone who can tell you.
Just get up on my back and I'll carry you thither.'

Yes, she sat up on his back, and away they went at such
a rate that the way didn't seem to be very long.

When they got to where the North Wind lived he was
so wild and unruly that cold gusts were felt a long way
off. 'What do you want?' he shouted from far away, but
still it made them shiver all over.

'Oh, you needn't be so very harsh,' said the South
Wind, 'it's I, your own brother; and I have with me she
who should have had the prince who lives in that castle
which lies east of the sun and west of the moon, and she
wants to ask you if you have ever been there and if you can
tell her the way. She is so very anxious to find him again.'

'Well, yes, I do know where it is,' said the North
Wind; 'I once blew an aspen leaf thither, but I was so
tired that I wasn't able to blow for many days after. But if
you really intend going there and you are not afraid to
come with me, I will take you on my back and try if I can
blow you so far.'

Yes, she was willing; she must go thither, if it were
possible, one way or another, and she wasn't a bit afraid,
go how it would.

'Very well!' said the North Wind, 'you must stop here
tonight then, for we must have a whole day before us and
perhaps more if we are to reach it.'

Early next morning the North Wind called her, and
then he puffed himself out and made himself so big and
strong that he was terrible to look at. Away they went,

high up through the air at such a fearful speed, as if they were going to the end of the world. There was such a hurricane on land that trees and houses were blown down, and when they came out on the big sea, ships were wrecked by the hundred. Ever onwards they swept, so far, far, that no one would believe how far they went, and still farther and farther out to sea, till the North Wind got more and more exhausted until he was scarcely able to give another blow, and was sinking and going down more and more; and at last they were so low that the tops of the billows touched their heels.

'Are you afraid?' said the North Wind.

'No,' she said, she wasn't a bit afraid.

By now they were not so very far from land either, and the North Wind had just sufficient strength left to reach the shore and put her off just under the windows of the castle which lay east of the sun and west of the moon; but he was then so tired and worn out that he had to rest for many days before he could start on his way home again.

Next morning she sat down under the castle windows, and began playing with the golden apple, and the first person she saw was the princess with the long nose, whom the prince was going to marry.

'What do you want for that golden apple of yours?' she asked, and opened the casement.

'It is not for sale, neither for gold nor money,' said the girl.

'If it isn't for sale for gold or money, what do you want for it then?' said the princess; 'I'll give you what you ask!'

'Well, if tonight I may sit in the armchair by the bedside of the prince who lives here, you shall have it,' said the girl who came with the North Wind.

Yes, she might do that, there would be no difficulty about that.

So the princess got the golden apple; but when the girl

came up into the prince's bedroom in the evening, he was fast asleep; she called him and shook him, and now and then she cried and wept; but no, she could not wake him up so that she might speak to him. Next morning, as soon as the day dawned, the princess with the long nose came and turned her out of the room.

Later in the day she sat down under the castle windows and began carding with her golden carding-comb, and then the same thing happened again. The princess asked her what she wanted for the carding-comb, and she told her that it wasn't for sale neither for gold nor money, but if she might get leave to sit in the armchair by the prince's bedside that night, she should have it. But when she came up into the bedroom she found him fast asleep again, and for all she cried and shook him, for all she wept, he slept so soundly that she could not get life into him; and when the day dawned, in came the princess with the long nose and turned her out of the room again.

As the day wore on, she sat down under the castle windows and began spinning on the spinning-wheel, and that the princess with the long nose wanted also to have. She opened the casement and asked the girl what she wanted for it. The girl told her, as she had done twice before, that it was not for sale either for gold or money, but if she might sit in the armchair by the princess bedside that night she should have it. Yes, she might do that.

But there were some Christian people who had been carried off and were imprisoned in the room next to the prince's, and they had heard that some woman had been in his room and wept and cried and called his name two nights running, and this they told the prince.

In the evening, when the princess came and brought him his drink, he made it appear as if he drank, but he threw it over his shoulder, for he felt sure she had put a sleeping draught in it.

So when the girl came into his room that night she found the prince wide awake, and then she told him how she had come there. 'You have just come in time,' said the prince, 'for tomorrow I was to be married to the princess; but I won't have that long nose, and you are the only one who can save me. I will say I want to see what my bride can do, and if she is fit to be my wife; then I will ask her to wash the shirt with the three tallow stains on it. She will try, for she does not know that it is you who dropped the tallow on the shirt and that it may only be washed clean by Christian folks, not by a pack of trolls like we have in this place; and so I will say that I will not have anybody else for a bride except the one who can wash the shirt clean, and I know you can do that.' And they felt very glad and happy, and they went on talking all night about the joyful time in store for them.

The next day, when the wedding was to take place, the prince said: 'I think I must see first what my bride can do!'

'Yes, quite so,' said the stepmother.

'I have got a very fine shirt, which I am going to use for my wedding shirt; but there are three tallow stains on it which I want washed out; and I have made a vow that I will not take any other woman for a wife than the one who is able to do that; if she cannot do that, she is not worth having,' said the prince.

'Well, that is easy enough,' said the stepmother and agreed to this trial.

Well, the princess with the long nose set to washing the best she could, but the more she washed the bigger grew the stains.

'Why, you cannot wash,' said the old witch who was her own mother; 'let me try!' But no sooner did she take the shirt than it got still worse, and the more she washed and rubbed the bigger and blacker the stains grew.

So all the other trolls tried their hands at washing, but

the longer they worked at it the dirtier the shirt grew, till at last it looked as if it had been up the chimney. 'Ah, you are not worth anything, the whole lot of you!' said the prince; 'there's a poor girl under the window just outside here, and I am sure she can wash much better than any of you. Come in, my girl!' he shouted out to her.

Yes, she would come in.

'Can you wash this shirt clean?' asked the prince.

'Well, I don't know,' she said, 'but I will try.'

And no sooner had she taken the shirt and dipped it in the water, than it was as white as the driven snow, if not whiter.

'Yes, you shall be my wife,' said the prince. At this the old witch flew into such a rage that she burst; and the princess with the long nose and all the trolls must have burst too, for I never heard of them since. The prince and his bride then set free all the people who had been carried off and imprisoned there and, taking as much gold and silver with them as they could carry, they moved as far away as they could from the castle which lay east of the sun and west of the moon.

❄

Ashiepattle who Made the
Princess tell the Truth

There was once upon a time a king who had a daughter,
and she was such an awful fibber that you couldn't find a
greater anywhere. So the king made it known that if
anyone could outdo her in telling fibs and could make
her tell the truth, he should have her for a wife and half
the kingdom into the bargain.

There were many who tried, for everybody would be
glad to get the princess and half the kingdom, but they
all fared badly.

Well, there were three brothers, who were also going
to try their luck, and the two elder set out first, but they
fared no better than all the others. Then the youngest,
Ashiepattle, thought he would try, so he set out for the
palace.

He met the princess outside the cowshed.

'Good-day,' said he.

'Good-day,' said she. 'I'm sure you haven't got such a
big cowshed as we have. When two boys stand, one at
each end, and blow their horns, they can't hear each
other!'

'Oh, indeed,' said Ashiepattle, 'ours is a great deal
bigger! If a young calf starts to go from one end of it to
the other, he is a big bull by the time he comes out.'

'Maybe,' said the princess; 'but then you haven't got so
big a bull as we have! Look, there he is! When two men

sit, one on each horn, they can't touch each other with a yard measure.'

'Why, that's nothing,' said Ashiepattle; 'we have a bull so big that when two men sit, one on each horn, and blow their horns, they can't hear each other.'

'Oh, indeed,' said the princess, 'but you haven't got so much milk as we have, for we milk our cows into great tubs and empty them into great big coppers, and make such awful big cheeses.'

'Well, we milk into great big casks, which we cart into the dairy, and put the milk into great brewing vats and make cheeses as big as houses. Once we had a cream-coloured mare that we put into the vat to tread the cheese together, and she had her foal with her, but one day she lost the foal in the cheese and we couldn't find it. But after we had been eating the cheese for seven years, we came across a great big cream-coloured horse who was walking about in the cheese. I was going to drive that horse to the mill one day and all of a sudden his back broke right in two, but I knew how to put that right. I took a pine twig and stuck it in his back, and he had no other back-bone as long as we had him. But that twig grew and grew so tall, that I climbed right up to the clouds by it, and when I got there I saw the North Wind sitting there spinning a rope of mutton broth. Suddenly the top of the pine tree broke off, and there I was, stranded. But the North Wind let me down by one of the ropes, and I landed right in a fox's hole; and who do you think were sitting there? – Why, my mother and your father of course! both mending boots; and all of a sudden my mother gave your father such a blow with an old boot, that the scurf flew out of his hair!'

'There you tell a lie,' shouted the princess; 'my father never was scurfy!'

And so Ashiepattle won!

An Evening in the Squire's Kitchen

It was a miserable evening; outside it was snowing and blowing, and in the squire's parlour the candle burned so dimly that you could scarcely distinguish anything in the room but a clock-case with some Chinese ornaments, a large mirror in an old-fashioned frame and a silver family tankard. The squire and I were the only occupants of the room. I sat in a corner of the sofa with a book in my hand, while the squire himself had taken a seat in the other corner buried in the perusal of the manuscript of a political treatise, which he had called: 'Attempts at a few well-meant Patriotic Utterances for the Welfare of my Country, by 'Anonymous', as he called himself out of modesty.

To the profound study of this intellectual gold mine, many shrewd opinions, as might easily be imagined, owed their birth. That he himself, at least, was convinced of their excellence, the cunning look in the grey blinking eyes which he directed towards me left me in no doubt; there was, however, no want of well-meant patriotic utterances in his conversation, the quality of which can best be judged by those who have had the opportunity of glancing over the above-named treatise, or his large unprinted essay about the tithes. But all this display of wisdom was lost upon me; I had it at my fingers' ends, having now heard it for the twenty-third time. I am not endowed with the patience of an angel but what could I do? The retreat to my room was cut off – they had been washing the floor for Sunday, and the room was no doubt steaming with vapour from the damp boards.

Having made a few vain attempts at engrossing my attention in my book, I was obliged to let myself be carried away by the impetuous torrent of the squire's eloquence. The squire was now on his hobby-horse, as we say; he had placed the old worn fur cap by his side on the sofa, leaving his bald head and grey hairs exposed. He became more and more excited; he rose from the sofa, walked up and down the floor with hurried steps, and fought with his hands in the air till the light flickered hither and thither, while the sweeping tail of his long grey homespun coat described long circles every time he swung himself round and raised himself on his longer leg, for, like Tyrtus and Peter Solvold of our parish, he was afflicted with a limp. His impassioned words buzzed about my ears like cockchafers round the top of the lime trees. He thundered away about lawsuits and judgments in the High Court of Justice, about disputes with the Court of Chancery, about clearing out the forests, about luxury, the rule of the majority in the National Assembly, and the blowing up of the rocks in the Horkefos, about the corn duty and the cultivation of the Jeedern district, about industries and centralisations, about the insufficiency of the currency, about aristocracy and all other 'ocracies' in the world, from King Nebuchadnezzar down to Peter Solvold's democracy.

It was impossible to endure the jargon and the affected pathos of the squire any longer. Out in the kitchen one peal of laughter succeeded another; Kristen, the smith on the farm, was the spokesman out there – he had evidently just finished a story, and another hearty laugh echoed through the room.

'No, I must go out and hear what the smith is saying,' I

said, interrupting the eloquent squire, and made a dart
for the kitchen, leaving him behind in the room in
company with the dimly burning candle and his own
disturbed reflections.

'Stuff and nonsense, and lying rigmaroles!' he growled,
as I vanished through the door; 'it's a disgrace to see
learned people . . . But well-meant patriotic words, no.' I
heard no more.

Light, life and merriment prevailed in the lofty airy
kitchen. A great fire blazed on the large open hearth and
lit up the room even in its farthest corners. By the side of
the hearth presided the squire's wife with her spinning-
wheel. Although she, for many years, had waged continual
war against rheumatism, her pleasant face shone like the
full moon from under her white head-gear, while she had
protected herself against any possible attack of the enemy
by a multiplicity of petticoats and jackets; and as an outer
fortification she had put on a monster of a frieze cloak.
Along the edge of the hearth sat the children, and cracked
nuts. Round about them was a circle of girls and wives of
the neighbouring tenants; they trod the spinning-wheels
with diligent feet, or were busy with the carding-combs.
In the passage outside the door, the threshers, who had
done their day's work, were stamping the snow off their
feet before they came in – their hair full of chaff. They sat
down by the big old-fashioned table, where the cook soon
brought them their supper, consisting of a large dish of
thick porridge and a bowl of milk.

The smith was leaning against the wall by the hearth;
he was smoking a long cutty-pipe, and on his countenance,
which bore traces of smithy-soot, lay a dry, serious
expression, which told he had been telling some story,
and that to his own satisfaction.

'Good-evening, Kristen,' said I; 'what are you telling
that creates such fun?'

'Hee, hee, hee!' screamed the youngsters, with great glee depicted in their faces; 'Kristen has told us about the smith and the devil, and then about the lad who got him into the nut, and now he says he's going to tell us about Peter Sannum, whose horse the fairies stopped on the Asmyr hill.'

'Yes,' began the smith, 'that Peter belonged to one of the Sannum farms north of the church. He was a wise man, and he was often fetched with sledge and horse to cure both man and beast, just like old Mother Bertha Tuppenhaug here. But somehow or other he could not have been clever enough for the fairies tied him up once in a field near his farm, where he had to stand the whole night with his mouth all on one side. And the time I was going to tell you about he fared no better either. You see, this Peter could never agree with people, he was just like – ahem, ahem! – well yes, he was a regular disagreeable fellow, who had lawsuits with everybody. Well, once he had a case before the Court of Appeal in Christiania and he had to be in court at ten o'clock in the morning. He thought he had better start from home the evening before to be in time, which he did; but when he came to the Asmyr hill his horse stopped.

'There is something not quite right thereabouts; many years ago someone hanged himself there, and there are many who have heard music there, played on fiddles and clarinets and flutes and other instruments. Yes, old Mother Bertha can tell something about that; she has heard it and she says she never heard anything so beautiful – it was just like the grand band which was over at the bailiff's in 1814. Isn't that true, Bertha?' asked the smith.

'Yes, every word of it, my lad,' said Mother Bertha, who was sitting near the hearth carding.

'Well, as I told you the horse stopped,' continued the

smith, 'and it would not move from the spot. For all he whipped and shouted, the horse only danced round in a ring and he couldn't get him to move either forwards or backwards. Hour passed after hour, but there the horse stood – and thus he stood the whole night through. He knew someone must be holding the horse, for although he cursed and carried on, he did not get a step farther. Towards the morning, just in the grey dawn, he got off the horse and went up to Ingebret Asmyr, and got him to bring a firebrand with him, and when he had got in the saddle again, he asked him to throw the firebrand over the horse. I should say he got a start then; away he went at full gallop; Peter could scarcely stick to the horse, and did not stop till he reached town, but then the horse burst.'

'I have heard of this before,' said old Bertha, and left off carding; 'but I would never believe that Peter Sannum didn't know better than that; but since you, Kristen, say so, I suppose I must believe it.'

'Yes, you may,' answered the smith; 'for I heard it from Ingebret Asmyr himself, who carried the firebrand and threw it over the horse for him.'

'He should have looked down over the horse's head between the ears, shouldn't he, Bertha?' asked one of the boys.

'Yes, that he should,' answered Bertha; 'for then he would have seen who held the horse, and then they would have had to let his horse go. I have heard that from one who knew more about such things than anybody; they called him "Hans Cheerful" at home in Halland. In other parishes they called him "Hans Decency", for he always used the expression, "everything with decency". He was taken into the mountain by the fairies, and had been with them for many years, and at last they wanted him to marry their daughter, who was always hanging about after him. But this he wouldn't, and when he had been rung for from several churches, the fairies took him at last and threw him from a high knoll far out into the parish. He thought he had been flung right out into the fjord. From that time he became half-witted. He was then put out on the parish, and went from farm to farm and told all sorts of wonderful stories, but all of a sudden he would laugh and say: "Hee, hee, hee! Kari, Karina, I see you!" for the huldre girl was always after him.

'While he was with the fairies, he told us, he had always to go with them when they went out to provide themselves with food and milk, for everything which the sign of the cross had been made over they had no power to touch, and so they would say to Hans: "You'll have to take this, for this has been crossed," and he would fill their bags with tremendous loads of all sorts of food; but if it ever began to thunder, they used to run away as fast as they could, so Hans could scarcely follow them. He was generally in company with one called Vaatt, and he was so strong, that he took both Hans and his load and carried them under his arms when such weather came upon them suddenly. Once they met the sheriff of Ringerike in a deep valley up in Halland, and Vaatt took hold of the horse and stopped him, and the sheriff shouted and whipped and pulled the poor horse about till he was pitiful to look at. But the sheriff's boy got off the sledge and looked over the horse's head between the ears, and then Vaatt had to let go his hold. "And I should say they shot off then," said Hans, "the boy had scarcely time to get on the sledge again, and we burst out with such laughter, that the sheriff turned round and looked behind." '

'Yes,' said a tenant from a distant part of the parish, 'I have heard something like that about a parson in Lier.

He was once on his way to an old woman, who was on her death-bed and who had led a wicked life. When he got into the forest his horse was stopped for him; but he knew what to do, he was a smart fellow that Lier parson – in one jump he was up on the back of the horse, and looked over his head between his ears, and then he saw an ugly old man, who was holding the reins. They say, it was Old Nick himself.

' "Leave go – you shan't have her," said the parson. He had to leave go, but he gave the horse such a smart blow at the same time that the horse took off at such a pace that the sparks flew about under his hoofs!'

'I just don't know what's the matter with the cows, ma'am,' said Mary, the dairy-maid, who came toiling in with a pail of milk; 'I do believe they're starving. Just look here, ma'am, what little milk we get.'

'You must take hay from the stable, Mary,' said the squire's wife.

'Yes, I ought to try that,' answered Mary; 'but if I go there, the men get as savage as wild geese.'

'I'll give you a good piece of advice, Mary,' said one of the boys with a sly look. 'You must boil cream-porridge and put it in the stable-loft every Thursday night, and you will find that the brownie helps you to carry hay to the cows, while the men are asleep.'

'Well, yes, if there only were any brownies here, I would do it,' answered the old dairy-maid quite innocently; 'but believe me, there is no brownie on this farm; why, our master and mistress don't believe in such – no, but that time I was in service at the captain's there was a brownie sure enough!'

'How do you know that, Mary?' asked the squire's wife. 'Did you see him?'

'See him? yes, of course; I've seen him, sure enough,' answered Mary.

'Oh, tell us, tell us all about it,' shouted the boys.

'Tell, yes! I can do that,' said the dairy-maid and she began: 'When I was at the captain's like I told you, the stable-boy said to me one Saturday night: "If you'll fodder the horses for me tonight, Mary, I'll do you a good turn someday."

' "All right," said I, "I'll do that for you," for he was going to see his sweetheart, you know.

'So towards evening when the horses should have their fodder, and I had given it to a couple of them, I took an armful of hay to give to the captain's own horse – he was always so fat and glossy, you could almost see yourself in his shiny coat – but just as I was going into the box to him, he fell right into my arms – '

'Who, who? the horse?' asked the boys.

'No, of course not! It was the brownie; I got so frightened, that I dropped the hay on the spot and ran away as fast as I could. When Peter, the lad, came home, I said to him: "I have foddered the horses for you once, my dear Peter, but believe me, I shan't do it again. The captain's horse didn't get as much as a straw, he didn't!" and so I told him all about it.

' "Ah, that didn't matter a bit," said Peter, "the captain's horse has got someone that looks after him anyhow, he has!" '

'What did the brownie look like, Mary?' asked one of the girls.

'Well, you see, I didn't see him exactly!' she said. 'It was so dark I couldn't see a hand before me, but I felt him as plainly as now, when I touch you; he was hairy, and didn't his eyes glisten?'

'Oh, it was only a cat!' objected another of the boys.

'Cat?' said Mary with the greatest contempt, 'why, I felt every one of his fingers; he had only four, and they were hairy all over! If that wasn't the brownie, may I never leave this spot alive!'

'Of course, that must have been the brownie sure enough,' said the smith, 'for he hasn't got any thumbs, and he's hairy on his fists – I've never shaken hands with him, but I've heard say so; and you know he minds the horses, and is about the best stable-boy you could have. There are a great many he is very useful to, but it's not only he that may be useful to the farmers. Up in Ullensaker,' he said, as he began a new story, 'there was a man who once found the fairies just as useful to him as the brownie is to others. He lived on Rögli Farm, and knew well enough that the huldre lives there, for once when he was going to town – it was in the spring just as the snow was melting away on the roads – and had got as far as Skjœllebvik and had watered his horses, he met a herd of red cows, so big and fat that it was a pleasure to look at them, and after them came several cart-loads of tubs and buckets and all sorts of things, with fine fat horses for the carts; but in front went a fine lassie with a snow-white milking pail in her hand.

' "Where are you going to this time of the year?" ' asked the Rögli man, surprised.

' "Oh, we are going to the Rögli pastures in Ullensaker," answered she who went in front; "there is plenty of grass there."

'He thought it was rather strange that they were going to graze on his pastures, but no one else but he either saw or heard anything of them. He asked several whom he met on the road, but no one had seen any cattle.

'At home on his farm several strange things happened too, sometimes. If he did any work after sunset it was always destroyed during the night, and at last he had to give up working after the sun had set.

'But now I must tell you about that time I told you they did him a good turn. One autumn he was walking about in his fields, feeling if his crop of barley was dry; it was very late in the autumn and he thought it wasn't quite dry enough to cart it in yet, but then he heard a voice over in a hill saying quite plainly: "You had better cart in your crops! Tomorrow it'll be snowing!" And he began carting as soon as he could, and carted till long past midnight, till he got his crop in; and the next morning the snow lay shoe-deep in the fields.'

'But it is not always that the fairies are so good,' said one of the boys. What about the huldre who stole the wedding fare?'

'Yes, I'll tell you all about that,' said the smith, who eagerly took this hint to begin a new story. 'There was once a wedding at Eldstad in Ullensaker, but as they hadn't any oven on the farm they had to send the joints to the neighbouring farm where they had an oven to get them roasted. In the evening, the boy on the farm, where the wedding was to take place, went to fetch them. As he was driving back over one of the moors, he plainly heard a voice shouting –

> ' "If you are going to Eldstad,
>   Just tell our Deld, from her sire,
>   That Dild fell in the fire."

'The boy was frightened, and drove so fast that the wind whistled in his nostrils, for the weather was cold, and the roads were in a splendid condition. He heard the voice calling after him several times, so he remembered the words well. He came safely home with his load, and went into a room where the servants were helping themselves to something to eat at the end of a big table while they had the chance to get a few mouthfuls.

' "Hallo, lad! has Old Nick brought you here already, or haven't you gone for the joints yet?" asked one of the people belonging to the house.

' "Yes, of course I have," said the lad; "there you see the joints coming in through the door. But I drove as fast as the horse could gallop, for when I came over the moor I heard a voice shouting after me:

' " 'If you are going to Eldstad,
        Just tell our Deld, from her sire,
        That Dild fell in the fire.' "

' "Oh, that's my child," shouted a voice from amongst the guests in the next room, and in an instant a woman rushed out as if she had lost her senses. She ran against one after the other, and nearly knocked them over, but suddenly her hat fell off, and it was then evident that she was a huldre; she had been stealing both meat and bacon, butter and cake, beer and brandy and all that was good. But she became so upset on hearing about the youngster, that she left behind her a silver cup in the beer bowl, and didn't notice that her hat had fallen off. They took both the cup and the hat and kept them at Eldstad; and the hat had this property, that whoever put it on was invisible to every other mortal, except to such as were gifted with second sight; but whether the hat is there still, I say for certain, for I have not seen it, nor have I had it on either.'

'Yes, these huldres are very smart at thieving, I have always heard that,' said old Bertha Tuppenhaug, 'but particularly in the summertime when the cattle are up in the mountains. It's regular holiday time for both huldres and other fairies then, for while the dairy-maids go about thinking of their sweethearts, they forget to make crosses over the milk and cream and other food, and then the fairies can take what they like. It isn't often they are seen, but it does happen now and then, as it happened once at the Neberg dairy up here.

'There were some woodcutters up there at work, and

as they were going towards the dairy for supper, they heard a voice over in the forest shouting to them: "Tell Kilde, both her sons fell in the soup-kettle and burnt themselves."

'When the woodcutters came to the dairy they told the girls: "As we were coming home to supper, just as we had shouldered our axes, we heard someone shouting over in the forest: 'Tell Kilde, both her sonnies fell in the soup-kettle and burnt themselves.' "

' "Oh, they're my children," someone shouted in the pantry, and suddenly a huldre rushed out with a milk-pail in her hand, which she dropped as she ran, splashing the milk all about the room.'

'Ah, well! you hear so many tales,' said the smith with a sneer, as if he had his doubts about the truth of this story; it was, however, perfectly evident that the remark was made out of vexation at being interrupted, when he was in the middle of his own stories. No one in the whole parish was richer than he in a stock of the most wonderful stories and tales about the huldres and fairies; and his belief in these supernatural beings was on a par with the credulity of the most superstitious. 'You hear so many things,' he continued, 'you cannot believe them all. But what has happened to your own kith and kin you are bound to believe! Now, I'll tell you something that happened to my father-in-law; he was a most serious and credible man, so what he said you may depend upon was true.

'His name was Joe, and he lived at Skroperud in Ullensaker. He built himself a new house there, and he had two or three fat cows and a horse, the like of which was not to be found in the whole parish; the horse was often used as post-horse between Mo and Trögstad, and Joe didn't seem to care much how the beast was used, for fat he was and fat he remained. Joe was a hunter, and a fiddler as well. He was often about in the parish playing, but at home it was impossible to get him to touch the fiddle; even if the room was full of lads and lasses he refused to play. But one evening some lads from the neighbouring farm came to see him, and they brought some brandy with them in their pocket-flasks. They treated Joe, and when they had made him tipsy, more lads came in, and although he refused to play at first, eventually he took down the fiddle. But after he had played for some time he put it away, for he knew that the fairies were not far off and that they didn't like the noise and disturbance. But the lads persuaded him to play again; and thus it happened two or three times that he put the fiddle away and that the lads coaxed him to play again. At last he hung his fiddle up on the wall, and swore he wouldn't play another stroke that night, and with that he turned them all out, lads and lasses! He was just going to bed, and was standing in his shirtsleeves by the hearth lighting his pipe for the night with a brand, when a large party of old and young people came in and filled the whole room.

' "Now, are you there again?" said Joe. He thought at first they were the same as had been there dancing, but when he saw they were strangers he felt a little frightened; he fetched his daughters, who were already in bed, and dragged them into the room – he was a big strong man – and demanded: "What people are these? Do you know them?"

'The lasses were sleepy, and didn't know what to answer. So he took his gun down from the wall and turned round towards the people who had come in and threatened them with the butt end of his rifle. "If you don't get out at once, I'll turn you out in such a way that you won't know whether you are standing on your heads or your heels!" Away they rushed, yelling, out of the door, the one on top of the other, and he fancied they all looked like a lot of grey balls of wools rolling out through the door. But when Joe had put his gun away and come over to the hearth to light his pipe again, he found an old man sitting on the stool by the fire; he had such a long beard, that it reached down to his knees – it must have been a yard long – and he also had a pipe, which he was trying to light with a fire-brand like Joe, but one moment it was alight and the next it went out.

' "And you," said Joe, "do you belong to the same gang of tramps, too? Where do you come from?"

' "Oh, I don't live far away, I can tell you," said the man, "and I would advise you to take more care and not make such a noise and disturbance in future, or I'll make you a poor man."

' "So," said Joe, "where do you live then?"

' "I live close by, under the corn-drying room," said the man; "and if we hadn't been living there, it would have been gone long ago, for you have been firing over much now and then, and it has been hot enough there I can tell you; and the whole building is not so strong but that it would collapse in a heap if I touched it with my finger. Now you know it, so you had better be warned!"

'There was no more dancing and playing to be heard at Skroperud after that; Joe parted with his fiddle, and they could never get him to touch another ever again.'

During the latter part of this story, the squire had been making a commotion in the parlour; cupboard doors were opened and shut; we heard keys rattle, and we knew he was busy locking up the silver plate and other portable property, from the silver tankard down to the leaden tobacco-box. Just as the smith had finished his story, the squire opened the door and popped in his head with his cap on one side.

'So you are at your cock and bull stories and lies again?' he asked.

'Lies?' said the smith very much offended, 'I have never told lies, sir! And this story is true enough, for I am married to one of the daughters. My wife, Dorthe, she was lying in bed and saw the old man with the beard. These girls were a little queer, to be sure, almost half-witted, but that came from their having seen fairies,' he added, with an indignant look at the squire.

'Half-witted?' said the squire, 'yes, I should think so; and that's what you are too, when you are not tipsy, and then you are raving mad. Come, boys! – Go to bed, and don't sit here and listen to such rubbish and nonsense.'

'I don't think that's kindly spoken on your part, sir,' answered the smith, with an air of superiority; 'the last time I heard rubbish and nonsense spoken, was when you made the speech on Neberg Hill the last anniversary of our independence.'

'Confounded rubbish!' muttered the squire, as he pushed his way through the kitchen with a candle in one hand and a bundle of Acts and some newspapers under his arm.

'Oh, wait a bit, sir,' said the smith, evidently with the intention of teasing the squire, 'and let the boys stay a little longer, too. You might like to hear a trifle yourself. It doesn't do you good to be always reading in the law books either. I'll tell you about a dragoon who was married to a huldre. I know it's true, for I've heard it off old Bertha, and she's from the very parish where it happened.'

The squire banged the door after him angrily, and we heard him tramping up the stairs.

'Well, well, since the squire won't listen, I'll tell it to you, my lads,' said the smith, addressing the boys, on whom all grandfatherly authority was lost when the smith promised to tell tales.

'Many years ago,' he began, 'there lived a wealthy old couple on a farm in Halland. They had a son, who was a

dragoon, and a fine big fellow he was. They had a dairy
up in the mountains, but it wasn't like the dairies you
generally see; it was a nice and well-built dairy, with a
regular chimney and roof and windows too. They stayed
there all the summer, but when they left in the autumn,
some woodcutters or hunters or fishermen or some such
people who knocked about in the mountains at that time
had noticed that the huldre people moved in there with
the cattle. And amongst them was a lass, who was so
lovely that they had never seen her like.

'The son had often heard people speak of this, and one
autumn when his parents had left the dairy he dressed
himself in full uniform, put the dragoon-saddle on his
horse and the pistols in their holsters, and off he started.
When he came in sight of the dairy, it was all ablaze with
light, and he guessed then that the huldre people were
there already. So he tied his horse to the stump of a pine
tree, took one of the pistols with him, and stole quietly
up to the window and looked in. In the room sat an old
man and an old woman who were so crooked and so
wrinkled with age, and so dreadfully ugly, that he had
never seen anything so hideous in his life; but then there
was a lass who was so lovely that he thought he could not
live if he did not make her his own. They all had cow's
tails, the lovely lass as well. He could see that they had
only just arrived, for the room appeared to have been
very lately put in order. The lass was busy washing the
ugly old man, while the woman was lighting a fire under
the big cheese-kettle on the hearth.

'All of a sudden the dragoon pushed the door open and
fired his pistol right over the head of the lassie, which
sent her rolling over on to the floor. But at the same
moment she turned just as ugly as she had been beautiful
before, and her nose grew as long as the pistol.

' "You can take her; she is yours now!" said the old

man. But the dragoon was spellbound; he remained standing on the same spot and could not move a step either forwards or backwards. The old man began to wash the lass, and she looked a little better after that; the nose decreased to about half the size and the ugly cow's tail was tied up, but it would be a sin to say she was anything like pretty.

' "She is yours now, my brave dragoon! Put her in front of you on the pommel of the saddle, and ride through the parish with her and celebrate your wedding. As for us, you can prepare something in the small chamber in the washhouse, for we don't care to mix with the other wedding-guests," said the ugly old one, who was the father of the lass; "but when the loving cup is passing round you may as well look in on us."

'He dared not do otherwise; he took the lassie with him on the pommel of the saddle and made preparations for the wedding. But before they went to church, the bride asked one of the bridesmaids to stand close behind, that no one should see the cow's tail fall off when the parson put his hand on her head.

'So the wedding was celebrated, and when the loving cup was being passed round, the bridegroom went across to the chamber where a table had been laid for the old huldre folks. He did not notice anything there that time, but when the guests had departed and he went in to see to the old folks again they were gone, but he found they had left behind quantities of gold and silver, indeed he had never seen so much treasure before.

'So everything went comfortably for a long time; and whenever they had any friends with them, the wife got something ready for the old couple in the little chamber, who always left so much money behind them that the young people did not know what to do with it all. But the huldre wife was ugly and remained ugly, and the young husband began to get tired of her, and I believe he was unkind to her now and then, and even attempted to strike her.

'One day late in the autumn he was going to town, but the early frost had set in and the roads were slippery, so he had to get his horse shod first. He went to the smithy to do it himself, for he was a clever smith, but whichever way he twisted and turned the iron, the shoes were either too large or too small, and he could not get them to fit. He had only that one horse at home on the farm, so he had no choice but to work away at the shoeing. But dinner-time came, and the afternoon wore on, and still the horse was unshod.

' "Will you never get those shoes ready?" asked his wife. "You are not much of a husband of late, and I think you are still less a smith. I see no help for it but to go myself to the smithy and shoe your horse. If I make the shoe too big you can make it smaller, and if I make it too small you can make it bigger." She went into the smithy, and the first thing she did was to take the shoe in her hands and pull the iron out straight.

' "Look here," she said, "this is the way you are to do it.' So she bent the shoe together as if it were of lead. "Now hold his foot up," she said, and the shoe fitted exactly; the best smith could not have done it better.

' "You seem to be very strong in your fingers," said her husband, as he looked at her.

' "Do you think so?" she said. "How do you think it would have fared with me, if you had been as strong in your fingers? But I care for you too much to use my strength against yours."

'From that day he was most kind and good to her.'

'Well I think we have had enough for tonight,' said the squire's wife, when the smith had finished this story, and she got up from her comfortable seat.

'Yes, I suppose we must be going, since the old man has gone to roost,' said the smith, and bade the children 'Good-night'; but he had to promise them to tell more the next evening, having made the condition that he was to have a 'quarter of tobacco'.

Next afternoon, when I went into the smithy, I found the smith chewing very hard, which was always the case when he had been drinking.

In the evening he went to some of the neighbouring farms to get more drink. When I saw him again some days afterwards, he was gloomy and chary of words. He would not tell any stories, although the boys promised him both tobacco and brandy. The girls whispered that the fairies had got hold of him and knocked him over in the Asmyr hill. A carter had found him lying there early in the morning, and said he was speaking incoherently.

※

Hans who Made the Princess Laugh

Once upon a time there was a king who had a daughter, and she was so lovely that reports of her beauty went far and wide; but she was so melancholy, that she never laughed, and besides she was so grand and proud that she said 'No' to all who came to woo her – she would not have any of them, were they ever so fine, whether they were princes or noblemen.

The king was tired of this whim of hers long ago, and thought she ought to get married like other people; there was nothing she need wait for – she was old enough and she would not be any richer either way, for she was to have half the kingdom, which she inherited after her mother.

So he made known every Sunday after the service, from the steps outside the church, that he that could make his daughter laugh should have both her and half the kingdom. But if there were anyone who tried and could not make her laugh, he would have three red stripes cut out of his back and salt rubbed into them – and, sad to relate, there were many sore backs in that kingdom. Lovers from south and from north, from east and from west came to try their luck – they thought it was an easy thing to make a princess laugh. They were a queer lot altogether, but for all their cleverness and for all the tricks and pranks they played, the princess was just as serious and immovable as ever.

But close to the palace lived a man who had three sons, and they had also heard that the king had made known that he who could make the princess laugh should have her and half the kingdom.

The eldest of the brothers wanted to try first, and away he went; and when he came to the palace, he told the king he wouldn't mind trying to make the princess laugh.

'Yes, yes! that's all very well,' said the king; 'but I am afraid it's of very little use, my man. There have been many here to try their luck, but my daughter is just as sad, and I am afraid it is no good trying. I do not like to see any more suffer on that account.'

But the lad thought he would try anyhow. It couldn't be such a difficult thing to make a princess laugh at him, for had not everybody, both grand and simple, laughed full many a time at him when he was a soldier and went through his drill under Sergeant Nils.

So he went out on the terrace outside the princess's windows and began drilling just as if Sergeant Nils himself were there. But all in vain! The princess sat just as serious and immovable as before, and so they took him and cut three broad, red stripes out of his back and sent him home.

He had no sooner arrived home, than this second brother wanted to set out and try his luck. He was a schoolmaster, and a funny figure he was altogether. He had one leg shorter than the other, and limped terribly when he walked. One moment he was no bigger than a boy but the next moment, when he raised himself up on his long leg, he was as big and tall as a giant. But he was very good at preaching.

When he came to the palace, and said that he wanted to make the princess laugh, the king thought that it was not so unlikely that he might. But I pity you, if you don't succeed,' said the king, 'for we cut the stripes broader and broader for everyone that tries.'

So the schoolmaster went out on the terrace, and took his place outside the princess's window, where he began preaching and chanting, imitating seven of the parsons, and reading and singing just like seven of the clerks whom they had had in the parish.

The king laughed at the schoolmaster till he was obliged to hold on to the door-post, and the princess was for a moment on the very point of smiling; but the moment past and she was again as sad and immovable as ever. And so it fared no better with Paul the schoolmaster than with Peter the soldier – for Peter and Paul were their names, you must know!

So they took Paul and cut three red stripes out of his back, put salt into them, and sent him home again.

Well, the youngest brother thought he would have a try next. His name was Hans. But the brothers laughed and made fun of him, and showed him their sore backs. Besides, the father would not give him leave to go, for he said he had so little sense it was no use his trying; all he could do was sit in a corner on the hearth, like a cat, rooting about in the ashes and cutting chips. But Hans would not take no for an answer – he begged and prayed so long they got tired of his whimpering and at last gave him leave to go to the king's palace and try his luck.

When he arrived at the palace, he did not say he had come to try to make the princess laugh, but asked if he could get a situation there. No, they had no situation for him; but Hans was not so easily put off; they might want someone to carry wood and water for the kitchen-maid in such a big place as that, he said. Yes, the king thought so too, and to get rid of the lad he gave him leave to remain there and carry wood and water for the kitchen-maid.

One day, when he was going to fetch water from the brook, he saw a big fish in the water just under an old root of a fir tree, which the current had carried all the soil away from. He put his bucket quietly under the fish and caught it. As he was going home to the palace, he met an old woman leading a golden goose.

'Good-day, grandmother!' said Hans. 'That's a fine bird you have got there; and such splendid feathers too! he shines a long way off. If one had such feathers, one needn't be chopping firewood.'

The woman thought just as much of the fish which Hans had in the bucket, and said if Hans would give her the fish he could have the golden goose; and this goose was such that if anyone touched it he would stick fast to it as long as Hans said: 'If you'll come along, then hang on.'

Yes, Hans would willingly exchange on those terms. 'A bird is as good as a fish any day,' he said to himself. 'If it is as you say, I might use it instead of a fish-hook,' he said to the woman, and felt greatly pleased with the possession of the goose.

He had not gone far before he met another old woman. When she saw the splendid golden goose, she longed to stroke it. She made herself very friendly and spoke nicely to Hans and asked him to let her stroke that lovely golden goose of his.

'Oh, yes!' said Hans, 'but you musn't pluck off any of its feathers!'

Just as she stroked the bird, Hans said: 'If you'll come along, then hang on!'

The woman pulled and tore, but she had to hang on, whether she liked it or not, and Hans walked on, as if he only had the goose with him.

When he had gone some distance, he met a man who had a grudge against the woman for a trick she had played upon him. When he saw that she fought so hard to get free and seemed to hang on so fast, he thought he might safely get his own back, so he gave her a kick.

'If you'll come along, then hang on!' said Hans, and the man had to hang on and limp along on one leg, whether he liked it or not; and when he tried to tear himself loose, he made it still worse for himself, for he very nearly fell on his back whenever he struggled to get free.

So on they went till they came into the neighbourhood of the palace. There they met the king's smith; he was on his way to the smithy, and had a large pair of tongs in his hand. This smith was a merry fellow, and was always full of mad pranks and tricks, and when he saw this procession coming jumping and limping along, he began laughing till he was bent in two, thinking to himself, 'This must be a new flock of geese for the princess; but who can tell which is goose and which is gander? I suppose it must be the gander toddling on in front. Goosey, goosey!' he called, and pretended to be strewing corn out of his hands as when feeding geese. But they did not stop. The woman and the man only looked in great rage at the smith for making game of them.

'It would be great fun to see if I could stop the whole flock, many as they are, thought the smith. He was a strong man and he seized the old man with his tongs from behind by his trousers.

The man shouted and struggled hard, until Hans said: 'If you'll come along, then hang on!'

And so the smith had to hang on too. He bent his back and stuck his heels in the ground when they went up a hill and tried to get away, but it was of no use; he stuck on as if he had been screwed there in the great vice in the smithy, and whether he liked it or not, he had to dance along with the others.

When they came near the palace, the farm-dog ran towards them and barked at them, as if they were a gang of tramps, and when the princess came to look out of her window to see what was the matter, and saw this procession, she burst out laughing. But Hans was not satisfied with that. 'Just wait a bit, and she will laugh still louder very soon,' he said, and made a tour round the palace with his followers.

When they came past the kitchen, the door was open and the cook was just boiling porridge, but when she saw Hans and his train after him, she rushed out of the door with the porridge-stick in one hand and a big ladle full of boiling porridge in the other, and she laughed till her sides shook; and when she saw the smith there as well she thought she would just die of laughter. When she had recovered herself, she looked at the golden goose again and thought it was so lovely that she must stroke it.

'Hans, Hans!' she cried, and ran after him with the ladle in her hand; 'just let me stroke that lovely bird of yours.'

'Rather let her stroke me!' said the smith.

'Very well,' said Hans.

But when the cook heard this, she got very angry. 'What is that you say!' she cried, and gave the smith a smack with the ladle.

'If you'll come along, then hang on,' said Hans, and so she stuck fast to the others too, and for all her scolding and all her tearing and pulling, she had to limp along with them.

And when they came past the princess's window again, she was still there waiting for them, and seeing that they had got hold of the cook too, with the ladle and porridge-stick, she laughed till the king had to hold her up. So Hans got the princess and half the kingdom, and they had a wedding which was heard of far and wide.

※

A Summer Night in a Norwegian Forest

The evening shadows now unfold
Their curtain o'er the lonely wold;
The night wind sighs with dreary moan,
And whispers over stock and stone.
Tramp, Tramp! the trolls come trooping, hark!
Across the moor to the deep woods dark.

ERIK GUSTAF GEIJER

When I was a boy about fourteen years old, I came one Saturday afternoon in the middle of the summer to Upper Lyse, the last farm in Sorkedale. I had frequently walked or driven over the main road between Christiania and Ringerike, and I had now, after having been at home on a short visit, taken the road to Lyse for a change, with the intention of making a short cut through the north part of the Krog wood.

I found all the doors of the farmhouse wide open, but I looked in vain in the parlour, in the kitchen and in the barn for a human being whom I could ask for a drink and who could give me directions.

There was no one at home but a black cat, who was sitting quite content and purring on the hearth, and a dazzling white cock, who was walking up and down the passage preening himself and crowing incessantly, as much as to say: 'Now I am the cock of the walk!' The swallows, which had been tempted here in great numbers on account of the quantity of insects to be found in proximity to the wood, and had established themselves in the barn and under the eaves, were gambolling, circling and twittering fearlessly about in the sunshine.

Tired with the heat and my walk, I threw myself down on the grass in the shadow of the house, where I lay half-asleep, enjoying a quiet rest, until I was startled by an unpleasant clamour – the jarring voice of a woman who was trying, by alternately scolding and using pet names, to pacify a litter of grunting pigs on the farm. By following the sound I came upon a barefooted old woman with a yellow dried-up countenance, who was bending down over the pigs' trough, busy filling it with food, over which the noisy little creatures were fighting, tearing, pushing and yelling with expectation and delight.

On my questioning her about the road, she answered me by asking me another question, not raising herself up from her task but turning her head half away from her pets to stare at me.

'Where might you come from?'

When she had got a satisfactory answer to this, she continued, while she repeatedly addressed herself to the young pigs: 'Ah, so! – you are at school at the parson's, eh! – hush, hush "little piggies" then! The road to Stubdale, do you say? – Just look at that one now! Will you let the others get something as well, you rascal! Hush, hush! Be quiet, will you! Oh, poor fellow, did I kick you then? – Yes, yes, I'll tell you the road directly. It's – it's straight on through the wood till you come to the big water-wheel!'

As this direction seemed to me to be rather vague for a road of about fourteen miles length through a forest, I asked her if I could not hire a lad who knew the road, to go with me.

'No, bless you! Is it likely?' she said, as she left the

piggery and came out on the slope before the farm. 'They are so busy now with the haymaking, that they've scarcely time to eat. But it's straight through the wood, and I'll explain it to you right enough, as if you see the road before you. First you go up the crag and all the hills over yonder, and when you have got up on the heights, you have the straight road right before you to Heggelie. You have the river on your left hand all the way, and if you don't see it, you'll hear it. But just about Heggelie there is a lot of twistings and turnings, and now and then the road is lost altogether for some distance – if one is a stranger there, it's not an easy thing to find one's way – but you are sure to find it as far as Heggelie, for that's close to the lake. Afterwards you go along the lake, till you come to the dam across a small tarn, just like a bridge, which is what they call it; bear away to the left there, and then turn off to the right, and you have the road straight before you to Stubdale in Aasa.'

Although this direction was not quite satisfactory, particularly as it was the first time I had started on an excursion off the main road, I set out confidently and soon all hesitation vanished. From the heights a view was now and then obtained between the lofty pine and fir trees of the valley below, with its smiling fields and variegated woods of birch and alder trees, between which the river wound like a narrow silvery streak. The red-painted farmhouses, peculiar to Norway, lay picturesquely scattered on the higher points of the undulating valley, where men and women were busy haymaking. From some chimneys rose columns of blue smoke, which appeared quite light against the dark background of thickly studded pine forests on the mountain slopes.

Over the whole landscape lay a repose so perfect that no one could have suspected the close proximity of the capital. When I had advanced some distance into the forest, I heard the notes of the bugle and the distant baying of hounds in full cry, which gradually faded, till nothing but a faint echo of the bugle reached my ear. I now heard the roar of the river, which rushed wildly past at some distance on my left, but as I advanced the road seemed gradually to approach it, and soon the valley in some parts grew narrower and narrower, till I at last found myself at the bottom of a deep, gloomy gorge, the greatest part of which was taken up by the river. But the road left the river again; there were certainly twistings and turnings, as the old woman had said, for at one moment it wound hither and the next thither, and at some places it was almost imperceptible. Now it went up a steep incline, and when I had passed the brow of the hill, I saw between the fir trees a couple of twinkling tarns before me, and on the margin of one of these a dairy on a verdant slope, bathed in the golden light of the evening sun. In the shady retreat under the hill grew clusters of luxuriant ferns; the wild French willow stood proudly with its lofty crest of gorgeous flowers, but the sedate monk's hood lifted its head still higher and looked gloomily and wickedly down on it, while it nodded and kept time to the cuckoo's song, as if it were counting how many days it had to live. On the verdant slope and down by the edge of the water, the bird-cherry and the mountain ash displayed their flowery garb of summer. They sent a pleasant and refreshing fragrance far around, and shook sorrowfully the leaves of their white flowers over the reflected picture of the landscape in the mirror of the lake, which on all sides was surrounded by pine trees and mossy cliffs.

There was no one at home in the dairy. All doors were locked. I knocked loudly everywhere, but there was no answer, no information as to the road. I sat down on a bench and waited a while, but no one appeared. The evening was setting in; I thought I could not stay there any longer, and started again. It was still darker in the forest, but shortly I came to a timber dam across a bit of river between two tarns. I supposed this was the place where I should 'bear off first to the left, and then to the right'. I went across, but on the other side of the dam there were only – as it appeared to me – flat, smooth, damp rocks and no trace of a road; on the opposite side, the right side of the dam, there was a well-trodden path. I examined both sides several times, and although it appeared to be contrary to the direction I had received, I decided on choosing the broader road or path, which was continued on the right-hand side of the water. As long as it followed the course of the dark tarn, the road was good and passable. But suddenly it turned off in a direction which, according to my ideas, was the very opposite of the one I should take, and lost itself in a confused net of paths and cattle-tracks amid the darkness of the forest. Inexpressibly tired of this anxious intricate search I threw myself down on the soft moss to rest for a while, but fatigue conquered the fears of the lonely forest, and I cannot now tell how long I dozed. On hearing a wild cry, the echo of which still resounded in my ears when I awoke, I jumped to my feet. I felt comforted by the song of the redbreast, and I felt less lonely and deserted as long as I heard the merry notes, too, of the thrush.

The sky was overcast and the darkness of the forest had increased considerably. A fine rain was falling which imparted renewed life to the plants and trees and filled the air with a fresh, aromatic fragrance; it also seemed to call to life all the nocturnal sounds and notes of the forest. Among the tips of the fir trees above me, I heard a hollow, metallic sound, like the croaking of a frog, and a penetrating whistling and piping. Round about me was a buzzing sound, as if from a hundred spinning-wheels, but the most terrible thing about all these sounds was that they at one time seemed close to my ear, and in another moment far away; now they were interrupted by frolicsome, wild cries and a flapping of wings, now by distant cries of distress followed by a sudden silence. I was seized by an indescribable fear; these sounds sent a chill through me, and my terror was increased by the darkness between the trees, where all objects appeared distorted, moving and alive, stretching forth thousands of hands and arms after the stray wanderer. All the fairy tales of my childhood were conjured up before my startled imagination, and appeared to be realised in the forms which surrounded me; I saw the whole forest filled with trolls, elves and sporting dwarfs. In thoughtless and breathless fear I rushed forward to avoid this host of demons, but while flying thus still more frightful and distorted shapes appeared, and I fancied I felt their hands clutching me. Suddenly I heard the heavy tread of someone who moved over the crackling branches of the undergrowth. I saw, or fancied I saw, a dark shape, which approached me with a pair of eyes shining like glowing stars. My hair stood on an end; I believed my fate was inevitably sealed, and shouted almost unconsciously as if to give myself new courage: 'If there's anybody there, tell me the way to Stubdale.'

A deep growl was the answer I received, and the bear, for such it was, walked quickly away in the same direction whence he had come. I stood for some time and listened to his heavy steps and the crackling of the branches under his feet. I mumbled to myself: 'I wish it was daylight and that I had a gun with me, and you should have had a bullet, Master Bruin, for frightening me so!'

With this wish and my childish threat all fear and thoughts of danger vanished, and I walked on again quite composed, on the soft mossy ground. There was now no sign of either road or path; but it grew lighter between the trees in front of me, the forest became more open, and I found myself on the slope leading down to the shores of a large lake, surrounded on all sides by pine forests, which on the distant shores vanished under the misty veil of the night.

By the red glimmering of the northern sky, which was reflected in the dark surface of the lake, over which the bats fluttered and circled, while large birds higher up in the air shot swiftly across with that croaking and penetrating whistle which not long ago had appeared so terrible to me, I found I had gone in a north-easterly direction instead of to the west.

While I was meditating whether I should remain here till the sun rose, or try to find my way back to the dam, I discerned to my inexpressible joy a glimpse of a fire between the trees on this side of the lake. I ran towards it, but I soon realised it must be farther off than it had at first appeared, because, after having walked about a mile, I found myself still separated from it by a deep valley.

When after considerable trouble I had forced my way through the chaos of fallen trees, which the wind had torn up in this exposed wild region, and had ascended the other steep hillside, I had still a good distance to walk across an open wooded heath, where the firs stood in rows like lofty pillars and where the ground resounded under my steps.

On the outskirts of this wood trickled a small brook, where the alder and the pine trees again sought to maintain their place, and on a small plot on the slope on the other side of a brook burned a great log-fire, which threw its red light far in between the trees. In front of the fire sat a dark figure, which, on account of its position between me and the blazing fire, appeared to me to be of supernatural proportions. The old stories about robbers and thieves in this forest came suddenly back to me, and I was on the point of running away when my eyes caught sight of a hut, made out of fir-branches, close to the fire, and two other men, who sat outside it, and the many axes, which were fixed into the stump of a felled tree, and it became evident to me that they were woodcutters.

The dark figure, an old man, was speaking – I saw him move his lips; he held a short pipe in his hand, which he only put to his mouth now and then to keep it alight by these occasional pulls. When I approached the group, the story had either come to an end or he had been interrupted; he stooped forward, put some glowing embers in his pipe, smoked incessantly and appeared to be attentively listening to what a fourth person, who had just arrived, had to say. This person, who apparently also belonged to the party, was carrying a bucket of water from the brook. His hair was red and he was dressed in a long jersey jacket, and had more the appearance of a tramp than a woodcutter. He looked as if he had been frightened by something or other.

The old man had now turned round towards him, and as I had crossed the brook and was approaching the party from the side, I could now see the old man plainly in the full glare of the fire. He was a short man with a long hooked nose. A blue skull-cap with a red border scarcely covered his head of bristly grey hair, and a short-bodied but long Ringerike coat of dark grey frieze with worn velvet borders served to make the roundness and crookedness of his back still more conspicuous.

The newcomer appeared to be speaking about a bear.

'Well, who would believe it?' said the old man, 'what did he want there? It must have been some other noise you heard, for there doesn't grow anything on the dry heath hereabout which he would be after. No, not Bruin, not he,' he added; 'I almost think you are telling lies, Peter! There's an old saying, that red hair and firs don't thrive in good soil,' he continued, half aloud. 'If it had been down in the bear's den or in Stygdale, where Knut and I both heard him and saw him the other day . . . but here? – No, no! he doesn't come so near the fire, he doesn't! You have been frightening yourself!'

'Frightening myself? Oh, dear no! Didn't I hear him moving and crashing through the undergrowth, my canny Thor Herberg?' answered the other, somewhat offended and chagrined at the old man's doubts and taunts.

'Well, well, my boy,' continued Thor in his former tone, 'I suppose it was something bigger than a squirrel anyhow!'

I now stepped forward, and said it must have been me that he had heard, and told them how I had lost my way, and the fright I had undergone, and how hungry and tired I was. I asked whereabouts I was now, and if one of them would show me the way to Stubdale.

My appearance created considerable surprise to the party, which however was not so much apparent in their words, as in the attention with which they regarded me and heard my story. The old man, whose name I had heard as Thor Herberg, seemed particularly interested in it; and as it appeared that he was accustomed to thinking aloud, I could, on hearing some of the remarks which he now and then mumbled to himself, participate in his reflections.

'No, no, that was the wrong way! – He should have gone over the dam there – Stubdale way – he went wrong altogether – he is too young – he isn't used to the woods – ah, that was the woodcock – and the goatsucker – yes, yes! it sounds strange to him, that hasn't heard him – oh, yes! the loon does shriek dreadfully – particularly when there's

fine rain – ah, ah! yes, that must have been the bear he
met – he is a brave boy after all!'

'Yes!' I said boldly, and gave vent to my awakening
youthful courage in about the same words as the man
who once came across a bear asleep on a sunny hillside:
'If it had been daylight, and if I had been a hunter and
had a loaded gun with me, and if I could have made it go
off, why, by my faith, the bear would most certainly have
lain dead on the spot.'

'Yes, of course, hah, hah, hah!' laughed old Thor, and
chuckled till the others joined in the laughter; 'of course
he would have lain dead on the spot – that's plain! hah,
hah, hah!

'But you are now by Storflaaten, the biggest lake in the
forest here,' he said, addressing himself to me, when I
had finished my story. 'Towards morning we'll help you
on your way, for we have got a boat, and when you have
got across the water you haven't far to go to Stubdale
then. But I suppose you would like to rest yourself a little
now, and get something to eat! I have nothing but some
pease pudding and rancid bacon, and maybe you are not
used to that kind of food; but if you are hungry, perhaps
you would like some fish? I have been out fishing, and
fine fish I caught too – yes, in this very lake!'

I thanked him for his offer, and he told one of his
companions to take a 'regular good 'un' off the string and
roast it in the glowing embers of the fire.

In the meantime the old man asked me a number of
questions about myself, and by the time I had answered
all these the fish was ready, and I began my meal with
great appetite. He now asked one of his companions to
tell us something about what he once said had happened
to his father, when he was out cutting timber.

'Well, that's very soon told,' answered the lad, a
strapping young fellow of a smart, undaunted appearance,

and not much more than twenty. 'Father was then working for the squire in Ask, and was cutting timber up in the squire's forest; he used to sleep at a cottage farther down the valley, at Helge Myra's place – you knew Helge, didn't you Thor? Well, one day he had been taking too long a nap after dinner – such a heavy sleep came over him – and when he awoke the sun was already setting behind the hills. But he would finish his day's work before he left off, and he began cutting away till the splinters flew about him in all directions; it grew darker and darker and there was still a small pine left which he was determined to have down, but no sooner had he given it the first cut, than the axe head flew off the handle. He set about looking for it and found it at last in a hollow.

'But suddenly he thought he heard someone calling him by name; he could not make out who it could be, for Helge Myra could not have any business thereabouts, and no one else lived there for miles around. He listened again, but did not hear anything, so he thought he might have been mistaken. He began cutting again, but all at once the axe-head flew off the handle again. He found it this time also after a long search, but when he was going to cut the tree on the north side of its stem, he heard plainly a voice shouting in the mountain: "Halvor, Halvor! Early you come and late you go."

' "As soon as I heard that," said my father, "I felt as if I had lost the use of my legs and I could scarcely get the axe out of the stem of the pine tree; but when I did take to my legs I didn't stop until I came to Helge's cottage." '

'Yes, I have heard that story before,' said old Thor, 'but that wasn't the one I meant; it was about the time he was at the wedding at the dairy on Kile Hill.'

'Oh, that time!' answered the indefatigable lad; 'that was in the spring, just before Easter Day. The snow wasn't gone yet, but my father had to set out for the forest to cut and drag home some wood. He went up in the Helling hill, where he found a withered fir, which he commenced cutting down at once. While cutting away at it, he thought he saw withered firs all around him, but while he was staring and wondering at this, up came a procession of eleven horses – all of a mouse-grey colour; it appeared to him to be a wedding-party.

' "What people are these, who are coming this way over the hill?" he asked.

' "Oh, we are from Östhalla," says one of them; "we are going to the Veien dairy to keep the wedding; the one who drives in front is the parson, next are the bride and bridegroom, and I am his father-in-law. You had better stand behind on my sledge and come along too."

'They came soon to a place which he thought he knew, and so it was. It was just north of Kile Hill, where the old dairy stood; but there was no dairy there then, but a great fine building, and here they all entered. Someone met them on the steps to give the guests a glass of welcome, and they gave father a glass also, but he said, "No, thanks!" he would not have anything he said, for he had only his old clothes on, and would not intrude on such fine folks.

' "Never mind this man," said one of them, "take a horse and see him on his way home," which they did; they put him in a sledge with a mouse-grey horse before it, and one of them sat up and drove the horse. When they got as far as the little valley north of Oppenhagen – where the land-slip took place – he thought he sat between the ears of a bucket; but shortly this vanished from under him and it was only then he really came to himself again. He began looking for his axe, and found it sticking in the same withered fir tree he had begun to cut down. When he came home, he was so confused and queer, that he could not tell now many days he had been away; but he was only away from the morning to the evening, – and for some time afterwards he was not himself – '

'Yes, many a queer thing happens hereabout,' said old Thor; 'and I for my part have seen some of it – witchcraft, I mean – and if you like to sit up a little longer, I'll tell you what has happened to me – in this here forest, I mean.'

Yes, they would all like to hear it; tomorrow was Sunday, and it didn't much matter if they went to bed late.

'Well, it might be about ten or twelve years ago,' he answered. 'I was burning charcoal over in Kampenhaug Forest. In the winter I had two horses there to cart the coals to the Bærum works. One day I happened to stop too long at the works, for I met some old friends from Ringerike there, and we had a good talk about one thing or another, and a little drop to drink too – yes, brandy, I mean – and so I did not come back to the kiln before ten o'clock in the evening. I made a fire, so I could see to load the sledges, for it was terribly dark and I had to get the carts loaded in the evening, for I had to be off at three o'clock next morning if I was to get to the works and back again the same day while it was light – back to the kiln, I mean. When I had got the fire to burn up, I began loading the sledges. But just as I was turning round to the fire again a drift of snow came sweeping down upon it and put it out entirely – the fire, I mean. So I thought to myself: "Why, bless me, the old witch in the hill here is vexed tonight, because I have come home so late and disturbed her." I struck a light and made a new fire. But, strange to say, the shovel would not drop all the coals into the basket – more than half went over the sides. At last I got the sledges loaded and I was going to put the ropes round them, but will you believe me, every one of them broke, one after the other – the ropes, I mean. So I went to get new ropes and at last had the sledges ready, gave the horses their fodder and went to bed. But do you think I awoke at three? No, not till long after the sun had risen, and still I felt heavy and queer, both in my head and my body. Well, I had something to eat and went then to look to the horses, but the shed was empty and the horses were gone. I got rather out of temper at this, and I am afraid I swore a little into the bargain, but I thought I had better try and find their tracks. During the night there had fallen a little fresh snow, and I could see they had not gone off in the direction of the valley or the works. I found, however, the tracks of two horses and of a couple of broad feet going in a northerly direction; I followed these for two or three miles, until the tracks parted, and the footprints vanished altogether; one horse had gone to the east, and the other to the west, and after following up one for five or six miles, I came upon him at last. I had to take him home to the hut and tie him up, before I could start looking for the other horse. By the time I got hold of him it was near upon noon, and so there was no use going to the works that day. But I promised I should never disturb the old witch any more – in the evening, I mean.

'But these promises are strange things; even if you keep a promise to Christmas you are pretty sure to break it before next Michaelmas. The year after, I made a trip to Christiania late in the autumn; the roads were in a fearful bad condition and it was already very late in the afternoon before I left town, but I wanted to get home that night. I was on horseback and took the road by Bokitad, which is the shortest, as you know – to Ausfjerdingen, I mean. The weather was wet and ugly, and it was beginning to grow dark when I started. But when I crossed the bridge by Heggelie I saw a man coming towards me – he wasn't very tall, but terribly big; he was as broad as a barn-door across his shoulders, and his hands were nearly a foot across the knuckles. He carried a leather bag in one hand, and seemed to be talking to himself. When I came nearer to him, his eyes glistened like burning cinders, and they were as big as saucers. His hair stood out like bristles, and his beard was no better; I thought he was a terrible, ugly brute, and I prayed for myself the little I could, but just as I came up to him, down he sank – into the ground, I mean.

'I rode on, humming an old psalm, but suddenly I met him again, coming down a hill, and his hair and beard sparkled with fire this time, like his eyes. I began praying again, and had no sooner finished than he was gone. But I had scarcely ridden a mile, before I met him once more as I was crossing a small bridge. His eyes flashed like lightning and sparks flew out of his hair and beard, and he shook his bag, till you could see blue and yellow and red tongues of fire shooting out of it. But then I lost my temper right out, and instead of praying I swore at him, and he vanished on the spot. But as I rode on, I began to be afraid that I should meet this brute again, so when I came to Lövlie I knocked at the door, and asked for lodgings till daylight – but do you think they would let me in? No. I could travel by day, like other folks, they said, and then I needn't ask for lodgings! So I guessed the old brute had been there before me and frightened them, and I had to set out again. But I started another old psalm, till the mountains rang with it, and I came at last safe to Stubdale, where I got lodgings – but it was almost morning then.'

The manner in which he told these stories was, like his speech, slow and expressive, and he had the custom of repeating single words, or part of his sentences, or adding one or another superfluous explanation. He generally applied these remarks after one of his many exertions to keep his pipe alight, and they had such a comical effect on me, that I had great difficulty in refraining from laughing outright. I was in a merry mood after having survived my nocturnal expedition, and to this I must ascribe the fact that his stories did not make the impression upon me which might have been expected.

The dawn of the day was now appearing and old Thor told one of his companions to row me across the lake and put me on the right road.

***

The Witch

On a hill, some distance from the main road in the middle of Gudbrandsdale, some years ago, stood a cottage. Perhaps it is there still. It was mild April weather – the snow was melting, the brooks rushed wildly down the mountainsides, the fields were nearly bare, the thrushes were scolding each other in the woods, all the groves resounded with the twittering of birds – in short there was every sign of an early spring.

In the mighty birch tree and lofty mountain ash, which stretched out their naked branches over the roof of the cottage in the glittering sunlight, some busy tom-tits whisked about, while a chaffinch, who had perched himself in the top of the birch tree, sang out at the top of his voice.

Inside, in the smoky room with the raftered ceiling, it was dark and dismal. A middle-aged peasant woman of a very common and unintellectual appearance was busy blowing into a blaze some branches and sticks of wood under the coffee-kettle on the open hearth. Having at last succeeded in this, she raised herself up, rubbed the smoke and the ashes out of her smarting eyes, and said: 'People say there's no use in this lead-melting – for the child hasn't got wasting sickness; they say it's a changeling. There was a fell-maker here the other day and he said the same, for when he was a youngster, he had seen a changeling in Ringerike somewhere, and that one was as soft in its body and as loose about its joints as this one.'

While she spoke, her simple face had assumed an expression of anxiety, which showed what impression the fell-maker's words had made upon her superstitious mind.

She addressed her words to a big bony woman, whose age might be about sixty. She was unusually tall but when she was sitting she appeared to be of low stature, and this peculiarity she had to thank for the nickname of 'Longlegs', which the people had added to her name of Gubjor. In the gang of tramps with whom she used to roam about, she had other names too, and was considered to be a sorceress. Grey hairs straggled out from under her head-gear, which surrounded a dark face with bushy eyebrows and a long knotted nose. The brutish expression of her face, which was characterised by a low forehead and great breadth between the cheekbones, contrasted greatly with the unmistakable cunning in her small sparkling eyes. Her dress betokened her as a straggler from some northern district; her whole appearance denoted that if she were not a witch, she was at least a tramp, who would be now impudent and audacious, now humble and cringing, according to circumstances.

While the peasant woman was speaking and attending to the coffee-kettle, Gubjor was keeping in motion a hanging cradle in which lay a child of a sickly appearance, by giving it now and then a push with her hand. She replied to the peasant woman in a calm tone of superiority, although her sparkling eyes and the quivering muscles round her mouth showed that she was not satisfied with the statement of the fell-maker.

'Folks will talk so much about things they don't understand, my dear Marit,' she said; 'they talk fast and loose, and, as for the fell-maker, he may understand sheep well enough, but sickness and changelings he knows nothing about, I say and maintain! – I should think I ought to

know something about changelings, for I have seen
enough of them. That changeling he spoke about must
have been the one Brit Solvold had in Gjerdrum, for I
recollect she had a changeling; she got it soon after she
was married. She had a very good and nice child, but it
was changed for a troll's brat as ill-tempered and unruly
as if it belonged to the fiend himself. He would never
speak a word – only eat and cry – but she hadn't the heart
to strike or ill-treat the youngster; at last somebody
taught her a charm to make him speak, and then she
found out what kind of a brat he really was. She got hold
of him one day and began to thrash him soundly and call
him all sorts of names; suddenly the door flew open and
somebody – whom of course she couldn't see – rushed
into the room, tore the changeling away from her and
threw her own child on to the floor with such violence
that it began to cry. Imagine how she rejoiced!

'Or perhaps it was the changeling that Siri Stromhugget
had? That was an old-fashioned, dried-up youngster, and
I don't think he had any joints at all – but he was no more
like your child here than this old cap of mine! I recollect
that youngster well. I served at the parish clerk's at that
time and I saw it more than once; and I also recollect how
she got rid of it. There was a great deal of talk about it at
the time, for Siri, as you know, came from this parish.
When she was quite young, she served at Kyam; after that
she moved to Stromhugget, where she was married to
Ola – the son there. Soon after her first child was born, a
strange woman came into the room and took the child
from the bed and put another in its place. Siri, who was
still weak, tried to get up and get her child back – she
struggled with all her might, but she could not move
from the spot – she was spellbound and quite powerless.
She was going to call her aunt, who was in the next room,
but she could not open her mouth, and she was just as

frightened as if they had been going to take her life. It was easy enough to see that the child was a changeling, for it wasn't like other children at all – it screamed and cried as if it had a knife stuck in it, and it flayed about with its arms like a huldre-cat and was as ugly as sin. It was always eating, and poor Siri didn't for the life of her know how to get rid of it. But at last she heard of a woman who knew something about these things, and she told her to take the youngster and flog him with a proper rod three Thursday evenings in succession. Well this, she did, and the third Thursday evening a woman came flying over the barn-roof, and threw a child away from her and took up the changeling. But as she rushed off she struck Siri across the fingers; and she carries the marks to this day – and I have seen them with my own eyes,' added Gubjor, as a further proof of the truth of her story. 'No, this child is no more a changeling than I am; and how could it happen, that they could change yours after all the trouble you have taken to prevent it?' she asked.

'Well, no! that's what I cannot make out either,' said the mother quite innocently, 'for I've put castor in the cradle, I have crossed him and put a silver brooch in his shirt, and I have stuck a knife in the beam over the door – so I don't know how they could have managed to change him.'

'Well then, they almost certainly haven't and they can't have had any power over him either. I know all about that, I should think,' began Gubjor again, 'for in a parish close to Christiania I once knew a woman who had a child, which she was so very careful about – she made crosses over it and used castor and everything else she had heard of, for there was plenty of witchcraft thereabout, I can tell you; but one night, as she lay in bed, with the child by her side near the edge of the bed, her husband, who was lying near the wall, awoke suddenly and saw such a red glare all over the room, just like when one stirs the fire – and sure enough, there *was* someone stirring the fire, for when he looked towards the fireplace, he saw an old man sitting there raking the logs together. He was an ugly brute – uglier than I can describe and he had a long grey beard. When he had got the fire to give a good light, he began stretching his arms out for the child, but he could not move from the stool he sat on. His arms grew longer and longer, till they reached halfway across the room, but he didn't stir from the fire, and couldn't reach the child. He sat thus for some time, while the husband was so frightened that he didn't know what to do. He then heard someone moving outside the window.

‘ "I say, Peter, why don't you come?" asked a voice outside.

‘ "Hold your tongue, woman!" said the old man, who was sitting by the fire, "they have been crossing and fiddling over this youngster, so I can't get it."

‘ "Well, you might as well give up, so we can be off," said the voice again. It was the old man's wife, who was waiting outside to receive the youngster.

‘But just look at this fine little boy,’ said the sorceress with affected kindness, as she took the child who had just woken up and who vigorously resisted the strange woman's caresses, crying at her apparently coaxing, but really repulsive, expression. ‘He is as white as snow and pure as an angel; he is rather weak about the joints, to be sure – but to say he is a changeling, that's a mistake! – No, it's wasting sickness,’ she added, as she turned round to the mother with a lofty air of conviction; ‘it's wasting sickness!’

‘Hush, I fancy I heard someone knocking outside. Mercy on me, if it's my husband who has come back!’ said Marit, terrified at being surprised by her husband in company with the sorceress over a cup of coffee. She ran to the door and looked out, but there was nobody there but a brindled cat, which sat on the steps licking her paws after a hunt in the neighbouring bush, and a woodpecker, which was pecking away at the sunburnt logs of the cottage wall, trying to wake up the drowsy insects from their winter sleep in the holes and crevices in the timber, and turning his head every moment, as if he was looking for someone, but it was only an April shower he was expecting.

'Is there anybody there?' asked Gubjor. On receiving an answer in the negative, she continued: 'Well, we had better leave the door open, so we can have the benefit of the sun and see when your husband comes home – for I suppose that's the way he'll come.'

'He went with his sledge to get a load of leaves for the goats,' answered Marit; 'but I'm so afraid he'll catch us together. Last time, when he heard that you had been here, he was that wild I didn't know what to say. He said he would give me money to go to the doctor – for he won't hear of any such things as magic curing; he is well read, and doesn't believe in the fairies any longer, since he went about with that schoolmaster of ours.'

'To the doctor's? Bah!' said the sorceress and spat upon the floor. 'I wouldn't advise anybody to go to that stuck-up grandee with his wee bit of a body. If one doesn't come with gold and fine presents,' she continued, with an affected air of superior knowledge, 'he bites and worries you as if you were dogs, and not people. Why, look what happened that time Gjertrud Kostibakken lay with the last gasp of breath in her body. He wouldn't go to a tramp, for he was at a Christmas party at the magistrate's, nor did he go either till he was threatened both with bishop and judge; and he might have saved himself the trouble, for when he came to the door the poor woman was dead. No! to go to the doctor's with a child suffering with wasting sickness, is madman's work!

But, dear me!' she said with a sneer, 'you may go to him for all I care, but if he can help you as much as I can, may I never be able to cure another in my life. They don't know anything about this wasting sickness, bless you! There's nothing about it in their books, and they don't know of any remedy for it! – and they know they don't know – that's the reason they don't give any powders or potions or other nasty stuff for it. No, there's no other remedy but lead-melting, but they don't know anything about that.'

'Let's put the ladle on, mother,' she went on in a different tone, 'it's getting on towards noon. If we have melted twice, we'll have to melt the third time as well, or we don't know what might happen. The child has the wasting sickness, but there are nine sorts of that disease in the world, as I've told you already. So far he has had the goblin-spell and the water-spell. The first Thursday the lead showed a man with two big horns and a tail. That was the goblin-spell. Last time it was a mermaid, you saw it as plainly as if it had been drawn. That was the water-spell. But now Thursday has come round again, and the question is what will it show this time? The third time is the most important, you must know. There, take the child,' she said, as she gave it to its mother. 'Let me finish this drop of coffee, and I'll set to at once.'

When the coffee was drunk, and the cup was put away with many thanks and blessings, she went demurely to the hearth, and pulled out a snuff-horn.

'Since last Thursday,' she said, 'I've been in seven parishes and scraped lead off the frames of church-windows at midnight, for I used the last of my lead last Thursday. It's trying both to mind and body,' she mumbled to herself as she shook out from the snuff-horn some of the lead, which, according to her statement, she had collected under such difficulties.

'I suppose you have brought some water from a brook running north at midnight?' she inquired further.

'Yes. I was down by the mill-stream last night; it's the only stream running north for a long way round,' answered the peasant woman, as she brought out a carefully closed pail and poured water from it into a large beer bowl. Across this was placed a thin oatmeal cake, through which a hole was made with a darning needle. When the lead was melted, Gubjor went to the door, looked up at the sun, took the ladle and poured the melted lead slowly through the hole into the water, while she mumbled some words over it which seemed to be to this effect:

'I conjure for sickness, I conjure for pain –
I conjure it off, and I call it again.
I conjure the weather, the wind, and the rain!
I have spells for the north, I have charms for the west,
And the south and the east must obey my behest.
I conjure in water, I conjure on land,
I conjure in rocks, and I conjure in sand,
I conjure pain into the alder-tree root,
I conjure disease into tiny foal's foot.
Where the flame of Gehenna comes bellowing forth,
Or where the charmed waters flow on to the north,
There, there shall pain wither, consumed by my spell,
And with the poor babe all shall henceforth be well!'

As was only natural, the boiling lead hissed and spluttered as it was poured into the water.

'Just listen to the wickedness of it – it must come out now,' said the sorceress to the peasant woman, who with a mixed feeling of fear and awe, stood listening with the child in her arms. When the oatmeal cake was taken off the bowl, a couple of figures formed by the melted lead were seen in the water.

The sorceress regarded them for some time, with her head on one side; she then began nodding and said: – 'Corpse-spell, corpse-spell! – first goblin-spell, then water-spell and now corpse-spell. One of them would have been enough,' she added, shaking her head. 'Yes, I now see how it has all happened,' she continued aloud, and turned round to the mistress of the house. 'First, you travelled through a wood and past a hill while the trolls were out, there you blessed the child. You then crossed a river, and there you also blessed the child; but when you came past the churchyard – it was before the cock crowed – you forgot to bless the child, and there it caught the corpse-spell.'

'Bless me – how do you know that?' exclaimed Marit with great surprise. 'Every word you say is true. When we left the dairy last summer, on our way home, it was rather late before we started as some of the sheep had gone astray, and it was growing dark by the time we got down into the valley. I thought I saw the glimmer of a light over in the forest and I heard something like a gate being opened in the Vesæt hill – they say there are fairies there – and then I blessed the child. When we crossed the river, I heard a terrible cry, and I blessed the child again – the others said it was only the loon, which screamed for bad weather.'

'Yes, that would have been sufficient, if there was nothing else but the loon,' said Gubjor; 'when it screams at a new-born babe, that child is bewitched.'

'Yes, I have also heard that,' said the mother; 'but when we came past the churchyard – it was just past midnight – then the bull got unruly and we had such trouble to keep the cattle together, that I forgot to bless the child there.'

'That's where the child caught it then, you may be sure, for the corpse-spell comes from the churchyard. Just look yourself in the bowl here: there stands a coffin and there is a church steeple, and in the coffin lies a corpse, spreading out its fingers,' said the sorceress with great importance, as she explained these mystic figures in the melted lead. 'Humph – but there is a remedy!' she mumbled to herself again, but sufficiently loud to be heard by the other.

'What remedy is that?' asked the mother, both glad and curious.

'There's a remedy – it does try one, but never mind,' said Gubjor; 'I shall make a dummy baby, which I shall bury in the churchyard, and then the dead will believe they have got the child; take my word, they won't know but what it is the real body. But we must have some family silver to go with it! Have you got any?'

'Yes, I have two or three old silver coins, which were given me when I was baptised, and I didn't want to touch them – but if life depends upon it . . . ' said the anxious mother, and she began at once searching in an old chest.

'Yes – one I shall put in the hill, the other in water, the third I shall bury in consecrated ground, where the disease was caught. I must have three in all,' said the sorceress, 'and some old rags to make a dummy of.'

She got what she asked for. A big doll was soon made up in the shape of a wrapped-up baby. The sorceress rose from her seat, took the dummy baby and her stick, and said: 'I'm going now to the churchyard to bury it. The third Thursday from today I shall be back again, then we'll see! If there is going to be life, you can see yourself in the pupils of the child's eye, but if he is going to die you'll see something black and nothing else. Presently I must be off to Joramo. I haven't been there for a long time; but they sent word to me to come and see a youngster who has got the troll-spell. But that's an easy matter! I'll push him under a piece of turf the contrary way to which the sun goes, and then he'll be a man again.'

'Dear me, dear me!' said the peasant woman admiringly, 'Joramo! Why, that's in Lesje! Bless me, are you going such a long way?'

'Yes, it is a long way off. I was bred and born there,' said Gubjor; 'I have travelled much, but gathered little, since I was there. It was better times for Gubjor then,' she added with a sigh, as she sat down on the settle. 'But in Joramo there was once a changeling,' she mused, as some legend from olden times came into her mind on recalling some of the memories of her childhood. 'My aunt's great grandmother who lived in Joramo had a changeling. I never saw it, for both she and the child were gone long before I was born, but my mother often spoke about it. The child looked like an old man with a weatherbeaten face, but his eyes were as red as fire, and glowed like an owl's eyes in the dark. He had a head as long as a horse's head and as round as a cabbage; the legs were as thin as a sheep's, and his body looked like last year's dried mutton. He was always crying and howling, and if he got hold of anything, he threw it right into his mother's face. He was always hungry, like the parish dog – everything he saw he must have, and he very nearly ate them out of house and home. The older he grew, the worse he grew, and there was no end to his howling and wailing. They could never make him speak a word, although he was old enough – in short, he was a perfect worry night and day. They tried for advice here and there and everywhere, and the poor woman was told to try this and that and everything. She hadn't the heart to thrash him till she was sure he really was a changeling, but then somebody told her how she could find it out. She was to say that the king was coming, and then she was to make a big fire on the hearth and break an egg in two. Half of the shell she was to put over the fire, and then a long pole down the chimney into the shell. Well, she did that; but when the changeling saw this, he sat upright in the cradle and stared at it. The woman went out of the room, but peeped in through the keyhole. He then crept out of the cradle on his hands, but left his legs stuck in the cradle, and he stretched himself out, till he was so long that he reached right across the floor to the hearth.

' "Well, well," he said, "I am now as old as seven generations of trees in the Lesje wood, but I have never seen such a big porridge stick in such a little porridge pot as this in Joramo."

'When the woman saw and heard this, she knew well enough he was a changeling; of course when she came in, he crawled back into the cradle like a worm. She then began to be hard on him. On the Thursday evening she took him out behind the cowshed and gave him a sound thrashing, and at the time she thought she heard someone whining and crying near her. The second Thursday night she served him in the same way, but when she thought he had had enough, she heard a voice speaking close to her, and she thought she could recognise the voice of her own child.

' "Every time you hit that Tjostul, the people in the hill hit me."

'The third Thursday evening she gave the changeling a thrashing again, and suddenly a woman, carrying a youngster, came rushing up to her, as if she had burnt herself.

' "Give me Tjostul back again – there's your own brat!' she said, and she threw the child at the woman who stretched out her hands to receive it; she got hold of one leg, which she held in her hand, but the rest of the child she never saw – so violently had the troll's wife thrown it from her.'

During this story the mistress of the house began to show unmistakable signs of uneasiness, and towards its end they became so apparent, that even the storyteller, who seemed to be fully taken up with her narrative, also noticed them.

'What's the matter?' said the witch, looking out through the open door. 'Oh, I see! – your husband is coming! There's no room here for Gubjor any longer; but don't you be afraid, mother,' she added in a grave tone; 'I'll go round by the churchyard, and then he won't see me.'

❄

DISTRIBUTORS
for Wordsworth Children's Classics

AUSTRALIA, BRUNEI & MALAYSIA

Reed Editions
22 Salmon Street
Port Melbourne
Vic 3207
Australia
Tel: (03) 646 6716
Fax: (03) 646 6925

GERMANY, AUSTRIA & SWITZERLAND

Swan Buch-Marketing GmbH
Goldscheuerstraße 16
D-7640 Kehl am Rhein
Germany

GREAT BRITAIN & IRELAND

Wordsworth Editions Ltd
Cumberland House
Crib Street
Ware
Hertfordshire SG12 9ET

INDIA

Om Book Service
1690 First Floor
Nai Sarak, Delhi - 110006
Tel: 3279823/3265303
Fax: 3278091

NEW ZEALAND

Whitcoulls Limited
Private Bag 92098, Auckland

SINGAPORE

Book Station
18 Leo Drive
Singapore
Tel: 4511998
Fax: 4529188

SOUTHERN AFRICA

Struik Book Distributors (Pty) Ltd
Graph Avenue
Montague Gardens
7441
P O Box 193
Maitland
7405
South Africa
Tel: (021) 551-5900
Fax: (021) 551-1124

USA, CANADA & MEXICO

Universal Sales & Marketing
230 Fifth Avenue
Suite 1212
New York, NY 10001 USA
Tel: 212-481-3500
Fax: 212-481-3534

ITALY

Magis Books
Piazza della Vittoria 1/C
42100 Reggio Emilia
Tel: 0522-452303
Fax: 0522-452845